Siân

Enjoy!

Next

Claire Highton-Stevenson

Claire

This is a work of fiction. Names, character, businesses, places, events and incidents are either products of the author's imagination or used in a fictitious manner. Any resemblance to actual persons, living or dead, or actual events is purely coincidental.

ISBN-13: 978-1978109124

ISBN-10: 1978109121

Facebook: Claire Highton-Stevenson writer
Twitter: @ItsClaStevOfficial
Website: www.ItsClaStevOfficial.co.uk

Cover Art: Claire Stevenson Photography

DEDICATION

For anyone that's ever loved another. It was always worth it.

ACKNOWLEDGMENTS

Special thanks goes to:

Michelle Arnold, for the many hours of encouragement, editing and proofreading. For little more than cake and pens!

Kelly Daniel, whose expertise and experience in the medical field was invaluable.

Chris Flynn, for her continued support and weekly lunch dates!

and

to my wife, Louise.

Without whom, none of this would be possible.

Part Two

Chapter One

When Janice Rashbrook arrived at dead on 10 a.m. as planned, she entered in a whirlwind of authority; this wasn't a woman who took any prisoners! With her power suit and briefcase, she was the epitome of Hollywood hardcore. What she hadn't seen, heard, or talked about wasn't worth knowing.

"So, lovebirds, let's talk, and while we're at it, I'll have a coffee, black, no sugar!" she demanded, not requested. Cam raised an eyebrow at Michelle and received a shrug and a smirk in return.

Cam could hear the conversation while she set up the coffee machine and gathered some mugs. There really was nothing nicer than the smell of fresh coffee brewing, as far as Cam was concerned. Her place was much like Michelle's: open-planned and spacious, with a lot of light streaming in from the windows and doors that faced the beach. Her kitchen, although a separate room, was just feet from where Michelle sat elegantly with Janice by her side.

"First we need to decide, are you in or out?"

"Huh?" said Michelle, her attention stuck firmly on Camryn's butt. The blonde seemed to have found some kind of rhythm in her head as she tensed each cheek. It was almost hypnotising as each side lifted and fell.

"Out!! Ya know, of the closet...no longer in Narnia, cruising the strip!" Janice used up her entire repertoire of LGBT retorts as Cam turned to join them in the room, carrying a tray of hot coffees, completely oblivious to the attention her girlfriend had been paying her.

"She means are you telling the world you're a lesbian," Cam deadpanned before grinning. She liked Janice. They sat on the same board for an arts foundation Cam was involved with and often had a giggle at someone else's expense. Though neither were ever mean or nasty, they couldn't help but see the humour in a lot of the things that went on in LA; it was a crazy place at times.

"Oh, uh…well, what happens if I wanted to come out? Officially? I mean people already know, so…" she inquired of her agent. She thanked Cam as she passed her a mug of hot coffee.

"Well first off, we get you booked on Ellen," she sniggered. The opportunity to play a little more with her client was just too much to ignore, especially as she clearly had Camryn's approval.

"Ha ha." A snarky reply came from Michelle, but she grinned anyway. "Could we take this seriously maybe?"

Cam smiled from her vantage point. She loved Michelle in all her guises, but she had a real soft spot for when she got a little riled.

"Ok seriously, I don't think there will be any issue with *Medical Diaries*, they have several gay cast members already and have had two gay characters so far, so I don't foresee any problems there. And it's been a pretty closed set in terms of gossip leaking, so I'm not worried. Plus, you only have a few more weeks of filming and then you'll be on hiatus, and any furore about it will hopefully have died down by the time you return."

"Ok well that's good." Michelle breathed a sigh of relief.

"But." She held up a finger. "It will probably stifle any prospective film parts. Right now you still get cast as the eye candy; once it's out that you're 'out,' the money men might be less likely to cast you as they do now!"

"Why?" Cam asked as she picked up her mug and sipped the dark nectar. "She's an actress, she got cast as a doctor without being one, why is there such an issue with playing straight sex sirens?"

"Because dear Camryn, the real world is full of assholes!" Never one to shy away from the truth, she wasn't going to start now. "And we haven't even got to the fans yet."

“Fair enough, but it’s still not fucking right.”

“Ok, so what about if we keep it quiet?” Michelle asked, resting her hand on Cam’s leg.

“Well then it depends on how quiet you plan to be. Silent? Nothing much changes. Out to colleagues? Again, no real change to your employment. However, bigger risk of some asshole outing ya, but it’s up to you Shelly. This is your career; it’s you that’s going to have to make the decision, and the fact that you say people already know may mean you have no choice.”

Janice and Camryn both gave their attention fully to Michelle. She looked between each of them and then burst into tears!

“I don’t know!” she cried. “What do I do?” Cam quickly placed her coffee down on the table and reached for her, guiding her into a hug that protected her from all the horribleness outside.

“Janice is right, this has to be your choice, but for now we stay silent and give you time to decide.” Cam spoke the words carefully, needing Michelle to know this was all okay.

“Really? You don’t want me to come out and acknowledge you?”

“What I want is for *you* to be happy and for *you* to acknowledge me. I don’t need your fans to accept me or for your boss to like me. I just don’t want you to feel ashamed of what we have.”

“I’m not, I promise you I am not ashamed of you or of us but, this is my dream! It has been my whole life, to act and be an actor. I don’t want to give that up, and it’s not fair that I have to consider not being able to do what I love just to be happy like anyone else.” She picked at imaginary fluff on Cam’s jumper, an overwhelming need developing inside her to just lock herself away in a room with only Camryn for company, where they could make love and be together without the pressures and judgement of the world.

"Life ain't fair honey, never has been," said Janice. "Like I said, I can keep this quiet, but you're going to have to get ya head around the idea that one misplaced hand," she nodded towards Michelle's hand on Camryn's leg, "kiss, or word, and you could be outed."

"You said that some people can come out and make it work for them. So, why can't it work for me?" Michelle spoke to Janice.

"It can, but it would mean possibly doing what I said earlier. Taking parts that are different from the ones you do now. It means advertising might drop off. You'll have to deal with the press and go on every talk show that asks. Put up with fans making comments you might not like to read. Or it could all go right and you'll become the biggest star on the planet."

"I don't care about the money Jan, I have enough money, it's never been about the money!" she said, looking to Cam who held her hand still.

"You say that now, but you've got a lifestyle you enjoy, and that costs money!" Janice emphasised.

"I have money, it's not an issue," Cam announced.

"Really?" Janice turned and looked right at Cam. "And what happens if this is just a little phase or you two have a fight like you've just had and decide not to be together anymore, what then? She gives up her whole career and you get to walk away. She has to live with any choice she makes now!" Janice glared at Cam. She liked the Brit, but at the end of the day she was paid to do what was best for Michelle, and what was best for Michelle was best for her too.

"We're not going to break up," Michelle whispered.

"You don't know that!" Janice replied gently.

"She's right, all the risk is on you Michelle, your entire life is going to change because of me!" Cam shrugged, realising just how much life could change for them both.

"Then so be it, I know what I want!"

"Do you? We haven't left this bubble for ten days. People already know, and as much as I trust them, all that it takes is one stupid comment to the wrong person. Once it's common knowledge, there is no taking it back."

"Ok Cam I get it, ok!" Michelle said sharply before she blew out a breath and checked her anger. She wasn't angry with Cam or Janice; it was the situation. How dare the world be so difficult just because she fell in love? "I'm sorry, I don't mean to shout, it's not your fault."

"I will support you in any decision you make. I'll walk 50 feet behind you to avoid a photograph, I'll stay home while you go on a 'date' with some stud from the studio, I'll keep on planning secret dates for us to enjoy in private, or I'll hold your hand with pride and stand on the red carpet with you; I'll do interviews and let them print any crap they like about me, but you have to decide which it is." She reached her hand for her lover once more and kissed her fingertips.

Michelle looked to Janice and said, "You see why I love her?"

"Oh I'm very aware of Camryn's attributes, Shelly. Look, let's leave things as they are, you two stay in your little bubble for a few more days and come up with an answer. I need to get going. Oh and Michelle, Saturday you have a charity event to attend. I'll text you the details later but you will need a date so, let's just say that whoever you turn up with will be the answer."

Cam saw her to the door, and when she returned she found Michelle still sitting on the sofa, her legs tucked up underneath her. Cam sat down, and Michelle climbed into her lap and curled up.

"Why does it have to be so hard? All I want is to do my job and love you, is that too much to ask?"

"No, in the real world it wouldn't really make any difference, but you are a story. Who knows, other actresses have come out, and the media doesn't hassle them."

"I just don't know if I want to live my entire life as a lie."

"You wouldn't be. We wouldn't be a lie at home, we would be able to tell our friends and family and enjoy a limited amount of freedom still."

"But why should we? I know I'm new to all this but I hate it, I hate that I have to hide you."

Cam smiled. How things had changed in just a few weeks. Michelle had gone from wanting to hide herself to now being angered by it, and Cam went from being out and proud to wanting to protect her lover with whatever it took, even if that meant pretending she didn't exist.

"I just think maybe things will work out," Michelle said. "We can keep our life private and still be a regular couple."

"Maybe, we still need to be careful though baby." Cam placed her hands on Michelle's waist and pulled her into her. She needed to make sure that she wasn't getting ahead of herself. "We can go out and do normal things, but we still have to keep our hands to ourselves just in case."

"I know," she whined, a little disappointed. "I just, I really love just being with you and doing normal everyday boring stuff."

"Good cos, I have *so* many really boring normal things for you to do, starting with the hoovering." She grinned.

"The what?"

"Vacuuming love, vacuuming!! The place needs cleaning, so let's get moving." She laughed at the look on Michelle's face. There was never going to be any cleaning needed doing in this house, not with Maria here anyway, but it was fun to mess with her a little.

"You seriously want to spend this evening cleaning house?"

"No I don't, that's why I have Maria, but she has the afternoon off and you said you wanted to do all the boring—"

She was cut off before she could finish by Michelle's lips crushing hers. "You are a bad, bad woman Camryn, making your girlfriend clean house when you should be making love to her."

"Oh, now you don't want to do the boring things, no?"

"You are such a funny woman. Now strip!" Michelle demanded.

If she thought sweet and lovely Michelle was sexy as hell, then Cam was completely undone by demanding and confident Michelle!

"You want me to strip?" she said, standing with a mischievous glint in her eye.

"Pretty sure that's what I said, you didn't seem to have a problem with it in the parking lot at OUT." She licked her lip before biting the lower one between her teeth. One leg crossed over the other, Michelle sat back and got herself comfortable for the show.

"I see," Cam said, as she wandered over to the Bose sound

system and flicked through some CDs, picking out the one she wanted. As the music kicked in and the bass picked up, she turned and locked eyes with Michelle, her hips started to sway as she reached up to the first button on her shirt, opening it as she sashayed towards Michelle, who sat open-mouthed at this impromptu strip show.

By the time she had crossed the room, dipping, swaying and twisting to the music, she had two more buttons undone. She pushed Michelle backwards with a firm hand on her chest until she was sitting on the couch, wide eyed and amazed.

"No touching," Cam stated, her lap dance commencing with a grin.

Chapter Two

Cam rolled over to the middle of the bed expecting, to find a warm body to wrap herself around. Instead she found the coolness of unoccupied sheets. One eye opened like a sleeping crocodile as she scanned the expanse of empty space. She cocked one ear, to add to the eye, and listened. The lyrics to Simon & Garfunkel's "Sound of Silence" popped instantly into her brain.

Clambering out of bed, she pulled an oversized fluffy white dressing gown around her naked form as she padded barefoot out to the hall, listening to hear if Michelle was downstairs, but – nothing.

She skipped down the stairs pretty much two at a time, calling out her name, but still, nothing!

As she wandered into the living room, she saw instantly where Michelle was: sitting outside on the sand, her face to the sky soaking up the early morning rays. *How did I get so lucky? Beautiful doesn't even begin to cover it*

Finding her clothes still lying on the floor and draped across the furniture from where they were scattered and discarded the night before, she quickly pulled them on (uttering a silent prayer that she had given Maria the day off). Barefoot still, she walked back into the kitchen and, noticing the coffee machine had a full jug, she did a happy jig and poured two cups before wandering outside herself.

~Next~

"Hey, I missed you!" Cam said, hovering over the woman sitting cross legged on the sand.

Shading her eyes from the bright sun with her hand, Michelle looked up. "Hey, I woke up early and you just looked so peaceful..."

"You ok?" Cam questioned, her eyes squinting in the bright light as she tried to fathom what Michelle was thinking about.

"Yes, yes I'm really ok." She smiled up at her.

"Good." Cam returned the smile but kept watch; something was definitely up.

"Is one of those for me!?" she asked, pointing towards the mugs of coffee Cam held.

"Oh, yes...sorry." She passed one over and flopped down next to her, two sets of long legs now lying parallel to one another. They sat sipping their drinks, enjoying the quiet of the morning. The beach wasn't that busy today, just a few people meandering along without a care in their world. It was a little breezy, but it was still warm, and Cam expected more people to arrive as the day went on, so it was nice to just sit and be. She glanced to her left, at Michelle. The woman she loved seemed to be lost deep in thought.

"I have made a decision," Michelle said suddenly, sitting up straighter and clasping her hands around the mug in her lap. Her voice sounded confident and bold.

"About what?"

"About me, us...life in general." She smiled again as she turned to face her lover.

"Ah, ok, going to share with the class?" Cam asked, tilting her head to the side. She could feel butterflies in her tummy, the feeling that Michelle was about to say something monumental. Something that would change everything.

"That is exactly what I'm going to do!" she replied cryptically.

"What do you mean babe?" Cam asked, a frown forming as she tried to understand.

"I have decided I don't want to spend my life hiding. I have no doubts about us Camryn, as a couple I think we can work. But, I've thought long and hard about what would happen if we broke up and well, the answer is I'd still be gay and I would still want to date women, so..."

"You're sure about this?" Cam asked, finally working out what it was that Michelle was really saying. "I mean I will support you whatever you decide, but are you sure?"

"Yes, when I woke up this morning in your arms, I realised that's what I want, every day! I don't want to be sneaking around, I'm 34 years old for fuck's sake. I'm a grown woman! This is my life and I don't want to be dictated to anymore. If it means I lose work then so be it, I'll go back to theatre. I just want to act. What I get paid or how the audience watches me do it doesn't make any difference, it's the acting I love." She was animated as she spoke; for the first time, it seemed as though she was finally at ease with not just who she was, but her place in the world. "I have all these young people that look up to me, how can I be a role model to them if I can't even be a role model to myself?"

Cam listened and drank her coffee. She was impressed with just how brave and strong this woman now was. Just a few months ago she was crying in her office about the idea that a drunken girl had recognised her, and now here she was, head held high, making a stand for what she wanted in life, and Cam loved her even more for it. She placed her coffee cup down on the sand and reached for her hand.

"Ok, then that's what we do."

"I love you Cam. I know that this will be hard for you as well, and there are going to be people wanting to know all about you, I know it will be a nightmare for a while..."

"Listen, if it means you are happy and we can just be who we want to be and not have to live in fear of always being found out, then I'll take all the crap they can throw at me!"

"Thank you." She leant forward and kissed her cheek.

They sat quietly for a moment longer, finishing off the coffee and contemplating Michelle's decision as the world around them continued to turn.

"So, how do you want to play it?" Cam asked, considering all the options. She could just picture Janice and her office of public relations on overdrive.

"I'm not going to make any announcement. I'm just going to do what I want to do. I will hold your hand, kiss you, be seen with you.... and you will be my date on Saturday, if you are up for it? If anyone asks the question then I will answer it truthfully. If they don't, I won't fill them in."

"Sounds like a plan then! When do we start?" She smiled.

"How about right now?" she said, grinning as she leant across again to kiss her full on the lips.

Cam stood breathlessly as the kiss came to an end, speaking as she came to her full height. "We had better get dressed and let Janice know your decision."

"And then I need to go see my parents."

Chapter Three

Entering the office of Janice Rashbrook's WRW talent agency the following day, Michelle and Cam were confronted with a room full of people. In addition to the producer of *Medical Diaries* and representatives of the network, there were also a stylist and several PR 'gurus' as well as a member of the actors' union.

"Ok, what is going on?" Michelle asked as she surveyed the room. She had known this was big, but she hadn't quite understood just how big until now.

"Michelle, these people are here to discuss the details of how and when you will be making any announcement. We need to get a handle on this as soon as possible in order to maximise any publicity as well as minimise any potential backlash," Janice replied, calm and steady as usual.

"I'm not making an announcement Janice, and in case anyone has failed to notice, this is my life we're talking about, not a TV show. And I won't be requiring a stylist, I'm not going to change how I look just because I'm fucking a woman now!" Michelle's voice rose considerably. Cam reached out, grounding her with a simple touch.

"If I may interject?" Doug Ramos, producer of *MD* raised his hand. "I think what Janice is trying to explain is that we need to co-ordinate anything you might want to say or do, so we're all talking from the same page." He looked around the room nodding. Everyone else nodded along with him. "As far as I am concerned," he continued, "there is no issue here; however, it would be foolish to assume that will be the case with the media, and because of that we will all be asked for our opinions."

"Agreed," the suit from the network added. "This network has always prided itself on our inclusivity of gay characters. We have promoted shows actively to include people from all walks of life so, for us this isn't an issue, but...I would be lying if I said that any negative impact from the press, and therefore the audience, wouldn't have a similar impact on your continued participation of the project."

Michelle listened to them speak. She had a great respect for Doug, he was gay himself, but since he was behind the camera, nobody seemed to care about that. She knew, however, that for her it would be different! For her, it would be exactly what the suit had just explained.

"First of all, I want to say on a personal level how happy I am for you both and that I fully support you and your decision today. So, how do you want to play this?" Doug smiled at her like a proud father.

"Well, I...We..." She looked towards Cam and smiled. "...have no intention of making an announcement, we plan to just be ourselves and if someone wants to write about it then let them, we would prefer that if asked for your opinions on it that everyone sings from the same songbook with an 'it's not my business' kinda reply. We understand that there will be things said and written about us, but we don't intend to add any flames to the fire. We don't want to make this issue any bigger than it needs to be."

"With all due respect." One of the PR suits sat forward to speak. "I think you could be missing out on some great publicity here!"

"I don't want the publicity and I certainly don't want Cam to have to suffer any more than she undoubtedly will."

"But Ms Hamlin if I can just—" This time Cam cut him off.

"I think you just had your answer. I have told Michelle that I am happy to do whatever she needs me to do, but I won't allow you or anyone in this room to bully her into changing her mind or doing something she isn't comfortable with."

Michelle took her hand and smiled affectionately at her, grateful for her support. It wasn't that Michelle was intimidated by anyone in this room, but they had a way of wearing you down and making you see things from their point of view, and she really didn't want to spend her day being exhausted by these people.

"When the time comes, I will be happy to do interviews if they are going to be done in the right way. I just don't think this is a big deal, or at least it shouldn't be, and if I make an announcement or treat it as something out of the ordinary then I'm telling the world that what we feel for each other needs explaining, and it doesn't, it really doesn't. We love each other, that's all there is to it, and if people don't like that then that's their issue, not ours!"

"Ok, can I take it that Cam will be your date on Saturday at the World Health Day event?" Janice asked, moving the conversation along. She had to admire Hamlin's stance even if it was going to be a pain in her ass to keep on top of. Hollywood wasn't in charge of this.

"Yes!" Michelle smiled widely. The thought of walking down a red carpet with her beautiful girlfriend by her side was extremely exciting to her and a little arousing. She imagined them both in long flowing dresses. Cam's hair would be up, and she would look so beautiful.

"We need to make sure you're both seen together in public for the first time looking hot to fucking trot," announced Janice. "So, yes you will be using Shawn here." She pointed at the stylist. "I don't care what you're wearing, just make sure it shouts sexy, hot, and happy."

"You're going to make me wear a dress, aren't you?" Cam said, a look of horror on her face at the thought of what kind outfit they would force her into.

Michelle laughed. "Only if you want to, but I think you would look really hot in a dress."

"I'll look like a man in drag!" Cam cried. "Seriously, I will not be comfortable."

"Ok. Ok princess, let's worry about that later, right now I need to go through a few things with these guys, so for now you can get lost and take Shawn with you." Janice chuckled and indicated the room was far more important than they were right now.

They both stood to leave, Shawn following. When they reached the lobby of the building, ready to exit into the world again, Michelle grabbed Cam's hand and said, "Ready?" Cam nodded and smiled.

"Never been more ready in my life!"

They walked out onto the street. Cam put her arm around Michelle and pulled her into her, kissing her hairline. People looked their way, but no one said a word to them. When they reached the car, Cam asked, "What do you want to do now?"

"I do know that I'm not ready to go home yet. I feel free Cam. I just want to do everything!" she laughed. "Does that sound silly?"

"Nope, sounds pretty good to me. Want to go and show me off?" She winked playfully with a sinful smirk.

"Hell yes!!" Michelle jumped around like an excited kid. The blonde laughed at her antics. It was sweet and real.

"I know just the place," Cam said, jumping into the Ferrari.

Chapter Four

It was obvious to Michelle where they were headed to as soon as Cam swung the car left at the lights and the ocean came into view: the same place they had enjoyed that very first date, that date that wasn't a date.

Cam parked in one of the hotel parking garages and they crossed the busy street hand in hand. The pier loomed out in front of them, cocooned with an uncountable number of people walking back and forth, left and right. It was a cacophony of noise as musicians took turns to hit a beat and advertise their talents, selling copies of homemade CDs to anyone who wanted one. There were kids on wheels of every kind: skateboards and rollers, cycles, and contraptions Cam had never seen before arriving in LA. It was vibrant, and they could blend in and mooch about just like any other tourist in Santa Monica.

Cam considered how different it was to be out in the daylight this time walking along Venice Beach with Shelly Hamlin by her side. Now people were looking, trying to decide if she really was the person they thought she was. Gone was the sunhat that she hid beneath on that first date. She still wore the sunglasses but hey, so did everyone else. It was a bright and beautiful day in LA, as usual, and heads turned.

"Hey, Shelly, hey can I get a picture?" A young woman called out exuberantly. She looked to be about 17; all hip and trendy, hanging with her friends who all looked just like she did, but in their own unique way. At first Michelle didn't hear her above all the other noise, but Cam did and made her aware of it.

"You ok?" she checked, searching her face for any sign that she had changed her mind.

"Yes, absolutely." She kissed Cam firmly on the lips before turning to the fan and becoming Shelly Hamlin in an instant. "Hi, how are you?" Michelle asked the girl as she posed for pics with her and her friends. It fascinated Cam to watch her when it happened. The two characters were not that much different, but she noticed the subtle changes: the larger-than-life character eclipsing the more private one, opening herself up and allowing her public to adore her.

"Wow, I can't believe it's really you! You're my favourite character on *Medical Diaries*," the kid gushed, her cheeks blushing instantly.

"Oh well I'm glad to hear it." Michelle laughed and signed her name across a random piece of paper the kid had dug out from her purse. She loved this part of the job: meeting the fans and getting to hear what they thought of her performance and the projects she was involved with. A small crowd had gathered as other people began to notice and wonder who it was that was so interesting.

"Is this your girlfriend? I didn't know you were gay," The teenager asked brazenly like only a teenager could do: without judgement or accusation, just a request for information.

"Uh yeah, yes she is," she replied, smiling at Cam, who looked about as proud as any person could be when her girlfriend just announced to the world who she was.

"Cool! You look great together," the fan enthused once more. She really was excited to meet Shelly, and for Cam it was a real insight into Michelle's world.

"Thank you, I think so too," she laughed, "Anyway, we have to get going now, so you have a great day and enjoy the rest of Venice."

"Thanks Shelly, you too."

The fans wandered off screaming and jostling with each other in their excitement at meeting a star on a day at the beach. The women watched them go and the crowd dispersed, but some lingered, taking photos on their iPhones, nudging one another at the commotion.

"Well, that went well," Cam said as she wrapped her arms around Michelle's waist and swung her around. When she came to a halt, Michelle placed her arms around Cam's neck.

"It did. Oh my God, can you believe it?" She kissed her once more. She could do this. She could actually touch and kiss her lover and just be herself.

"Ya know if we keep walking along this road, we can be at the yacht in a few minutes." Cam suggested with a wink.

"The yacht huh?"

"Yes, the one I own, remember? With the bed, the big comfortable bed." She winked and drew her tongue across her bottom lip.

"Oh *that* yacht, with the bed? Only you and I onboard along with the big bed?"

"Indeed so, can I interest my gorgeous girlfriend in spending the next few hours naked with me in the big bed?" she asked, grabbing her hands and leading her backwards toward the marina.

Michelle answered with a kiss that said, 'you can have me naked anywhere you like'.

Chapter Five

Having dressed and showered, Cam stepped out onto the deck to find Michelle already sitting on a sofa, legs tucked underneath her as she usually did. Chewing a thumbnail, she glanced up at Cam but remained silent.

"Everything ok sweetheart?" Cam asked as she swaggered towards her lover with a bottle of champagne and two glasses. "Michelle? What's wrong?" Watery eyes glistened in the late afternoon sun as they looked up. "Baby? What is it?" She moved toward her, placing the bottle and glasses on the deck next to her, dropping to her knees in an instant.

"Janice called me," she sniffed, "She said it's out." Cam frowned. Wasn't that what was supposed to happen? "Cam, I'm out." She smiled now. "It's all over social media already."

Cam pulled her own phone from her pocket and flicked open the Twitter app. Scrolling to search, she typed in 'Shelly Hamlin' and up came with hundreds of tweets that all seemed to stem from several sent by @PinkPocket two hours ago that said, *'Just met @realShellyHamlin and her GF on Venice beach! She is so beautiful'* and *'Yeah, like she's completely gay, met her GF too, both Hot!'*

The replies ranged from, *'Wow lucky you'* to *'OMG her GF is so lucky'* to the less-than-favourable, *'what? Hamlin's a fucking dyke? No way man, she is way too hot to be a beaver basher.'*

Cam chuckled. "Beaver basher?"

"I know, well, I knew not everyone was going to be excited about it."

Cam sat beside her, her arm snaking around her to hold her

closer. There were several tweets that could be considered offensive. Most, however, were positive and supportive of them, and Cam was relieved it wasn't that bad a reaction, so far.

"You're ok though, right?" she asked. Reaching down for the glasses, she passed one across to Michelle before filling both with the chilled bubbles.

She nodded. "Yeah, I'm good, these are happy tears." She laughed and slid happily against Cam's side.

~Next~

"I need to go see my parents, I can't tell them this on the phone," Michelle said quietly to Cam as they sat peacefully together watching the sun start to drop in the distance over Malibu and Santa Monica. "Or leave it and they find out from the papers."

"Where do they live?"

"Arizona, they moved there to be closer to me."

"Ok, we can fly out tomorrow then, but for now, let's go out to dinner," Cam said.

"Ok, where?"

"I can get us into Rafael's," Cam said, referring to the latest premier Beverly Hills restaurant with the longest waiting list for a table. It was renowned for its celebrity appeal and audacious menu, not to mention it was pricey, but the reviews were outstanding, and anyone who was anyone wanted to go there.

"At this short notice?"

Cam nodded. "I'm on the list."

"The list?"

"Uh huh. The List! You're not on the list?" Cam asked, dumfounded, mischief in her eyes as they locked together with Michelle's.

"I never knew there was a list." Michelle was incredulous; she had never even bothered to try and get a table there simply because she knew how difficult it was to get in. Cam pulled out her phone and made the call as Michelle listened in, intrigued.

"Hi, this is Camryn Thomas...good thank you yes...I'd like a table for this evening if possible please." The person on the other end of the line was obviously speaking again while Cam listened, grinning. "Uh huh, that's perfect...Yes thank you." She winked at Michelle and gave a thumbs-up. The person on the other end said something else that Michelle couldn't hear, before Cam replied with, "No, that's not necessary. I'll have my own driver, but thank you. It will be just the two of us this evening." They spoke again, but just briefly this time. "Ok thank you, good day." Cam closed the phone off and smiled to Michelle. "Eight o'clock."

"That is so cool, I need to be on the 'list'."

Chapter Six

Gavin collected them at seven thirty and promptly delivered them to Rafael's. Climbing out of the car, Cam walked slightly behind Michelle, her hand placed protectively on the small of her back as she guided her up the steps and into the entrance of one of LA's finest eateries.

The maître d' welcomed them in with a huge smile and a few words in greeting. Fellow diners turned to observe the striking couple as they walked through the busy restaurant and took their seats. Michelle had chosen to wear a lavender pant suit with three-inch killer heels that for once allowed her to almost tower over Cam, and she looked stunning.

"I should own up. I know Pierre, the maître d'. I don't know if there really is a list," Cam laughed as they took their seats and got comfortable. It was one of the many things she could thank Amanda for. She had introduced Camryn to everyone who was anyone in this town, the doers and the people in the know. Cam's list of 'useful' people was quite extensive, and it worked well for her. Once Amanda had introduced her and, no doubt, let them know her worth, she found she had an 'in' anytime she needed one.

It didn't matter how much time had passed, she would always feel the guilt for the way things ended with Amanda.

"Oh, you had me fooled," Michelle giggled as she picked up the menu and began browsing. Her hand reached out and found its mate without either of them looking up. They ordered cocktails while they continued to browse the menu. Everything about the restaurant was beautifully done. Tables were neatly arranged to give a limited amount of privacy to guests, but it was still packed, and the sound of chatter as diners enjoyed their night out was a buzz. The menu offered a six-course taster option, and it seemed as though that was suitable to both of them. They picked a wine to go with each course and then spent an evening of absolute bliss. Occasionally, one or the other would glance up and catch someone staring at them, clearly wondering what they were witnessing. Michelle wondered if things could get any better as she looked across at the smiling face opposite her.

The meal was outstanding, the wine delicious, and the company exceptional. Cam couldn't think of a time she had been this happy or this comfortable with anyone, and it calmed her soul to know that Michelle felt the same way. They continued to hold hands and talked of things they wanted to do together in the coming weeks. Both knew that they wouldn't have this amount of time together for much longer. Work would get in the way soon enough for both of them. Cam had neglected the club for too long now, and Michelle was due to finish off this season of Medical Diaries and then go straight into filming a small part in a movie around Thanksgiving. She would then be in the studio leading right up to Christmas.

When they left the restaurant, before they had even reached the steps that took them down to the waiting car, a photographer popped up and snapped a few shots of them together.

Gavin had the door already open for them both, but Cam waited for Michelle to get in first before following her onto the back seat. Settled behind the safety of darkened windows, Michelle reached for Camryn.

"I guess we should have expected that," she said, looking back over her shoulder at the guy with the camera who was now focused on somebody else.

"Paparazzi? Yeah, I didn't even think about it to be honest. You ok?"

"I am, I am very clear on that Cam. I will take whatever the consequences are if it means I can be happy, with you."

~Next~

Passing the long queue of excited revelers all waiting to get into OUT and start enjoying the night ahead, they walked straight into the sound of the bass pumping loud. It never failed to get Cam in a good mood, nor did the loud cheers coming from Angie and Fran. "Well howdy stranger, decided to return to us I see, and ya brought Dimples with you too." It was Angie who spoke as Fran giggled.

'Dimples' smiled at Angie and Fran. "Hi, I'm Michelle, and you guys must be Fran and Angie, right?" she said, holding her hand out to one and then the other.

"That's right honey, I'm going to assume you and the boss here have been enjoying your time away?" Angie inquired.

"Nosey. Nosey. Nosey," said Cam, passing out the round of drinks she had just ordered at the bar. "Babe, will you be ok if I just pop upstairs and speak to Erin?"

"Sure Cam." She kissed her mouth just a little longer than was respectable. "Don't be long though sweetheart, I want to dance with you."

"Oh I won't," she said, unable not to kiss her once more. "I will be right back."

Angie and Fran both stared in disbelief; did Cam really just kiss Shelly Hamlin in full view of anyone who wanted to see? And she just kissed her right back!

"*So*," Fran spoke to Michelle, "how's things in the movie business?" It was a little surreal to them all still. Hanging out with a movie star was not something that just happened on a daily basis.

"Pretty slow right now thankfully, how's it been at the club with Cam gone?" She could tell just by looking around that everything was under control here with Erin in charge.

"Not the same, but Erin has done a great job, you guys hanging around tonight or…?" She let the question hang.

"Oh I think we're going to be hanging around, I feel like dancing." Michelle smiled, "Want another drink?" she asked, receiving nods all around.

Chapter Seven

Upstairs, Cam knocked on the office door and opened it. "Erin, hey."

"Cam, you're back. Good flight?" Cam blushed a little, which gave Erin her answer, but she let her off the hook and waited for the reply.

"Yes." She laughed, knowing full well Erin had read her like a book. "And I wanted to say thank you in person. I know we spoke on the phone but, what you did took balls and though I have some concerns with regards to my boundaries being breached quite so easily…I am grateful that you cared enough to want to help."

Erin sat back in her chair and contemplated everything Camryn just told her. Relief finally washed over her completely. Even with Cam's assurance not to fire her already, she still felt apprehensive about everything.

"Wow, the great Camryn Thomas brought back into the real world and all it took was a movie star." She chuckled. "Hey I'm glad for you both. You needed this, and I got a great car out of it."

"Yeah, so I heard." Cam laughed. She noted the hair colour had changed once again. Blue now. One day it would all fall out Cam had told her, but Erin didn't care.

"I'm glad you're happy Cam. Happy looks good on you…so now what?"

"Well, for now we are just enjoying each other, spending time together ya know. How's things been doing here while I was away?" Cam asked, sitting down in front of Erin's desk.

"Things are good Cam, no problems at all really. I had to let

Jenny go, she either didn't turn up or, when she did, she spent most of her time flirting with the guests. But, other than that profits are up on Saturdays since Jose started and the staff I did hire are working out well so far."

"Great, I never had any doubts Erin, that's why I left you in charge. Thank you," she said sincerely. She was just so grateful for all the people in her life right now. She had come a long way, and things were on the up. Life had never been better.

~Next~

Coming back downstairs, she expected to find her lover and both friends at the bar. They were nowhere to be seen. As she scanned the crowd however, she soon discovered exactly what they were all up to. All three were on the dancefloor. Michelle was bouncing and gyrating with the best of them as her arms moved in sync with her hips, waving high above her head. She was smiling like someone without a care in the world. She spotted Cam and wagged a 'come hither' finger in her direction. Without a thought, Cam started to move. Sauntering in rhythm, she moved between bodies until she found herself face to face with the brunette beauty she was head over heels in love with.

"Hey beautiful," she said with a shit-eating grin on her face, wrapping her arms around her waist and kissing her as the world around them whirled and spun. "Did I tell you just how much I love you today?" Michelle's arms moved to take their place around her lover's neck.

"No you did not." She smiled, knowing what was coming next.

"Oh that's very remiss of me." She kissed her neck. "I love you."

"I love you too gorgeous," Michelle replied, enjoying the kissing of her neck. "And I really want to dance with my girlfriend in a hot lesbian club with all the other hot lesbians."

"Oh, well who am I to deny your desires?" Cam grabbed her hand and began to spin her around. Watching her laugh and enjoy herself meant that Cam relaxed, and as people around them began to notice and understand what they were witnessing, she didn't care.

Their bodies melded as one. Fingers teased as kisses were shared. It was hot to watch and obvious to anyone who had recognised her that Shelly Hamlin was going home with Camryn for some hot action between the sheets that night.

Chapter Eight

Cam's cheeks were already smiling before she had even woken up fully. Memories of the previous night were still vivid in her mind's eye. Hours of dancing had turned into hours of love making and had left a delicious ache in her muscles as she had stretched out on her side of the bed before finally snuggling up against the naked body next to her.

"Wakey wakey sleepyhead," Cam whispered against Michelle's ear as the actress mumbled something unintelligible and pulled the cover up over her head. "Sweetheart. You gotta get up, we're going to see your parents, remember?" She sniggered at her lover's antics as she clambered out of the bed herself.

"Just another hour," Michelle pleaded from under the blanket.

"Nope, come on. The jet is waiting for us." Inch by inch she pulled the comforter until every part of her gloriously naked girlfriend was on display. It was an image that burned into Cam's memory as she pounced and began to tickle.

~Next~

In all the time that she had been in the States, Cam had never been out this way before, and she was intrigued with the beauty of it. It was rugged in many ways with its huge red rock formations, and the way the light played with the shadows was an artist's dream.

"Would you mind if I spoke to them by myself first?" Michelle asked Cam as she drove them out of the airport and onto the freeway.

"Of course not, drop me off in town at a coffee shop and I can wait for you there. How do you think they will react?"

Michelle considered the question; it was a valid one. "I'm really not sure. I never had to give it any thought before. They don't pester me about my love life." She checked left and right at the junction before pulling out and continuing her train of thought. "I would like to think that as long as I'm happy they will be happy but, they come from a different generation and grew up in a different environment than we did so, who knows?"

"Then let's think positive and hope for the best, eh?" Cam said, giving Michelle's thigh a comforting squeeze as she pulled onto the side of the road to let Camryn climb out. "I'll be here waiting, ok?"

~Next~

Michelle's parents' home was modest compared to her own. She had offered to buy them a house anywhere they chose, but they wouldn't hear of it; they were very happy with what they had in life. Their daughter being rich and famous was wonderful, for Michelle, but it wasn't about them and they wouldn't be found holding their hands out to her.

Walking up to the huge oak door, she was greeted before she could even ring the bell. "Oh my goodness! Michelle baby, what are you doing here? Why didn't you tell us you were coming?" She was grabbed by the shoulders and pulled into a real motherly hug as the questions kept coming. Her mother, the image of what Michelle would look like in thirty years.

"Hey Mom, is Dad home too?"

"Of course, where else would the old coot be?" she chuckled. "Bob, Bob, get in here, Michelle's come to see us," she hollered out to her husband in the yard.

Bob Hamilton was tall and solid for a man in his early sixties, and his long strides brought him into the house in seconds. He hugged his daughter like his wife had just done: with vigour. "Good to see you Pumpkin, it's been far too long."

"Yes, Daddy, it has, and I'm sorry about that...things have been a little hectic lately," she explained, smiling at her expectant parents. It was good to see them, but still she couldn't quite quieten the nerves that tumbled within her.

"Well, it doesn't matter; you're here now. How long are you staying for?" He looked around her and noticed the lack of baggage. Their daughter didn't visit often, but when she did it was with more bags than would ever be needed. "Bags still in the car?"

"No, not this time Dad, I can only stay for a few hours; we have a jet waiting to take me back. I uh, I need to talk to you both."

"What's wrong?" her mother interjected, worried. Her mother tended to find the negative before she found the positive in anything, and she was pretty good at picking up on Michelle's moods.

"Nothing is wrong mom, in fact quite the opposite." She tried to smile and watched as her mother's eyes widened knowingly.

"You're pregnant? I didn't know you were even dating anyone! Is it Tom's? Such a nice boy." Her mother rambled on with questions that had Michelle wondering how on Earth she had come to *that* conclusion. "Where is he?"

"No, no Mom, I'm not pregnant...please, I need to tell you something and I need you to promise you will let me finish before you say anything," she implored gently, guiding her mother to the couch.

"Go on Pumpkin, you know you can tell us anything," her father said, throwing his wife a warning glare to be quiet and let their child speak. He sat on the arm of the sofa beside his wife and held his daughter's gaze.

"Thanks Dad. Well...I don't really know where to start so I'm just going to say it, ok?" She looked to them both. "I...Ok, I have met someone, that is part of it, yes, but what I need to tell you is that I...well, the person I've met...is a woman." Both of her parents sat in front of her in silence, just staring. She let them digest the information for a few moments more. It was a lot to take in, she understood that. It wasn't as if they had had any clue from a past liaison or any rumours. She had done nothing in her life to give them even the tiniest inkling that she would fall in love with a woman.

The silence was louder than any noise she had ever heard. She gave in. "Please say something, anything."

"Do you love her? I mean…this…it's not just a phase or some weird thing that everyone in Hollywood is doing?" her father asked her seriously. He had seen plenty of fads come and go with the people his daughter mixed with and so nothing would surprise him anymore.

"I do, I love her very much…Her name is Camryn, or Cam." Her mother was still yet to speak, so she continued talking about Cam, hoping that if she could just bring her to life with description then her parents would fall in love with her just as easily as she had. "She's British and she's the nicest, kindest person I've ever met and she loves me. She is sincere and honest, she's funny and gorgeous…" She waited but still there was nothing coming from either of her parents. "Mom?"

"I…I'm…, I don't really know what to say Michelle. I can't say that I'm shocked, that would be a lie. You never have shown any real interest in anyone you've dated before. I just…I never assumed it was because you were a lesbian." Michelle cringed internally at hearing her mother label her. She was still finding it a little difficult when other people pigeonholed her – not that she was ashamed, but because it was just so unnecessary. What did it matter? "I…I'm going to just need a little while to process it all Michelle," she said honestly. "Are we going to meet her?"

"Yes." Her eyes lit up at the thought of Camryn. "She's in town waiting for me. I wanted to make sure that when I spoke to you first it was just me, I didn't think it would be fair on you or her to just spring her on you."

"Then I suggest you go and get her and introduce us," her mother said calmly, much to Michelle's relief. At least she wasn't being banished just yet!

Chapter Nine

Cam was half way through a café latte and reading her Kindle when the car they had hired pulled up outside and parked. She watched Michelle enter the shop and, glancing at her watch, she worried that it hadn't been very long. *I hope this has gone well.*

"Everything go ok?" she asked, tentatively. She placed her cup back down on the table in front of her, the electronic book dropping to her lap as Michelle bent at the waist to kiss her.

"Hmm not sure, I think so. I mean they didn't throw me out or shout or anything." Cam reached out to take her hand, and Michelle felt the calmness enter her being in an instant.

"Ok, what next then?"

"They want to meet you," she said simply. Her shoulders shrugged and then sagged a little.

"Ok, I'm good with that." Cam smiled, boosting her confidence. "Would you like a coffee first, or shall we just go?"

She was feeling a little nauseous. "Finish your coffee, but I don't want one." All she wanted was for her parents to see this woman the way she did, well not quite that way, but to see all the things that meant this was the best relationship she had ever been involved in. She was risking everything to be with Camryn because she loved her, but she couldn't deny that it would be a huge heartache to have her parents turn their back on her over it.

~Next~

Michelle parked on her parents' drive and took Cam's hand in her own. Turning in her seat, she found herself lost in blue eyes that held her gaze with adoration.

"I love you," Cam whispered. "No matter what they say today, we will be ok and they will either like me or they won't. I'm a big girl, I can deal with it. So, try not to worry ok?" Michelle nodded and their lips met briefly before parting too soon. "I'll be right by your side. Come on," Cam urged. Opening the door to the car, she jumped out. While Michelle wasn't looking, she blew out a breath and composed herself, prepared herself for whichever reaction she got from Mr and Mrs Hamilton.

They found her father sitting in his favourite armchair and her mother hovering around him, tidying things and wiping at imaginary dust. Her mother always did like to clean when she had something on her mind. Hand in hand, they stood together as Michelle introduced her.

"Mom, Dad, this is Camryn Thomas. Cam, my parents."

"Hello, it's lovely to meet you Mr Hamilton, Mrs Hamilton." She reached out her hand to shake. Michelle's father took it immediately and her mother followed suit, but Cam was definitely aware of the glare.

"Please take a seat, and it's Bob," her father offered, using his hand to point towards a spot on the sofa for them both. The room was cosy and cool, a nice balance to the dry heat that rained down outside. Cam had been to the desert a few times and was always amazed at the heat; it was unbearable, and she wondered why people chose to live in places this hot. Looking around the room she could see that Michelle and her brother were the highlight of their parent's lives. Photographs lined the sideboards and walls. Posters from Michelle's films were framed and hung proudly. This was a good family with love in its heart, and it gave Cam hope that maybe she would be invited into it willingly.

"Ok, thank you Bob." She wanted to make sure she impressed these people and let them know that she loved their daughter. Manners were the start.

"So, how did you meet?" he asked Cam, smiling at her warmly. There was a jug of lemonade on the table with four glasses. He picked up the jug and began to pour, a silent question of whether she would like one or not. She nodded her assent and reached for the glass.

"Thank you." She remembered he had asked her a question. "In a club actually, I was working." She returned the smile and took a sip. Homemade and slightly tart. She liked it.

They spent a few moments chit chatting about general things like where she was from, what Michelle's next project was, and how Bob's golf swing was coming along. Getting to know each other a little whilst sticking to safer topics was pretty much how the afternoon was panning out, and it suited Michelle just fine. She had just begun to relax, finally feeling a little at ease with how her parents were reacting, when her mother found the target.

"Are you with my daughter for her money?" An intense stare at Camryn reminded her very much of Michelle. She looked a lot like her mother. They were both tall and lean, and she had the same dark hair and olive skin. But her eyes were green; Michelle got her darker eyes from her father.

"Mother, really?" Michelle shouted. "I can't believe you would even ask that!"

Cam touched her arm and spoke gently, stopping her in her tracks before her anger with her mother grew any more. "It's ok." There was nothing to hide. She took a moment to consider her reply. She had the opportunity now to maybe take the upper hand, because nobody in this room was expecting to hear what she was about to throw at them. Even Michelle had no real idea. So, she turned to Mrs Hamilton and spoke directly to her. "Mrs Hamilton, the simple answer is no, I am not with Michelle for her money. Maybe she is with me for mine!" Cam smiled, trying to ease the tension just a little bit.

"What is that supposed to mean? She's a movie star, she earns a lot of money," her mother continued, a little bit peeved at the nonchalant attitude towards Michelle's wealth from this wandering tourist.

"I guess that's true. To be honest, I have no idea what Michelle earns. She hasn't told me and I haven't asked. However, I do have my own money and I—" She was cut off again, this time by Bob.

"I think my wife makes a valid, if impolite, point. We never had to worry when she dated people in the business, but this is a somewhat different circumstance, you said you met in the bar you work in?"

Cam calmly turned her attention to Michelle's father. "Sir, if you will allow me to finish?" He nodded at her to continue. Michelle sat silently seething beside her, but she smiled a little when her father mentioned working in the bar. "As I was saying, I couldn't give you an exact figure, but my own worth is most definitely over a hundred..." She was cut off from her monologue once more, Michelle's mother again.

"A hundred thousand dollars is not really on a par with our daughter, now is it?" Mrs Hamilton jumped back in again, scornful and full of disdain. It was a substantial amount of course, but her daughter was earning that per episode on *Medical Diaries*. She made more than that every time she advertised something. Michelle was a wealthy woman, and Martha Hamilton wasn't going to just sit back and let anyone walk into her life and sweep her off her feet.

Cam took a deep breath and reminded herself that they only had Michelle's best interest at heart, but she really was trying very hard to not be annoyed by the constant interruptions. She wouldn't allow herself to become irritated by it; she would be everything Michelle needed her to be, to show them that she really was worthy of their daughter.

"Million." She spoke quietly and stared at the floor, waiting for their reaction. It came quite quickly, and she stifled the smirk that threatened to race across her face. If this was the one time she had to use her wealth to win someone over, then so be it.

"Sorry? What did you say?" Bob said incredulously. He looked at the blonde woman sitting opposite him and contemplated the idea that she was a millionaire. She didn't look like a millionaire; she didn't look like someone with money at all at first glance. But now, as he studied her some more, he could see where they had gone wrong. The watch for one, he was pretty sure that was a Rolex. Her clothes fit her perfectly; they might look like off-the-peg items, but he had been watching his daughter dress for years and even he could tell made-to-measure clothing. But it was her demeanour more than anything, the way she held herself with all the confidence in the world. She wasn't fazed by any of it. She took everything in her stride, clearly someone who was used to getting what she wanted.

Michelle twisted in her seat to face her, squinting as she too tried to decipher what Camryn had just said. Cam just nodded at her; she had heard correctly, but just to be clear she confirmed it. "My net worth, it's over one hundred million…" She was no gold digger and she needed these people to understand that money had nothing to do with this relationship.

"Dollars!" exclaimed Michelle's mother.

"No."

All three heads spun to look at her quizzically as they all spoke in unison. "No?"

"No, not dollars. One hundred million pounds." She spelled it out. "I don't want or need Michelle for her money. The one thing I have more than enough of, is money." They all sat in silence for a minute as Cam let it all sink in. They could hate her for many reasons, but being a gold digger wasn't going to be one of them. "So, as I said, I can get you an exact figure if you want it, but it might take a few hours for my accountant to work it out. I assume it's around

130 million dollars if it helps or makes a difference." She sat back in her seat and took another sip of her lemonade. It seemed something as crass as her fortune was going to be the winner today. "I won the European lottery. I have used that money to my advantage and spent it wisely on ventures that have helped to grow my bank balance and my portfolio. I own several businesses. I met your daughter in a club, that's correct. It's my club, I own it along with its sister club back in London. I have a lot of other investments that I can get you the details of if you really need me to, but I leave my broker to deal with most of that." She took another sip of her drink and gave them the opportunity to ask any questions. They remained quiet and so she continued. "I own a lot of property. Other than my beach house in Malibu I own apartments in Paris and Milan, villas in Greece and Spain, and a penthouse on the Thames in London. I own a yacht! It's moored at the marina in LA. I have several fast cars and a motorbike. I'm a shareholder in a winery. I considered buying a jet, but well, to be honest, it just wasn't worth the hassle." She took a breath and waited to allow all of that information to sink in. All three of them still sat in complete silence, so she continued again. "I'm in love with Michelle because *she* is a beautiful human being that enriches my life in ways I cannot buy. Because *we* have a connection that doesn't need quantifying and because when I am with her life is better, *she* makes everything better." A light blush crept up her neck as she finished her speech and chanced a glance at Michelle, who was smiling at her like an idiot in love.

"Camryn, I'm so sorry, I think my parents have forgotten the morals they embedded in me as a child," Michelle said, quickly glaring at her parents to apologise right this minute.

"Yes, I'm sorry Camryn, that was out of line for me to pry," Michelle's mother said sorrowfully. "And it's Martha, not Mrs Hamilton."

Cam smiled tightly. She wanted to be angry and annoyed, she should be, but they were just being good parents. Caring about their child the way a mother should, sticking up for her and defending her.

There was a tiny piece of Cam that was jealous about that.

"It's perfectly okay."

"It's not ok! Mom, I love Camryn. I don't care if she has money or not, we haven't even discussed that! I can't believe you would even ask!"

"I'm sorry Camryn," Martha reiterated. The truth in her eyes told how sorry she was.

"Its fine, it really is, it would be something we needed to discuss at some point anyway." She felt Michelle's hand slip softly into her own.

"Maybe so, but not like this," Michelle concurred.

"You didn't know?" Bob asked.

"No! And I have never asked," Michelle added, her eyes hardened. "And I'm not asking for your permission to do this. I'm telling you because you are my parents and I love you and I want you to love the person I love. But if you can't support this...us, then I'll just have to accept that," Michelle said sadly, her grip on Cam's hand tightening.

Her parents looked suitably told off. It had been so much easier with their son Robbie; he had met his wife Jennifer while at college and they had been inseparable ever since. He had a normal career in sports psychology, and his life had always revolved around his family, whereas Michelle had never shown any real interest in settling down with anyone. She hadn't seemed that interested in dating at all, everything had always been about work, and yet here she was sitting in their living room effortlessly describing how in love she was with another person. A woman yes, but that didn't matter so much; it was just so out of character, and Martha wanted to make sure her baby was ok.

"There will probably be some interest in the media. Michelle wanted to make sure you had the heads up on that, so you wouldn't be blindsided by articles or reporters," Cam explained, trying to relieve the tension between them all.

They only had a few hours, and Bob made the decision that for today they would spend those precious moments enjoying each other, Camryn included. When it was time to leave, it felt to Camryn as though they might have turned a corner.

"Mom, Dad, we have to get going, but maybe you can come and visit soon?" Michelle smiled at them both. The visit wasn't long enough.

"Why don't you both come over for Thanksgiving? It's just a few weeks away, it would be lovely to have you...both," her mother made clear.

"I'll let ya know Mom, I am filming around that time so it will all depend on if I am on set or location." They hugged, and Martha held on for just a little longer than she might normally have.

"Michelle?"

"Yeah Mom?"

"No matter what happens, we will always love you. It might take us some time but we will support you, you're our child always," her mother said to her as Cam looked on. For another microsecond she was jealous. Here were a mother and father who loved their child regardless of anything she told them. Even if they couldn't understand it, they understood their love for their child, and that was all that mattered. Her own parents had been unable to do that, and it burned a little.

"Thanks Mom, I love you too."

~Next~

Outside in the car, Michelle sat silently for a moment as Cam fumbled about putting the key in the ignition, but she didn't move to drive away. It had been an odd kind of day, and they both needed a moment to process things.

"Well, I thought that went well," Cam finally said, a smile threatening to grace her lips. She turned slowly to her right hoping to find Michelle equally as amused. She still wasn't quite sure if Michelle's parents had taken to her or not, but things were at least civil.

"130 million? You won 130 million dollars?"

Cam laughed at her reaction as she pulled the vehicle off the drive and pointed them in the direction of the airport and the waiting jet. "Something like that." She smirked; she still didn't like discussing things like her wealth, but it had been pretty satisfying to see the look on Michelle's mom's face when she gave her all the details.

"Fuck."

Chapter Ten

When it finally came around, Saturday was a blur of hairdressers, facials, and every other bodily pampering that Cam had ever heard of. She had never been so indulged in her entire life! And Shawn had come up trumps too. He had arrived at Michelle's place with two dress bags, one for Cam and one for Michelle. Cam was dreading it, but Shawn hadn't let her down. He uncovered a classic white Armani tuxedo pant suit. The trousers fit perfectly, clinging in all the right places, accentuating her long legs and, according to Michelle, '*her firm butt*'. The jacket, she discovered, was to be worn with *nothing* underneath it and was open from the neck, all the way down to the valley between her breasts. He set it all off with some fancy bling and black pumps. Cam had to admit, she looked sexy in this outfit, even if she did feel completely out of her comfort zone. However, the fact that Michelle could barely keep her hands off her only emphasised the point that she did look good.

Michelle, on the other hand, was dressed to equal her in the sexy stakes. She wore a long and sleek black ankle-length sleeveless gown that split down from her chest to her belly button and then split again from just below the crotch to the floor! Set off with 3-inch heels, she looked like an Amazonian. Her hair was pulled up into a simple ponytail, giving the illusion of an elongated neck. She looked stunning. Yin and yang in perfect harmony with each other.

"You look amazing. You do know that, right?" Cam spoke in hushed tones. These were the moments when she really did have to ask herself how she ever got this lucky. The woman in front of her was just stunning.

"Thank you," she replied. Taking a step closer to her lover, she placed her palms on her shoulders and slid them down slowly to rest on her chest, her eyes following her hands. "You look quite amazing yourself!"

"Hmm, I scrub up ok, I guess." She leant forward and kissed her cheek, not daring to mess with her lipstick. "You sure you wanna do this with me?"

"More sure than I have ever been of anything. Look at you!" Michelle took a step backward and looked her over once more. "You are gorgeous Camryn." The blonde blushed, but accepted the compliment and held out her arm.

"Let's go then."

They looked amazing individually; together they looked stunning. The car had arrived and they were at the venue in no time. Cam had barely become comfortable in her seat when it pulled up and the door was opened for them. As she was about to climb out, Michelle pulled her back quickly and kissed her lightly on the cheek.

"It's going to be fine," she said, instantly wiping the lipstick mark away with her thumb. Cam nodded with a nervous smile and a deep breath. She had never done anything like this before, but for Michelle she would put her own fears and nerves on the back burner and do or say whatever she needed her to.

Cameras flashed. With Michelle leading the way as they walked the red carpet, her happiness was evident for all to see. It gave Cam immense pride to be the one standing by her side, hand in hand with her. Coming to a halt, Cam realised they had reached the bank of photographers. She stopped and stood casually, one hand in her pocket, trying her best to look confident and happy to be there. Michelle could feel the tension emanating from her and leant in, whispering against her ear, "Just smile and look in the direction they call me from."

At least fifty photographers stood in front of her. It was something Cam never expected to see in her life. The contorted faces behind the continuous flashing called out for Michelle to look this way and that. She gripped Cam's hand harder and stroked her thumb over the back of it, letting her know she wasn't alone.

Some of the reporters shouted questions, one of which Cam was sure was, 'is this your girlfriend?' and there were several requests for them to kiss. The women both ignored the questions, smiled, and moved on when the next celebrity arrived.

"Jesus that was intense." Cam gasped in relief and grabbed two glasses of something fizzy as the waiter passed her. "How do you deal with that?"

"You did great," Michelle said, taking one of the glasses from her. "Let's go and mingle and then we can get out of here and go home," she whispered seductively.

Inside the party, Michelle was instantly set upon by some of her fellow actors. Cam never really understood the whole glitz and glamour of Hollywood until now. Any party she had been to, no matter how upscale the address had been, was nothing compared with this.

"So, it's true!" a woman in a short red dress screamed in delight, clapping her hands together like a burgundy-clad seal. "I can't believe you didn't say anything." Michelle had been filming on *Medical Diaries* with both of these women all week. There had been the paparazzi pictures already printed and so rumours were already rife, but she had held back from making any announcements.

"I couldn't believe it when I heard but oh wow, you two look just great together," said the woman in the blue dress giving Camryn the once over. Michelle laughed, and Cam smiled like the cat that got the cream this time, but she had no idea who these women were.

"Cam, this is Pamela Michaels." She nodded to Red Dress Woman. "And Margo Hunter," she added as she acknowledged Blue Dress Lady. "Ladies, this is Camryn Thomas, my partner."

"Hi, lovely to meet you both," Cam said confidently as she

shook each woman's hand.

"So, how did you meet?" "We want all the details," they said at the same time. Raucous laughter ensued and Cam decided that now might be just the perfect time to escape. Let Michelle enjoy telling her friends their love story.

"Uh, I'm going to go and find some proper drinks while you tell these lovely ladies what they want to know." Cam winked at her before leaning in and whispering with a smile, "You can keep some of the details to yourself though, huh?"

Moving through the crowds and making her way to the bar, Cam couldn't help but overhear a conversation being had by three good-looking guys that she didn't recognise. They stood in a huddle discussing Michelle and the '*hot piece of ass*' that she had shown up with. She slowed up and listened in as they got straight to the point.

"Did you hear that Shelly Hamlin has gone gay for some dyke?" Blondie said to the group, puffing up his chest as though he were someone more important than the rest. The wine glass in his hand looked oddly out of place, his fist far too big to hold it gracefully.

"I know but fuck, did you see her? I'd flip too, I bet they're hot together." Chiselled laughed along with the others. She rolled her eyes but moved a little closer; she didn't want to miss the good bit. "I just wanted to pop that button open." Her fingers instinctively moved to the button of her jacket, checking it was still in place.

"I know one thing, a threesome would be awesome," Blondie replied again, still laughing and preening like a cock on heat. Cam couldn't ignore it any longer. Coughing gently, she got their attention. Chiselled spun around first, his cheeks at least having the decency to blush. Realising instantly who she was and what she had just overheard, he nudged his pals.

"Ya know I'm pretty sure had I not just heard your disgusting, sexist, and quite frankly vulgar description of two women that are in a loving relationship, I'd still guarantee that neither of us would be interested in a threesome with any of you. Now, if being in a threesome is so intriguing to you all, I suggest you learn to count..." She pointed at each of them as she spoke. "One, two. Oh look, three. Go fuck yourselves huh!" Turning to walk away with a smug smile on her face, she walked straight into Michelle.

"Oh, hi there." The smiled dropped from her face in an instant. Causing a scene had not been her intention, but she couldn't just stand by and listen to these morons talking such trash about them.

"I wondered what was taking you so long."

"I'm sorry, I got a little distracted along the way." She glanced back at the men who stood there sheepishly gawping at each other.

"So I see." She glared at them and smiled as they one by one turned with their tails between their legs and walked away. "Did you know just how fucking arousing it is to watch you defend my honour like that?" She fingered the lapel of Cam's jacket slowly.

"Uh well..." She swallowed, her mouth suddenly dry.

"Indeed." She leant in really close to make sure nobody else heard her. "It makes me really hot hearing you tell those assholes where to go."

"I see." Cam drew a deep breath. "Well, in that case I do hope I will be the beneficiary at some point this evening."

"Oh, you can count on it," she said as she kissed the blonde's earlobe and walked away. It took Cam a few seconds to regain her self-control. Spinning to follow, she watched as the most perfect rear sashayed away from her. *Holy hell, she is going to be the death of me.*

Chapter Eleven

The evening was going well. Cam had met a lot of people that Michelle knew from work and other charitable events. They were the couple everybody wanted to talk to, mainly to get the gossip and find out if it really was true that Shelly Hamlin had gotten herself a lesbian lover and was happily flaunting it. It was nice to be a part of Michelle's world for a little while, to gain a better understanding of what she did, who she was when she went to work; but she wouldn't be unhappy to finally get out of there, which she hoped would be soon by the look on Michelle's face.

"Meet me in the bathroom in two minutes," Michelle whispered to Cam as she passed. Placing her empty glass on a nearby table, she sauntered off knowing full well that her blonde lover was watching.

Cam swallowed down her drink, excused herself from the conversation she was having with one of the many women she had been introduced to earlier, and decided it was probably going to be in her best interest to just do as she was instructed.

A woman stood at the sink washing her hands, but otherwise the bathroom was all but empty. Cam smiled at her through the mirror's reflection as she passed. With five cubicles to choose from, it wasn't difficult to work out which one Michelle was waiting inside. She tapped gently with her knuckles on the only door that appeared to be locked. The sound of the lock sliding across was the only noise before the door opened. She was eye to eye with dark pools intently laid upon her, desire evident. Without a word, Michelle grabbed Cam's hand and pulled her inside the cubicle with her.

"Do I need to tell you what I need?" She spoke urgently in a whisper.

This dress, Cam decided, was perfection. The actress was already way ahead of her as she guided her lover's fingers to part the skirt, revealing a lack of underwear. She smirked at the realisation on her lover's face as Camryn's deft fingers stroked lightly back and forth.

"We don't have time for romance Camryn! Fuck me!" she hissed in a half whisper that had Cam's knees almost giving way.

Her fingers engaged the depths of her lover. Hearing Michelle whimper as her climax began to build in this illicit connection was beyond exciting. She held her gaze intently as she drove into her hard and fast, following the instructions to the letter. At the sound of the bathroom door opening, click clacking of heels nearing, Cam's mouth engulfed Michelle's, absorbing her moans and whimpers until her head was thrown back in a silent scream, her body releasing the pent-up tension she had been holding onto from the moment Cam had stepped into that suit.

"I'll be outside, you might wanna...clean up a little." Cam smirked as she left the cubicle. She stopped to wash her hands at the sink, smiling through the mirror at the latest woman to enter the small room, and then left the bathroom feeling like she could take on the world!

~Next~

The bar was a beautiful white countertop, stocked with almost every beverage you could ask for. Cam had ordered a vodka with lime and soda for herself and glass of white chardonnay for Michelle. She took a sip of her drink and savoured it; she needed to drink this more often, she reminded herself.

"Hello." A silky voice purred against her ear, sending a shiver down her spine. Turning slowly, she found a very attractive brunette standing next to her, smiling. The women took a long moment to look the blonde up and down; Cam had been undressed in somebody's bedroom in less time than it took this woman to divest her of metaphorical clothing.

"Uh, hi?" Cam almost stuttered. She didn't want to appear intimidated at all, but the way this woman was looking at her was quite unnerving. Not that she hadn't ever come across women who wanted to just devour her before; she had rarely turned them down either, but she hadn't expected it here.

"I'm sorry, I saw you standing here all by yourself and I thought I'd introduce myself." She held out her perfectly manicured hand. "Lisa Marconi." The name rang a bell, but Cam couldn't quite place it.

"Camryn Thomas." A lifetime ago and she would have been very interested in someone like Lisa Marconi. She was everything and more than most people dared to dream about. Slightly older than Cam was, but sexy as hell, and clearly interested. She was too late, of course. Cam had no interest in anyone else but Michelle, but that didn't mean she couldn't enjoy the attention.

"Camryn, such a beautiful name, it suits you well." She pronounced her name perfectly. It caught Cam's attention.

"Well I didn't get much say in it, my parents chose it." Her smile was warm as she glanced about the room for Michelle. *What was taking her so long?*

Laughing, Lisa added, "I have to say you look absolutely stunning in this suit, I almost want to devour you right here." Cam blushed and coughed slightly. This woman seriously had no shame, and Cam kind of had to admire that. What didn't help, however, was that she was aroused as hell after Michelle's little escapade in the bathroom.

"Well, I'm flattered of course. However, I'm with someone right now so…" she let it hang in the air. Lisa was not giving up just yet though. Her dark eyes swept back and forth between Camryn's blue eyes and her mouth as the tip of her tongue moistened her own lips.

"I'm sure that's something that we could work around, don't you think?" she said, trailing her finger down Cam's bare chest until she reached the point at which the first button held tight.

"I'm sure there are plenty of women out there that would be interested in working around anything to be with you," Cam replied, diplomacy the only way forward as she placed a hand on the lingering finger and stopped any further movement.

"But not you?" she asked, a little indignant, but the smile lingered. Clearly not a woman used to being told no.

"Not me, no."

"Damn, my gaydar isn't normally this off."

"Your gaydar is working just fine." Cam smirked. If she were single, this woman would be in a hotel room by now, but right now all she could think about was the other brunette in her line of sight.

"Then what is the problem, we could have a lot of fun you and I." The finger was back to trailing; her cheek this time.

"The problem is me!" Michelle stood just behind Lisa. She turned slowly at the voice.

"Shelly darling, how are you?" Lisa's attention instantly moved from Cam to Michelle. Cam awkwardly moved between the two women as they eyed one another.

"I am wonderful thank you Lisa, but you are wasting your time with Camryn." The brunettes stared at each other from their positions either side of the blonde.

"Oh darling, it could never be a waste of time with someone as handsome as this one is." She looked at Cam once again like she was going to devour her. Cam raised an eyebrow, a plea of help on her face that only brought forth a further smirk from Michelle.

"Very true my dear…which is why I'm fucking her!"

Lisa was momentarily speechless. "You're fucking her? Is that what you just said?"

"Yes, often and at *every* opportunity."

Cam smirked; she loved possessive Michelle. There was nothing sexier than the woman you loved staking her claim.

"Well aren't you the lucky one," Lisa whispered conspiratorially with a gentle chuckle. "Tell me, is she *everything* she looks to be?"

Cam was a little taken aback by this woman's candour, no better than the three guys she had told off earlier for their crude conversation, but the shock she felt when Michelle continued was doubled.

"Oh everything and more, I have *never* been so fulfilled in my entire life, and what she can do with her tongue…" Michelle's facial inflections told Lisa exactly what she could do with her tongue!

"Ok, ok that's quite enough thank you." Cam spoke urgently, her cheeks burning. Both women smiled at Cam before they both burst into laughter. Unsure as to what exactly was so funny, Cam waited them out.

"Oh Cam, I'm so sorry." Michelle was still laughing, though she had managed to get herself together enough to explain. "Lisa is a friend of mine from *Medical Diaries* and she loves to tease everyone, luckily for you she is happily married."

"Really?" Cam exclaimed. She took a sip of her drink and watched the two women as they flustered; unsure if they had gone too far. "So you think you're funny huh?" They both looked suitably ashamed of the prank. Cam could barely contain her own laughter. The bubble of giggles rattled up from somewhere deep and escaped in a rather high-spirited chuckle. "That was pretty mean, you do know I will be getting you back, right?"

Chapter Twelve

The party had ended with the same short limo ride back home, a ride that seemed to take much longer in reverse. They were slightly tipsy from the copious amounts of alcohol offered and accepted, but they were far from sleepy. Michelle had been fantasising about this very moment all evening. From the instant Cam had walked into the room in that suit, she had been envisaging taking it off of her, but over the course of the evening she had had a lot more ideas and most of them now included her staying dressed.

Barely through the door, Michelle made her move and, side-stepping the blonde, she found herself in the perfect position to press Cam back up against the wall, her lips ghosting over those in front of her.

"You get two choices," she whispered, her breath fluttering across Cam's lips as she spoke. The blonde listened intently. "I fuck you right here…or I do it upstairs."

Camryn smirked. If she was honest, she didn't care where they did it. She would push all of Michelle's boundaries if she could; every inhibition, every hang-up. "Here," she answered, trying to capture escaping lips that smiled mercilessly at her. Michelle had her body pinned, but she eased off a little.

"Undo all of the buttons," she urged, "but…leave it all on." She took another step backwards to watch as trembling fingers fiddled with the two buttons that held the jacket in place. When undone, Michelle stepped forward once more. Her palms moved easily to slide beneath the silk material and against the warmth of skin. She breathed easily as she explored the expanse of Camryn's shoulders and chest, exposing her breasts as she moved the jacket aside. "Now the other one." She gestured to the button on Cam's trousers as she stepped back once again, enjoying every moment of this self-control.

Never one to look a gift horse in the mouth, Camryn kept her gaze on the brunette and did as she was told, but she wouldn't be rushed. She watched Michelle become enthralled with her fingers slowly, teasingly unbuckling her belt, which made her more aroused than she thought possible. Michelle was taut, a loaded spring. Ready to pounce, but holding herself back until the perfect moment to seize the opportunity. "I know what you're doing," Michelle accused, her vision maintaining its vigil.

Cam chuckled to herself. "Yeah? What am I doing?"

"Making me wait." Michelle allowed her gaze to wander higher. Slowly her eyes lifted to fix on Cam's ice blues. "You can take as long as you want, but I *am* going to get what *I* want," she whispered. "Do you understand me Camryn?"

"Oh, I understand perfectly, sweetheart," she countered. The button popped and Michelle's eyes were drawn back down to the area she was so explicitly interested in. With her gaze firmly fixed, Michelle reached behind her and tugged gently on the hidden zip. There was a silence only broken by heavy breathing and zippers as Camryn teasingly dragged her own zip downward and slipped her hand inside the opening. In a second Michelle had shimmied out of her dress, the material nothing more than a heaped ring of black pooling on the floor behind her as she moved panther-like toward her prey, all underwear and high heels.

Cam leant nonchalantly, shoulders against the wall while her fingers slowly eased their way inside her open trousers. She wondered just how far Michelle would let her go. The answer came in an instant when lips crashed firmly against her own and her jacket was dragged off her shoulders and down her arms, acting like cuffs as her hand was hauled unceremoniously away from the prize that Michelle clearly, greedily wanted all to herself. She didn't have to wait long before she felt deft fingers slide between her folds and begin to manipulate her in the most exquisite of ways. One hand, the right, held her resolutely by the throat as the other continued its exploration. There was a need for oxygen and yet, somehow she didn't feel the urge to break the kiss that was claiming her. But as Michelle shifted her attention, delving lower and deeper until she was able to thrust, Camryn threw back her head and succumbed to every stroke, her cries of pleasure dwarfed only by the constant filth being articulated against her ear.

~Next~

Cam was enjoying a small dip on the back of her lover's shoulder. It was nothing remarkable, not outstanding like other parts of her body might be described. No, nothing like that, but it was a tiny part of Michelle that Camryn just adored, mainly because it was something that only she got to appreciate.

Anyone else would be staring at her front. So this dip, this small perfect dimple of imperfection that was hidden from the world, was all Cam's.

"What are you doing?" Michelle mumbled into the pillow as she lay in blissful peace. They had finally made it to the bedroom by the early hours. The hallway had just been the first of many stops along the way. Once she had ridden herself of the jacket she was restricted by, the stairs had been the perfect place for Camryn to peel away her girlfriend's underwear and ravish her with just her heels for company. By the time Michelle had recovered enough to allow herself to be virtually carried to the top, she had found a way to stop Camryn in her tracks. She stripped her of her pants, and with her mouth she made light work of Cam's second orgasm. Getting to the bedroom had been the last act of an otherwise exquisite adventure.

"Adoring you, why?" she replied, her lips warm and gentle in the press against her skin.

The actress chuckled sleepily. "Adore me tomorrow. I'm too tired for another round.

Chapter Thirteen

Getting back from her mid-morning run the next day, Cam came bounding into the house with a pile of papers and magazines under her arm. With Michelle in the shower, she flopped down on the bed and picked the first one off the pile to flick through.

Page 18 was a full-blown article on "Shelly Hamlin's Big Gay Adventure." Photos of them both coming out of Rafael's and again in Venice were printed, with pictures of them kissing and laughing alongside a brief body of writing.

'Beautiful actress Shelly Hamlin was literally *out* and about this week with a rather surprising addition. *A woman*! Spotted walking around Venice Beach, the star of *Medical Diaries* was seen to be romantically involved with an as-yet-unnamed blonde. They spent more than an hour walking the boardwalk, kissing and holding hands with each other. Stopping to chat to fans and posing for pictures, the sultry brunette seemed quite at ease.

'Shelly's last reported relationship was with actor Tom Reynolds, whom she met on the set of *Riders without Shame.* They dated for several months last year until it was announced that he was taking on a part in a Canadian TV show, *The Catalyst.*

'We're wondering who the lucky woman that has won Shelly's heart might be? Whoever she is, she is putting a *big* smile on Shelly's face. Good luck girls!'

Michelle came out of the bathroom wrapped in a white towel, her face flushed from the heat of the water. "Good run?" She leant down to kiss her. Her mind instantly went to other things, but she was stopped in her tracks by a palm to the chest as Camryn held up the newspaper.

"We're in the paper," she said with a grin. Michelle raised a brow as she continued to towel dry her hair.

"That was fast! What did they say?" She took a seat on the edge of the bed while Cam read the article aloud.

Picking up her phone, Cam Googled Shelly's name and came up with several other photos and articles about their relationship, many from the previous night. She flicked back and forth through a few before picking up the paper Michelle was reading from. "Oh I love this photo." She held the phone out at arms-length so that her lover could see what she was talking about.

"Camryn, are you taking this seriously?" Michelle couldn't help but giggle at her lover's positive outlook. She took almost everything in her stride, and it was infectious.

"Yes, look it's a fabulous picture!! I'm going to ask for a copy and have it framed."

"You will not." She laughed and flung her wet towel at her.

"Oh wow, they got us kissing! I love this, there is nothing better than photos taken when the subject is not aware," Cam said as she rolled over onto her stomach. Resting on her elbows, she let her legs kick up and down as she spoke.

"I really think you're not taking this seriously." Michelle smiled and rolled herself closer. "What? What is it?" she asked urgently as Cam continued to read the tweets, her brow knitting together in a tight frown.

"Nothing," she tried to smile, but Michelle wasn't buying it. "It's just a few morons, that's all."

"Show me." She held her hand out for Cam's phone. Reluctantly, Cam passed it over and watched silently as she read. "I'm coming for you… What does that even mean?"

"Probably nothing, I wouldn't worry about it." Cam took the phone before she could scroll back and see the filth that came before it. "Most people are happy for us."

"Ok, well so far so good, what time is it?"

"Nearly midday," Cam answered, her eyes firmly fixed on the article about them as she re-read it again.

"God, I can't believe I slept this late." She was naked now, the towel left in a puddle on the floor.

"Would you prefer I woke you earlier?"

Michelle flopped backwards, feeling the bruises on her shoulders and lower back, a tender reminder of the previous evening's escapades. "God no, you completely wore me out." She smiled lazily, her mind right back to that moment when Camryn...Her thoughts were interrupted when she felt the soft sweep of a warm tongue wash across her abdomen. "Really?" she chuckled, her eyes seeking out her lover as soft kisses circled her tummy. She watched the blue eyes intently as they moved closer, travelling upward as lips kissed a trail through the valley between her breasts. Left, then right, she eclipsed each nipple with open lips before continuing higher. Camryn hovered above her, intensely watching the brown darken and dilate as Michelle registered the intrusion. Her hips began to rock, a rhythm slow and sensual as both worked toward the ultimate prize. "Camryn." Her voice was a whisper as she repeated her lover's name like a song of prayer. Her eyes fluttered shut as once more she succumbed to the delightful thrusts of her lover's fingers. When she opened them again to find the ice blue orbs still intently observing her, she realised there was nowhere else she ever needed to look again. Everything she needed was right there, looking back at her. Loving her just as intently.

Chapter Fourteen

By the following week, they had appeared in over thirty magazines and newspapers, usually as photographs with a small caption reiterating the 'lesbian' aspect of the romance, and Cam's name had finally been printed. On several occasions, there had been reporters at the studio or the club, mingling in with party goers to see if they could get the scoop, or hanging around both of their homes, trying desperately to get a quick interview with the woman who was bedding Shelly Hamlin.

So far they had both managed to avoid anything too problematic, but they both understood that eventually someone was going to talk. Janice suggested it might be a good idea to just give them an interview, on the condition that it then stopped the constant questions at every event Shelly attended, but Michelle was steadfast in her decision to keep Cam away from it all. She gave enough of her own life to the media, and she wasn't prepared to share Camryn any more than she had to, especially as Cam had never shown any interest in the fame side of things. She had managed to live her life out of the limelight until she met the actress, and Michelle intended to help her continue that way of life for as long as was possible.

There had been several so-called '*sources*' that claimed to know everything about their relationship or about Cam, but obviously they were just people who had spotted them at the club or at another venue, because nobody printed anything of any real interest.

The most interesting article was in an international magazine with the headline, '*Who is Camryn Thomas*?"

All they seemed to know was that she was British, had grown up in London, and had arrived in LA two years ago. She was extremely rich, but no one knew how she had come to have such wealth. So, they wrote about her business ventures: the club OUT and another club in London's Soho. They mentioned a few investment options and the Thomas Foundation for the Arts. She was described as a lesbian Lothario who enjoyed sexual conquests with no strings. Nothing that wasn't true, though she took offense at the term Lothario. She had never once been a selfish or irresponsible lover, nor had she ever gained financially from any of her sexual encounters. So she slapped them with the threat of a lawsuit if they didn't retract the term and apologise. On the whole though, the world hadn't turned upside down in those first few days and weeks of being 'out,' and Michelle only grew in self-confidence.

~Next~

Friday night found Cam back behind the bar. She had missed these nights, and with Erin successfully building the business, another pair of hands was never going to be turned down. In the uniform black shirt, she wandered back and forth behind the bar serving drinks and sharing jokes with customers all intent on having a good time. Every now and then she would catch Michelle glancing her way, especially when a particularly cute girl would start to openly flirt with her. Jealous Michelle was pretty damn sexy, so she allowed the flirtatious nature of the night to continue.

For a change, the actress was the one being entertained. Angie and Fran had both taken the brunette under their wings while she navigated her way through lesbian life and all the added attention it got her at the club now. Security had been beefed up somewhat just to make sure nobody was harassed by anyone wanting to get too close to Michelle. Unofficially, Gavin had been placed in charge of keeping Michelle safe from any unwanted attention or harassment while Cam was working. Michelle barely noticed him as he kept to a safe distance and allowed her the freedom to just enjoy herself.

Working her way along the bar, serving each customer that

waved a dollar bill or threw a smile in her direction, Cam stopped in her tracks. Looking across the bar at her wasn't the face of a random stranger wanting a drink. Green eyes smiled at her, familiar green eyes that once had looked at her in the manner of which they were now: adoringly. It actually took Cam a few seconds to really grasp whose face she was looking at, whose eyes they were that now bore in to her.

"Hello Camryn." The voice was calm, different from the hundreds of other voices she heard throughout the day now. This voice sounded very much like her own.

"Jessica?" Her jaw tightened. What had she done to karma to warrant this episode? "What are you doing here?"

"Looking for you, what else would I be doing here?" She kept smiling, that same smile that Cam had fallen for years ago but that now had no hold over her. She looked tired; her skin was deathly white with a tinge of pink from too much sun. She was thinner and smaller than how Cam remembered her. Her hair was longer, but still the same mousy brown that had no real style to it.

"Then you came a very long way for nothing," Cam replied coldly, turning away to take the order from the customer along from her. People jostled each other to take up position at the bar, but Jessica held firm.

"Camryn please, can we at least be civil? I just want to talk to you." She was always a manipulator, always so convincing when she needed to be, and Cam had to remind herself of that. She passed two beers across the bar and took a twenty from the guy.

She handed the man his change and turned back to face Jessica, aware now that people either side of them were interested in the conversation she was trying not to have. "I don't think we have anything to say to each other." She moved to the end of the bar; another customer. Jessica followed.

"Erin? I'm taking a quick break."

The colourful manageress looked back and forth between her boss and the woman clearly waiting to speak to her, eyes narrowing as she scrutinised her and tried to fathom who she was and why Cam looked distinctly pissed off about it.

"*Ok*," she replied, her eyes locked with Cam. "All good?" Her boss nodded, so she took her at her word and accepted her request for a break. Cam smiled tightly, but while her lips moved, the smile never reached her eyes. Erin retreated and left her to it, one eye on the situation.

Stepping out from behind the bar at the opposite end to where Michelle sat laughing with Fran, she stood in front of Jessica, arms folded across her chest, her face impassive. The music was loud and there were people all around them, but Cam wasn't bothered; she had nothing to hide or say, and once Jessica had got whatever it was she needed to say off her chest, they could go their separate ways once again.

"You look good, Cam," Jessica said, taking a step toward her ex-lover. The blonde stepped backward, reiterating the need for distance. Jessica, seemingly acknowledging that, remained still. "I realise you didn't expect to see me, but I have come a long way just to see you. The least you could do is hear me out surely?" Her head tilted to the side, her signature manipulative move. It was cute and she knew it, and it had always worked with Camryn before. When she wanted something, or just plain wanted to seduce her, she would do the head tilt and bite her lip. Cam had fallen for it every time. But, not this time. It irked her, but she wouldn't show it.

"Hear you out? I think I heard all I needed to the day I left you, don't you?" She grimaced at the memory, but felt a little better when she noted the sharp barb hitting home.

"I admit that wasn't one of my finest hours." She recovered quickly and had the decency to at least blush at the reminder of having been caught naked and in the midst of an orgasm she should never have even contemplated.

"Because you fucked my best friend or because you got caught fucking my best friend?" The question was a fair one, wasn't it? There was a heat rising within her, anger that bubbled just below the surface waiting to erupt. An anger that she had suppressed for so long now that she had forgotten all about it, and when Michelle had come along and penetrated her heart, she thought it had gone. It caught her by surprise to feel it now. She could see Erin out of the corner of her eye, watching the situation, and reigned herself in; the last thing she needed was a public slanging match to get the attention of any would-be journalist.

Jessica smiled sadly before she composed herself. "I was selfish Camryn, I realise that, I truly do. But, I've never gotten over you, you were it for me." Coy, she was going to play coy. Camryn laughed almost hysterically. She thought of several sarcastic replies she could use, but decided not to prolong this torture any longer than she needed to. She rubbed her palms over her face, bringing them to prayer over her lips as she spoke.

"Just say what you have to say and then leave ok, I don't have time for this."

Jessica grinned triumphantly and once more composed herself to speak, as though she had been rehearsing her lines all day.

"I want you back, Camryn! There I've said it, that's the truth of it. I have spent every day since that awful one regretting what I did and looking for you, but you just disappeared so I had no choice but to give up and then, as if by fate, I was on a bus and I picked up a discarded magazine and there you were. *Who is Camryn Thomas*?" She dramatically moved her hand through the air to illustrate the imaginary headline. "And I thought to myself, I know who she is! So, I got some leave from work and flew straight here." Cam was astonished. One lousy magazine had so far been the only one to cause her any complications, and it had to be the very issue that

Jessica had found by, supposedly, complete coincidence.

"I am sorry you've wasted your time, but I am not interested in resurrecting our relationship. It's over Jessica, it's been over for a long time now, and I am happy. I am really happy now. So, please, just go home. Go home and find someone who wants to be with you."

"LA obviously suits you, and I understand that you won't want to leave all this and come back to London. Which is why I'm willing to stay here and work things through." She continued as if Camryn hadn't spoken a word.

"Jessica, you're not hearing me. I'm not interested in you. What you did cannot be undone nor forgiven, do you understand? I am happy here, I have a girlfriend and she is a decent, beautiful, caring, and selfless human being that adores me, and I adore her, so there is nothing you can offer me."

Jessica just stood there, smiling, her sight fixed intently on Camryn as she took a hesitant step forward. Her head tilted again as she considered her next move. "Oh come on Camryn, you know just what I can offer you." Her voice became huskier, the way it had always done when they were in bed together. "Don't you remember how good we were together?" Grabbing a hold of her shirt, she pulled her closer and leant in to kiss Cam's lips.

Cam pushed her away and wiped her mouth in disgust. "Don't touch me again Jess." Sex with Jessica had been good, she could admit that much, but it wasn't enough, and she certainly wasn't going to give up what she had now for a woman who just didn't get her, a woman who had no respect for her.

"Camryn, is everything ok?" Cam glanced up, and behind Jessica stood the impressive sight of her girlfriend. In an instant her eyes softened and she calmed, but it was obvious to Michelle that she was hurting, that same hurt that had been there before they had gone to Greece.

"Who is this?" Jessica asked, suddenly aware of the most stunning woman; she was absolutely gorgeous. It took a moment to place her, but recognition dawned almost as quickly as she had finished asking the question. The actress from the article. Camryn's latest plaything.

"I'm Michelle, and you are?" she asked politely enough, though her thoughts were anything but. She didn't like the way this woman was looking at Camryn, and she absolutely did not like it that she had placed her hands, let alone her mouth, on Camryn.

"Jessica, Jessica Montgomery," she said, confidently holding her hand out. Michelle didn't take it, instead she moved to position herself by Camryn's side. The name Jessica was instantly recognisable, and she felt the sudden lurch in her stomach as she considered what she was here for. There could be only one answer: Camryn.

"Camryn, do you want me to get Gavin?" Cam shook her head no. She could deal with this; she just wished she didn't have to.

"No, it's alright. Jessica is leaving," she said unquestionably as she felt Michelle slip her hand in her own and let their fingers entwine, giving her the strength and fortitude to deal with the hurt from her past.

"Camryn please, we need to talk," Jessica pleaded quietly. Her gaze, however, never left Michelle as she tried and subsequently failed to assert herself back into Camryn's life.

Shaking her head, Cam answered once more. "No, we don't Jess, we really don't." This was a situation she had never considered happening, and now she was contemplating the need to have Gavin deal with her, but she hadn't reckoned on Michelle.

"You need to leave Jessica." Michelle spoke quietly but authoritatively. She took a step forward and used her full height to her advantage. Intimidating had never been a word used to describe

Shelly Hamlin or Michelle Hamilton until now, and under other circumstances, Camryn would find it extremely arousing.

"Camryn, I would prefer to speak with you in private," Jessica insisted, glaring at Michelle with an intensity that sent a shiver down Cam's spine.

"And Cam would prefer it if she never saw you again," Michelle insisted, her demeanour now that of a woman defending what was hers. "Leave now." She could see the conflict in Jessica's mind. Backing down wasn't something she was used to doing, but this wasn't the time or place to continue the conversation she needed to have with Camryn.

"Fine, I'll leave." She picked up her bag and noticed several people looking their way. "But I won't give up Camryn. We were meant to be together, I realise that now, and you will too." She threw one more glare in Michelle's direction before she turned and walked away. Camryn shook her head and watched her go, making sure she left.

"You ok?" Michelle took her face in her palms, focusing her attention back on her. Their eyes fixed on one another as the world around them slipped away.

"I am now," she said. Taking a deep breath, she smiled at Michelle. "Thank you."

"For?"

"For being everything she isn't."

Chapter Fifteen

When Thanksgiving finally came around, Michelle had finished filming on *Medical Diaries* for this season and was away on location working on a film in Hawaii. It was a big part in a film that was expected to be a summer hit the following year and was one of those jobs that she loved: a few weeks filming on location before returning to LA to complete in the studio. They were fun and usually she had a great time, enjoying the 'family' that being part of a cast and crew could sometimes create. But she'd never had anyone to miss before.

"I know, but it's just a few more days and then you'll be home and—" Cam held the phone in the crook of her neck as she listened to Michelle. Settling back against the leather seat inside the limo she was travelling in, she smiled as the outside world sped past in a blur.

"It's already been way too long. I am never signing up for another film away from home again," Michelle groaned, interrupting Cam's flow.

"Yes you will, because that is what you love doing," Cam assured her. "But hey listen, I got a few things I need to do right now. So, you around to talk later?"

"Where else will I be?" she said sadly, and for a minute Cam felt badly. "Ok well, I love you."

"I love you too sweetheart." Disconnecting the phone, she couldn't hold it in any longer and laughed out loud. "She has no idea!" From the seat opposite her, Bob and Martha joined in with the laughter.

It wasn't a holiday that Camryn had ever really celebrated. British people had Bonfire Night, celebrating the gunpowder plot of Guy Fawkes and his fellow conspirators, at the beginning of November, and then it was Christmas, but she understood just how important it was to Americans to be with family and friends at this time of the year.

"She is going to be so excited when she finds out what we've done," said Martha from underneath her designer sunglasses. She herself was still giddy with everything. Arriving on a jet like a superstar had really made her day.

The idea had come at the last minute from Cam. Over dinner the night before Michelle had left, she had made a brief comment about how she wished she could spend time with those she loved this year. Her mother had reiterated her invitation for them both to join them for Thanksgiving during a phone call just days prior, and Michelle had been saddened to have to turn it down. She wanted her parents to know Cam and to see them as a couple that were in love and happy, so they could understand that she was content with how things were now.

When Cam had called them up and put her idea to them, they jumped on it. So she began planning and sent a private jet to pick them up, meeting them in Hawaii, having taken a flight from LA herself. They were now in the limousine and heading straight to the hotel.

Michelle and the cast were all staying at the Ritz-Carlton. Cam had managed to make a last-minute booking for a suite for Michelle's parents (she planned on sleeping with Michelle obviously), and during innocent chitchat it wasn't difficult to find out which room Michelle was in. She could have insisted on a huge suite, but she was no diva and instead asked to be placed in the same type of room that everyone else would have. Of course, it was a still a great room, and she had no complaints.

"Thank you for doing this Camryn, Michelle will be so surprised to see us, and you of course." Martha smiled at the blonde woman who seemed to be everything her daughter said she was and probably more.

"Martha, you must know by now that I would do anything for your daughter's happiness. If it's within my power to, I will get it done; she deserves nothing less than the very best of me." Cam spoke sincerely and from her heart.

"I really believe you would, Camryn. I just hate that we got off on such a bad footing!" Full of remorse, Martha had been hoping for the opportunity to apologise properly to Camryn.

"We did nothing of the sort, you asked a question to protect your child. I'm ok with that." Cam nodded, constantly reminded of her own parents' failings. It was good to know not every parent was so slack in their total commitment to a child they created.

"Well, thank you for being so forgiving. Now, how will we be doing this?"

~Next~

The hotel was just as Cam expected it would be. The lobby was large and open, all dark wood and comfortable chairs. This was going to be the most difficult part of the plan: getting inside their suite without Michelle finding out. Like Martha, Cam wore her aviators and a cap. Bob too wore a cap and all three of them huddled together at the desk waiting, trying to be as inconspicuous as they could. Cam wasn't quite so sure they were succeeding with Martha loudly reminding Bob to 'keep his head down,' but she figured even if they were caught, the surprise would still be pretty awesome.

Cam stood with her back against the desk, her eyes scanning the area anyway, just in case Michelle happened to wander by. She really couldn't wait to see her, to have eyes on her again and be able to touch the woman she so desperately missed. She was lost in thought when Martha poked her, the older woman nodding behind her to the receptionist trying to gain her attention.

"Good afternoon and welcome to the Kapalua," said the voice from behind Cam. Pulling her shades from her face as she turned,

Camryn looked straight into the eyes of Amanda.

"Camryn?"

"Amanda! Hey. Hi." She stumbled and had to take a moment. "Hi," she tried again, adding a smile. The last time she had seen this woman, she had been walking out of her hotel room, having just slapped her face. She still carried that sting with her. "How are you?"

Amanda seemed to hesitate for a moment before she noticed that Camryn wasn't alone. Reminding herself that she was a professional with a job to do, her hands flew to the keyboard and she began tapping details into the system. She found the booking (C Thomas, Suite 3) in an instant, plastered a smile on her face, and replied to the question.

"I am...well, thank you. So, I see you have a suite booked with us today." She still dazzled, though maybe more so with other customers, Cam considered. She couldn't blame her.

"Uh yes. Yes I do." Her confidence returned in an instant as she felt the unintentional nudge of her lover's mother against her shoulder as Martha moved to ensure they were not spotted by Michelle. Amanda printed off some details and passed them across the desk to Cam, much like she had when Cam had arrived in LA the day they had met.

"If you could just sign here...and here." She pointed to two spaces that she had marked with a tiny red cross. "Here is your key card and some essential information on the hotel and surrounding areas. I understand your stay is for just the one night, but I am sure you might find something to entertain you while you're in town." She smiled sweetly, but Cam accepted the slight undertone of sarcasm. She deserved it.

"Thank you. Is there anyone that could maybe show my..." She didn't quite know what to call Bob & Martha. "...friends up to our suite?" Amanda nodded and summoned a young man, who instantly took Martha's bag and led them away from the desk towards the elevators. "Amanda? Do you...?" she was about to ask if maybe they could get a drink but reconsidered. This was probably not the time or place to be fixing the errors of her previous recklessness. "I really am sorry for how things turned out."

Amanda checked the surrounding area before speaking again. She didn't wish to be overheard or reprimanded for speaking out of turn; however, she might not ever get this opportunity again.

"Don't flatter yourself Ms Thomas." She spoke quietly, but the intensity was there. "We both know exactly how you saw me. I've no illusions, especially now that you're so brazenly happy and flaunting your *relationship* with Shelly Hamlin." The fake smile remained; if anyone were to observe them then they would see a pleasant exchange between them.

Contrition was all Cam had in her armoury right now. "I understand, but whatever you may think of me, I really didn't intend for things to turn out the way they did."

"I haven't thought of you a day since. Now, if you don't mind, some of us do have to work for a living." She turned her attention back to the keyboard and did her best to look indifferent, but Cam saw the tremor in her fingers as they typed and the difficult swallow in her throat. This was not a woman who was over it, and Cam would not make it any worse by trying to force her to accept her apology.

"Camryn, are you coming?" Martha called out in a hushed tone. She had been watching the interaction and noted the sadness that washed across Camryn's face as the receptionist turned away from her. A small smile instantly replaced the frown as she walked away and toward the elevator. "Everything alright?" Martha asked when Cam reached them. She nodded. It would be of course, but she still felt badly about it.

~Next~

"I have organised with the hotel for them to deliver a complete Thanksgiving dinner to your suite, where you and Bob will be waiting. I will go down to Michelle's room and pretend to be room service. Then I'll bring her up here thinking it's just me and well, that's where you guys will come in." She smiled as she checked her watch. They had spent the last hour settling in. They'd all taken quick showers and redressed, ready for the big reveal.

Room service arrived on time, and every possible dish ever served for Thanksgiving was wheeled in and set up on the elegant table. Bottles of champagne and wine had been added to the refrigerator as requested and the staff were tripping over themselves to help when Cam tipped them all the equivalence of a week's wages.

~Next~

Outside in the corridor of room 402, she raised her hand and knocked twice. "Room service," she called out, trying to put on her best American accent and giggling a little at how bad it was. She could hear Michelle Hamilton stalk towards her door. "I didn't order anything," she said as she opened the door and stared straight into the eyes of her lover.

"Camryn? Oh my God." Without hesitation, she pulled her into the room and into her embrace, wasting no time in pressing her firmly against the wall and kissing her. She had a desperate need to feel her; touch her.

"Well hello to you too," Cam said as she broke the kiss, in need of some air. She realised though just how much she missed kissing those lips and went back in again. "That was worth the trip, ok got to go now!" She turned and pretended to leave.

"What?!! No! Not a chance, get in here and get naked right now!" Michelle demanded, her eyes darkening with pent up desire. Since they had returned from Greece she could count on her hands how many nights they had spent apart, and she didn't like it much when it happened.

"Uh nope, as much as that idea really appeals to me right now—" She stroked a finger down her cheek, "—and I do mean *really appeals*, I have something I need to do first. But, you can come with me if you like?" Michelle studied her face and smirked.

"Camryn Thomas, you are being devious, aren't you? I can tell, you get this look on your face and I just know you are up to something." She narrowed her eyes before grinning widely. She was such a fan of Cam's deviousness; so far it had been extremely alluring and satisfying.

"Me? Oh I'm hurt that you would think of me as so duplicitous!!" She kissed her, a simple and tender peck. "I'll have you know that I do have something up my sleeve, and if you follow me I will show you," Cam admitted with a smile as she bit her lip and took Michelle's hand, ready to turn and leave.

"Does it involve getting naked and having my way with you? Because I'm only going if I'm coming." She laughed at her little play on words.

"Michelle Hamilton, you have a filthy one-tracked mind, and right now I'm too busy to deal with it, but I will be coming back to this conversation later and you will be dealt with, thoroughly! Am I clear about that?"

"Absolutely." She purred seductively as she ran her finger down Camryn's arm and followed her down the hallway.

~Next~

The ding of the elevator let them know they had reached their destination. Following Cam out, Michelle took a moment to check out her girlfriend's ass. *I missed that too.*

"Are you coming or are you just going to gawp at my arse all day long?" Cam said over her shoulder, the grin on her face spreading as she looked at her girlfriend, caught red-handed.

"I like to gawp; it's a pretty hot ass!"

Cam turned to look at her, squinting her eyes at her hornier-than-usual girlfriend. "Two hours and I promise, you will be naked," she said before turning back to the door. Michelle raised an eyebrow and Cam opened the door to the suite.

"I'll hold you to that," she said as she stepped inside the room, straight into her mother's arms!

"Oh my God. Mom, Dad! When? How?" she floundered, searching for the right words. "Camryn. How did you manage to do all this?"

"Wasn't too difficult." She smiled. "Happy Thanksgiving darling."

Chapter Sixteen

They sat down to the most amazing meal – the hotel had really outdone itself. Cam had never tried half of the dishes on the table before, so she got stuck in and gave everything a try, much to Michelle's amusement. It was a great time to just talk and catch up with each other, and the delight on her lover's face made it all the more special as Camryn enjoyed her first family meal. When the meal was finished, Martha and Bob retired to their bedroom for a long overdue nap. It had been a lengthy day for them already, and they were not oblivious to the fact that the two lovebirds might want a few hours to themselves. They would be meeting up again later to enjoy a light evening meal together and possibly a few drinks in the bar. There would be plenty of time to see their daughter.

Michelle took the opportunity to make a move on her lover. She wore her dark hair down today, framing her face, her eyes shining with emotion and desire as she moved in closer. "You really are something else, aren't you?" she said, placing her arms around Cam's neck and straddling her lap. "Every time I think I love you more than is possible, you do something to prove I love you more."

"I just want you to be happy," Cam replied, looking her in the eye and bringing her arms around her waist, pulling her in closer.

"I am, so very happy." She smiled.

"Ok, I will meet you in your room in ten, I just need to do something first. Will you bring some of those leftovers with you, I have a feeling we will work up an appetite." Michelle nodded and set about preparing leftovers on a plate while Cam left to do whatever she had to do.

She made her way down to her room. Balancing the plates in one hand, she fished into her purse for the key card, but it wasn't there. Groaning, she realised she must have left it in the room in the excitement of Cam's arrival. She had to go down to reception in order to get a new key.

Excited to get back to her room and to Camryn, she ignored the slight rudeness of the women dealing with her request, putting her attitude down to perhaps being upset at having to work on such an important day. She could understand the desire to be anywhere but where she was, and it was unimportant in the grand scheme of things. She had somewhere else to be.

Michelle entered the room in virtual darkness. She didn't remember closing the curtains before she left, but she must have; the room was lit only by a small lamp. She placed the plates down on the side table and then entered the bedroom. Another lamp, this time by her bed, was on low and pointed to the bed. She moved to switch the main light on, but was stopped in her tracks.

"Don't." She froze. *Was that Cam?* "Leave the light off," the voice commanded.

Michelle breathed a sigh of relief. *It was Cam; how had she?* It dawned on her then just where her key card had gone. She smiled wryly.

"Lock the door," Cam demanded quietly. Michelle did as she was told and paused. The air around her stilled as the waiting extended and she felt herself tense low in her stomach, the way she always did when something turned her on. "Come further into the room," Cam ordered gently. Michelle took a few more steps further into the room, nearer the bed. She couldn't see Cam fully, just a figure sitting in the darkest corner. It definitely turned her on. Every nerve of her body twitched and pulsed at the mere thought of what her lover had planned. She knew Camryn wasn't shy when it came to sex and her imagination. Being with someone like Camryn was like an awakening.

The silence in the room was palpable and created a sexual

tension Michelle hadn't ever felt before. She realised she was holding her breath, awaiting Cam's next instruction, and slowly released it. Being made to wait like this was almost torturous in its arousal. Most of her previous lovers, actually all of her previous lovers, had not been able to control themselves once she had invited them into the bedroom. The idea that she might want or need something other than their cock inside of her didn't enter their minds. Foreplay to them had been undressing her. But with Camryn everything was different, and she would wait for as long as Cam asked her to because she knew that any and all outcomes would revolve around pleasing her and making this an experience she would enjoy.

"Take off your dress." The command was firm, and yet it still held the respect and love that Michelle was used to hearing from her lover. Somehow the voice was sexier, low and confident, and that accent—god how she loved that accent when they were in bed.

Biting down gently on her bottom lip, Michelle hesitated and for a second, Cam thought she wouldn't do it. She was relieved, however, when Michelle reached behind herself and tugged at the zipper, slowly pulling it downwards until it would go no further. She then shrugged the dress off her shoulders. Slowly, seductively she let it fall to the floor to pool around her feet in a puddle of blue.

Stepping out of it, she stood still in just her underwear and heels. She felt completely exposed, but at the same time she revelled in the fact that it was Cam who was watching her. She felt herself becoming more aroused than ever; her underwear would give her away any moment, she was sure.

She completely trusted in Cam and whatever sexual adventure she was being taken on. So, she stood still and waited.

Commanded to remove her bra, she acquiesced in an instant. When Cam leant forward, still silhouetted in darkness, and whispered, "Turn around and take it all off," Michelle almost came there on the spot at Cam's voice. Her whimper was loud and clear; she had to bite her lip again to stop herself from downright moaning in pleasure, but she did as she was instructed and, bending at the waist with her heels still on, she gave Camryn the show she desired.

She was so concentrated on doing as she was told, she didn't hear the soft shuffle of footsteps that moved quickly from the corner of the room to right behind her. It was only the feeling of strong arms wrapping around her waist as kisses peppered her shoulders and neck that grounded her. Cam's hands moved in an instant to cup her breasts, pulling her closer against her own naked flesh as her fingertips tweaked hardened nipples.

"Even when we're apart, I am always in a dark recess of your mind," she whispered against the shell of her ear and felt the shudder of excitement and anticipation work its way down Michelle's spine. "All you have to do is imagine me and I'll be there with you." Her fingers slipped lower. "Touching you." Her lips moved against her cheek. "Kissing you." She spun her and pushed her backwards so she landed on her backside on the bed, then climbed on the bed with her, hovering over her as her mouth dipped lower to suck gently on a rigid nipple as her fingers homed in on her. Teasing her, she let her fingers play before she added, "Inside you." Her digits following the plot. The brunette gasped and arched all at the same time as her lover increased her pace, creating a rhythm that she knew would bring Michelle to her peak.

"I am in here." She kissed her forehead, "In here." She kissed her chest, right above her heart. "And in here." She changed up her position to use her thumb, pressing against her sensitive nub of nerves as she continued the same rhythm. "All you have to do is think of me and touch yourself." And with those few words Michelle crested and soared in a cacophony of whimpers and pleas.

Chapter Seventeen

With Christmas just around the corner, things had quieted down on the media front. They had only been in a couple of magazines after attending an event that Michelle was obliged to go to. Now and then a newspaper would print a picture of them out and about, and in one magazine they were even voted seventh in the "Hottest Couple of the Year" section, which made Cam blush and gave Angie and Fran plenty to joke about. But mainly the news was now following the latest marriage and divorce of another actress and her affair that had led to it.

Michelle had finished filming in Hawaii the previous week and was now back in LA. Although she still had some work to do in the studio, she was happy to be back and looking forward to her family finally being together for the holidays. Her parents were coming to stay, as were her brother and his family. It was exciting, and Cam loved her enthusiasm.

"Are we going to hold Christmas at yours or mine?" Cam asked Michelle one afternoon, latte in hand as they sat together in a coffee shop catching up. There was nothing better than just being together and doing the simple things. People rarely bothered them, and when they did it was usually only for an autograph or a photo opportunity. Just part of the job, Michelle had told Cam, part of the job she enjoyed, and it was something that Cam was getting used to.

"Hmm? I hadn't really thought about it. I guess your place has the room, would you mind?" Michelle said, tilting her head back against Cam's shoulder. The comfortable couch allowed for them to sit huddled together like any other couple would be. Her own home was probably large enough too, but the idea of spending Christmas with Cam at the beach just seemed perfect.

“I don’t mind, no, but I did want to talk to you about something.” There was a light pink tinge appearing on the blonde’s cheeks that delighted Michelle. The actress put down her cup and turned to give her attention fully to Camryn.

“What is it?” Camryn was nervous, and it put Michelle a little on edge.

“Well, I know it’s only been four months, which in the grand scheme of things isn’t very long I know, but...well, what I was thinking was...” She paused to make sure she worded this correctly. “Ok, so what I was thinking was...”

“Camryn, spit it out baby.” Michelle laughed, touching her face with her delicate fingers. “Whatever it is, the answer will be yes.”

“You don’t know what it is yet!”

“I don’t need to.” She smiled, knowing that if Camryn asked her to give everything up and move to the ends of the earth and live in a mud hut with no running water, the answer would be yes. Though maybe on the condition that they dug a well!

“Ok well. I was thinking that...I don’t want to have a *‘your place or mine’*. I, well...I would like, no...I want, I most definitely want *our* place.” She finished speaking only to find Michelle staring at her open mouthed, eyes wide.

“Camryn, are you asking me to move in with you?” Her fingers flew to cover her mouth.

“Yes, or I can move in with you, or we could, well we could buy somewhere together...I just, I want—” she was cut off mid-pitch from her ramble.

“Yes, absolutely yes! I want to wake up every morning with you in *our* bed, in *our* room, in *our* house. Yes Camryn, my answer is yes.” She grasped her face in her palms and kissed her quickly, her dimples on full display as she grinned at Camryn.

"So, that's a yes then," Cam stated with a wide grin.

"I said yes!" She kissed her lover once more, "I will always say yes." She exhaled and, grasping her lover's chin, she brought their eyes in line with one another and held her gaze.

"Always yes."

~Next~

Michelle hadn't been back to her own home for weeks. The nights leading up to Hawaii had been spent with Cam at the beach, and then she had been away filming, only to return back to Cam's. It was a pretty easy decision to make when Camryn invited her to move in with her; they were practically living together as it was anyway.

She also still hadn't bought a new car. Since returning from Greece she had been using Cam's Audi. She loved it, and she loved that they were so completely a couple in every possible way. Even the hooded sweat top she was wearing was Camryn's. As she pulled up to the gates of her home, she hit the button that would open the gates. The big wooden gates opened slowly, and she reminisced about the time when Cam drove through on her motorbike. An awakening had taken place on that bike, and Michelle couldn't hide the smile that those memories brought back.

But as she drove through the gates, her heart almost leapt from her mouth as she registered the words painted in red on the white wall of her home: '*Dyke Whore.*'

She glanced around quickly; it was daylight, but it still freaked her out. Who would do this and why? Everything had been going so well. She understood that not everyone would like her choices in life, but to invade her home to make the point?

Her phone sat in its hands-free cradle. She hit the call button for Camryn and waited as the loud ringing erupted from the speakers like a rabid heartbeat. Feeling alone and vulnerable was not an emotion she enjoyed. What if the perpetrator was still here? It felt like hours had passed as the phone continued to ring.

"Yo," said a happy voice. Camryn had been spending the day clearing out the things she didn't need anymore in order to make room for Michelle's stuff. She had already made space in her heart; now as she moved about her home creating literal space, she realised how big the changes were in her life. And she loved every bit of it!

"Camryn." Her voice was shaky and she realised she was trembling. "Camryn, I need you to…I don't know what to do."

"Huh? What's up?" She could hear the distress in an instant. "Michelle?"

"I…I got home but, someone has…there is writing on the wall, someone has been here." Cam didn't quite understand what she was talking about, but she did know that Michelle was distressed.

"I am on my way now, ok?" She grabbed her keys and was running out of the house in seconds. Her heart was racing as she climbed onto the bike.

"Ok, hurry please." She could feel the tears sliding down her cheeks as she continued to gaze at the words on the wall, trying to make sense of them and why anyone would call her that.

"I'm coming, stay on the line ok." The phone connected to her own hands-free inside her helmet. It didn't take long to get there as she weaved through the traffic, the sound of Michelle crying quietly in her ear keeping her focused.

~Next~

The police officer wrote up the details of the complaint. Crime scene techs took photographs, dusted the area for prints, and searched the surrounding area for anything disturbed to indicate an intruder. They found barely anything. Whoever had done this had been smart and fast.

Her neighbours were spoken to and asked if they had seen anything or noticed anyone suspicious hanging around, but other than the intermittent on and off of the lights that were on the sensor, nobody noticed anything out of the ordinary.

Cam organised a cleaning company to come down and go through the house once the police were finished with it. It didn't matter that Michelle was moving out; it was still her home, and Camryn wanted to make sure it felt that way whenever Michelle needed to return here. She found a local decorator who was happy to come along and repaint the outside of the house; in twenty-four hours, it would be like nobody had been here. But Michelle knew differently, and that was going to be something Cam couldn't fix quite so easily.

"I'm going to pack some things, will you stay with me?" Michelle asked. She was nervous and on edge, and Camryn was angry on her behalf.

"Yes, of course. I'll help." She made a call to Gavin and had him organise a truck to come straight to Michelle's. Room by room they went through things, packing items that she wanted to take with her immediately. Cam already had the Audi filled with cases and bags by the time Gavin arrived with the truck. He had had the foresight to buy packing boxes, and the three of them went through the house like termites. Michelle piled the things she wanted to take with her, while Cam and Gavin got on with packing it all.

All her personal files were packed into cardboard boxes and loaded into the truck, along with several boxes of awards and photographs she had accumulated over the years. Her memories.

Last to be loaded was the large canvas of the naked women that Cam had admired that first night she had stayed here. Both women enjoyed it, and Cam knew exactly where to put it.

~Next~

"I can't believe anyone would do that." Cam spoke calmly, but inside she was seething still. "I mean, how dare anyone actually do that to your home?" She had a glass of crisp, cold white wine in her hand, twirling the stem between her fingers as she considered the events of the day.

"Baby, don't let it upset you." Michelle pressed a finger to Cam's lips to stop her from interrupting. "It's just a...these things happen to people like me. It isn't right, and 99% of the time it turns out to be nothing to worry about." She settled down on the couch next to her lover. "But, it happens."

"But, it shouldn't. You shouldn't have to tolerate this crap just because you're an actress." She placed her glass down on the side table. "Or because you love me." Cam's gaze drifted away from Michelle towards the floor.

"No, it shouldn't, but that is the world we live in right now. I'm ok babe, nothing happened that can't be fixed." Michelle lifted her chin and made eye contact again. "Loving you is the best thing to ever happen to me. Don't you dare let anyone make you feel badly for that!" The blonde nodded. She knew that Michelle was right; self-doubt wasn't going to make any difference. "It will blow over. Whoever is doing this will get bored and move on but, until then we have to deal with it."

"I don't like it." Cam mumbled.

"I know you don't."

Chapter Eighteen

It was still early when a Detective Gomes arrived at the house to discuss the case with Michelle. He seemed like a straight-up guy in Cam's opinion. He was tall and broad, his ebony skin lined and creased, like a man who had seen his share of crap in the world and was a little tired from it all, but his smile was warm and honest.

"Can I get you a drink Detective?" Cam asked. She had already shown him into the lounge and offered him a seat. She could hear Michelle walking down the stairs and looked around to catch a glimpse. *Beautiful.*

"No, thank you Ms Thomas. I just had one on the way over, but thank you." His voice was deep and silky. A voiceover actor couldn't have sounded any better. He turned at the sound of Michelle entering the room. "Ms Hamlin, good morning."

"Hello…"

"I'm sorry, Detective Gomes," he answered, his hand held out, which she took. "I've been placed in charge of your case. As I understand it, this is the first attack on you?"

She nodded. "Yes." She took a seat on the couch opposite him.

"So, you're unaware of some of the comments on social media?" he asked gently. Cam moved across the room and took the seat next to Michelle.

"No, I mean… there were so many messages since we announced our relationship that I… I turned off the notifications and I haven't even looked at it, I've just been so busy." Her hand reached out for Cam and was found in an instant.

"Well, there was that one weird one…'I'm coming for you'? Or something like that." Cam spoke quickly as the detective scribbled into his notebook.

"Ok, well then I need to inform you that not everybody is happy about your relationship status." He placed the case file he was holding onto the table between them and slid a page out. "Do you know anyone using the name Trickcity220?" Michelle shook her head. "Ok, do you know anyone by the name of James Cantrell?"

"No, I don't think so. I mean, I meet a lot of people and it's possible I have met him, but I don't recall the name."

Detective Gomes nodded and slid another piece of paper from the file. "What about a... Tom Reynolds?" He looked up and at Michelle and held her gaze.

"Tom? Yes, we, uh...we dated last year for a while." Her grip on Cam's hand tightened. The thought of someone she knew being behind this was abhorrent. "I can't imagine Tom would do this."

"Your social media has given us quite a few leads." He passed the first piece of paper across to Michelle. "As you can see, Mr Cantrell seems to have an issue with your relationship." The white sheet was covered in print, all of it a copy of several messages sent by the man using Trickcity220 as a name. He called her a dyke and a whore. He ranted that she needed a real man to guide her back to the light. It was upsetting to read, but these were the kind of things she had accepted she would receive once they announced their relationship. She didn't expect them to take it further and become a reality.

When it was clear she had finished reading, Gomes passed her the second sheet, the one with Tom's messages. She read the private message that had been sent just a few weeks ago.

What the fuck? Seriously Michelle? You're a dyke now? Do you have any idea how upsetting this is!! Have you seen the shit people are writing about me? The guy whose girl went gay!! I can't fucking believe you would do this to me... you didn't seem to have any complaints riding my dick!!

I really hope that you have the decency to come to your senses and dump this wannabe man or at least have the fucking decency to make it clear I wasn't the reason you turned to pussy!

"I am not suggesting that either of these guys are responsible for the break-in at your home. However, I do think it's worth looking into, and that's exactly what I am doing. What I would suggest is that you continue to have no contact with anyone from social media or that you don't know and trust, keeping in mind that this may well be somebody you do know."

"Thank you, for taking this all seriously," Cam said as they all stood and began walking towards the door.

"We take anything like this seriously, but I need you to understand that so far, all anyone has done is vandalism and although I can arrest them, they will probably get a slap on the wrist."

"So, what do you suggest we do? Wait until one of these loonies actually tries to hurt her?" Cam's question was a valid one, and one that Michelle was a little worried to hear the answer to.

"I don't like it any more than you do, but that's about the crux of it."

Chapter Nineteen

It felt like an age waiting for Michelle to come home. Camryn had spent the last thirty minutes sitting by herself on the stairs watching the door. She saw the shadows of two people moving closer and her heart beat faster. She was up and down the last two steps, opening the door before Michelle could even get her key out. Gavin nodded, a small sign that all was ok, and without a word she pulled the brunette through the door and into her embrace.

She could barely keep her hands off of her lover; for once it wasn't a sexual instigation, but one of need. She needed to make sure that every inch of her was intact, alive and well. She ran her hands over her, kissed her gently, and then as the fear left, the emotion twisted into a passionate frenzy as her kisses became more forceful, the impact of the day finally catching up with her.

They made love on the stairs, half naked and desperate. Mouths pressed firmly against each other as clothes were pulled apart or pushed out of the way. Michelle's underwear was ripped aside as Cam searched her soul from the inside out. It was frantic and fraught as each woman tried to convey their feelings for the other with a touch, a kiss.

They had to prove to one another that they were both fine and nothing or nobody would stop that. Especially a maniac with a warped mind, because today there had been photographs. Left in an envelope for Michelle at the bar. In each of them, Michelle's face had been scratched out. But that wasn't the worst of it.

"Camryn Thomas, this is Lindsey from the studio. Ms Hamlin would like you to come right away and meet with her." The peppy operator chirped down the phone line.

Wasting no time, Cam drove as quickly as was lawful, knowing full well that Michelle wouldn't have asked for her unless it was important.

~Next~

"How are you feeling?" Michelle asked Cam later as they cuddled together on the sofa. They were wrapped together, Michelle naked under the blanket. Her clothes were still scattered around the stairs and hallway. The normality of lying here, wrapped in her lover's embrace and cocooned underneath a blanket, meant she finally felt safe.

"Unprepared and uneasy. Someone is out there watching us, watching you! I expected the usual paparazzi or a reporter, even fans to be taking pictures of you of course, but this, this is creepy; unhinged. What kind of weirdo would do this, and if they can go this far, then just how far are they willing to go?!" She tightened her hold. Michelle remained silent. She didn't dare to think about it.

"Where did this come from?" Cam asked nobody in particular. Blank stares all around. "It's come from somewhere!!"

A short black woman in her thirties spoke up. "It was delivered by hand this morning and placed in the internal mail."

"And nobody checks these things before they are delivered?" Cam's inquiry was more than a little aggressive.

"Usually yes, unfortunately today we had a new member of staff who isn't quite so…jaded as the rest of us and his lack of experience meant that it was passed along to Ms Hamlin…unchecked."

Cam was the big spoon to Michelle. It was comfortable, and they both relaxed into each other a little as the evening progressed, enjoying the closeness, their home a sanctuary away from all the craziness.

Michelle had never lived with anyone before. She had always assumed she was too set in her ways to ever compromise enough to feel comfortable sharing every facet of her life with someone else and yet, she couldn't imagine it any other way now. Now that she had Camryn to come home to, all of that had changed. She wanted to share everything. She wanted nothing more than to have this woman's opinion, to have this woman's arms holding her tightly.

"I don't want my parents to know about this Cam, they don't need to be frightened by it," she said, turning in her arms to face her. Cam searched her face, the images from earlier playing over and over in her mind.

The box was nothing more than a filing box. Brand new. But, what it was filled with was anything but new. More photographs. Hundreds of them. Every single one of them had Michelle's face scratched out. The words whore and dyke were scribbled across them in bold red marker pen.

"Ok, we won't talk about it when they are here but, you promise me if there is anything else, then you tell me, don't try and protect me like you want to protect your parents."

"I promise you I will not do that."

"Is this all of it?" Cam asked the room. Everybody nodded apart from one man. Tall and unassuming in any other circumstances, but right now he looked as guilty as anyone ever could.

"Actually..." he began. His eyes flitted from one face to another as a blush rapidly made itself at home. "There was...there, I mean we had several..."

"Just spit it out Paul."

"There were letters." Every person in the room stood staring at him. "I'll...I'll get them." He returned a few minutes later with a file that held a dozen or so pieces of paper filled with a typed diatribe of vile hatred, threats and promises of things to come if this disgusting relationship didn't come to an end.

They sat together like that until the sun finally dropped to the horizon. It was quiet, peaceful, the heat of the day rapidly changing to the coolness of night. Another hour or so and Cam would need to get up and build a fire.

"What was that?" Cam suddenly sat up and stared out through the window into the night.

"What?" Michelle said anxiously, her head turning to look over her shoulder in the direction Cam was staring.

"Stay here." Cam said urgently. Clambering over Michelle, she walked across to the window to get a better look. It was hard to see anything – dusk brought with it shadows; places to hide.

"Cam? Seriously, you are freaking me out right now." Michelle was now sitting up on the couch, watching her girlfriend stare at something or someone outside.

"Wait here, I'm going to go outside and check. If I am not back in five minutes, then you call the police! Ok?" She didn't wait for a response. Her long limbs were already on the move, striding out through the patio doors with purpose.

"No, Cam don't be stupid. Please don't go out there." Michelle stood by the window watching, fear building that this wasn't just a crazy fan writing messages.

Chapter Twenty

Camryn ran around the exterior of the house before moving towards the beach. Her eyes adjusted somewhat to the lack of light and she could make out the shapes of sun loungers and trees. There was nobody there. Just as she was about to give up and come back inside she saw it: a shadow moving behind the palm tree that sat to the left of the beach. The shadow moved fast and sprinted at full speed away and towards the alleyway that would lead them to the road and an escape route.

"Hey!" Cam shouted, giving chase. Her feet pounded into the soft sand, slipping and sliding underneath her when they couldn't get a good enough purchase to give her speed. Running on sand was not easy. She wouldn't give up though. The figure was still ahead, but with effort, she was gaining on them. "Hey, stop." She was out of breath and about to give up when the figure ahead came to an abrupt halt. It took seconds for her to catch up. "What the hell are you doing?" she gasped. Her lungs burned with the effort, and catching her breath was only hindered when the figure turned around. "Amanda?"

The dark-haired woman was herself breathing heavily as she tried to catch her breath, her face partially hidden under the dark hood of her sweater.

"Amanda? What are you doing here?" Instantly suspicious now, Cam studied the woman she had once been intimately involved with. She appeared nervous, and that only heightened Cam's concerns.

"I...I've come home for Christmas and..." She ran a hand through her hair in frustration and pushed the hood from her head. "Look, I just wanted to apologise...for the way I behaved." Her breathing was almost back to normal now. "I should have been more gracious and accepted your apology, but I was...I was just so *pissed off* at you." Cam stood quietly, her gaze falling to the sand beneath her feet. It didn't matter how sorry she was; she would always feel badly for the way she treated Amanda. "You let me fall in love with you and then..." Cam's gaze rose in an instant at that admission. She always thought that they had had a lot of fun together, cared for each other. It had never occurred to her that Amanda felt more than that. Love? "And then you just tossed me aside because you didn't want a *relationship*. I was just angry, I read about you and *Shelly Hamlin* and then she walked into the hotel and I was just...it hurt Cam. It hurt to know I wasn't good enough for you." There was a tremor in her voice. She was on the verge of tears, and Cam felt like a complete and utter asshole.

"I'm so sorry Amanda, I really didn't ever...I met you when I was in a really different place, a bad place, and I could never have been the person you wanted me to be. I never wanted to hurt you. I didn't want to hurt anyone, I had been hurt...that's why I couldn't..." She looked to the stars for inspiration, for some words that would help Amanda feel better. To help herself feel better about it all. "I wish there was something I could say or do that would make us both feel better..."

Amanda shuffled from foot to foot as she considered Cam's words and wondered herself if there was anything that Cam could say that would make her feel better. When Camryn Thomas had walked into the reception that first day and smiled at her in that way she had of making you feel like the only person on the planet, it hadn't taken much more for Amanda to take her up on the offer of dinner, and from then on it had been easy to allow herself to ride along on the wave of excitement Camryn created. Cam took her everywhere. The hotel had even released her to act as an unofficial tour guide once they realised just how well off the British woman was. They wanted her to feel comfortable with staying at the hotel for as long as possible, and Amanda hadn't been against the idea if it meant she got to spend more time with Ms Thomas. And the more time she spent with her, the easier it was to fall for her. Her only mistake? She had made the assumption that Camryn felt the same way. She was tactile and generous. When they made love, it was with respect and passion. Even their more rampant couplings had always ended with cuddling and laughter. She felt comfortable with Cam and enjoyed their budding relationship. Only it wasn't a relationship, not for Camryn Thomas. For her, it was just fun. Amanda was nothing more than someone to pass the time with, and it hurt!

"Why did you come here?" Cam asked. "How did you even know where I lived?"

"This is LA Cam, everyone knows where anyone lives. Tourists pay for that kind of information," she explained before adding, "I came to the beach to apologise, but then I wasn't sure and I was going to leave, that's when you saw me and I…I panicked and ran." She smiled sadly. "Does she make you happy?" she asked, referring to Michelle.

"Yeah, she does. I never—" She paused to consider her words before continuing. "I didn't look for love Amanda, it found me. I tried to avoid it…I didn't think…I didn't think I could ever love anyone again, but I was wrong, and it has nothing to do with her being better than you or her being an actress…it's just her. I never understood soul mates before, I didn't get it, but I do now." Amanda nodded. A single tear slid slowly down her cheek and Cam reached forward to wipe it away. "Your soul mate is out there and when you find them you're gonna realise that…"

"It's ok Cam, I get it." Amanda took a step forward. For a brief moment, Cam thought she was going to kiss her, but she didn't. Instead Amanda focused her stare more intently on the blue eyes that watched her. "I don't have to like her."

"You don't know her so, you can have no feelings about her either way," Cam replied. "You don't have to hurt her though, to get back at me." She studied her some more. Was Amanda really capable of being Michelle's stalker? She would never have considered it until that last comment, but now, she had to consider that it could literally be anyone.

"Why would I hurt her?" She frowned at that, studied Cam herself now as she tried to understand where she was coming from. "I think I should go," she said, suddenly turning to leave. "Have a good life Camryn," she called over her shoulder. Cam watched her leave before turning on her heels and jogging back to the house.

"What took you so long? I was just about to call Gavin."

Cam closed her eyes as she flopped down onto the couch. "It was someone I know…from my past." She was a little sheepish, if anything, and the panic that had initially flooded Michelle gently dissipated.

"Another one?" Michelle joked, her face turning serious when Cam didn't smile. "Who was it?"

"Amanda. She was the first woman I met when I got to LA."

"The one you hurt by not being clear about your intentions?" Michelle asked, remembering the story. Cam nodded. "What did she want?"

"To apologise." Cam rubbed a palm across her face. "While you was in Hawaii…When I brought your parents to see you?" Michelle nodded; she obviously remembered. "By coincidence, Amanda was working on reception. I tried to apologise to her and explain again, but she blew me off and told me I shouldn't flatter myself." She thought she detected a small smirk slip across Michelle's face before she got herself together again.

"Brunette? Beautiful? Your type?" Michelle inquired with a raised brow.

"I don't have a type," she scoffed, "But yes, she is a brunette and very pretty. Why?"

"She was quite rude to me when I needed a new key card that day because a certain someone had stolen mine." She raised a brow again and giggled. "I just put it down to a bad day. No American wants to work on Thanksgiving if they don't have to."

"Why didn't you say anything?"

"Like I said, I just put it down to someone having a bad day...You don't think..." She left the question unasked, and Cam shook her head.

"No, I don't think she would be the type to send those kind of photos, but we have to consider it could be anyone. Especially somebody we know."

Chapter Twenty-One

Christmas morning arrived and Cam woke early. Her eyes focused across the bed to the long dark hair fanned out on the pillow as the beauty sleeping next to her breathed deeply. In and out, in and out. It was soothing, and Cam spent a few minutes just observing her.

If it hadn't been for Michelle's family arriving the previous evening, she would have considered just hunkering back down under the duvet and wrapping herself around that warm torso, letting her fingertips explore. Still, she was tempted.

They had had a wonderful meal together the previous evening and there had been a lot of laughter. The children had been so excited to see all the presents under the tree, and now Cam wanted to put the finishing touches to their first Christmas as a family together. Seeing Michelle in her element, enjoying herself with her family around her, was something Cam loved to see. She'd spent the evening showing off and being the Hollywood drama queen they all loved as she regaled and entertained them all with stories and jokes from her time on sets and locations over the previous few months. She really was a great actress, Cam thought, as she amused them all without the slightest hint that anything was wrong.

As they all slept quietly in their beds that morning, Cam forced herself from the comfort of her lover's arms and got dressed. She snuck outside, finding all the equipment in place that she expected to be there. It didn't take long as she went about switching it all on.

Rushing back towards the house to set the coffee machine running and to get breakfast on the go, she found herself face to face with someone that definitely shouldn't be there. Jessica!

She placed her hand over her heart. "Jesus Christ, again!

What are you doing here?" She was beginning to think she was going to have to physically put Jessica on a plane back to the UK herself, just to get rid of her. *Maybe if I just pay her off?*

"Camryn, it's Christmas. I have a gift for you," she said, smiling as she held out a small box wrapped beautifully and tied off with a bow.

"Jessica please just leave, I don't want any gifts from you, ok?" She tried to walk past her, but her ex pushed out a hand to stop her.

"I can't just leave Camryn, don't you understand that? I love you! Please just stop this now, ok? I get it, I hurt you and now you're punishing me, I understand baby, and I forgive you," Jessica said, continuing to smile at Camryn.

Astonished by what she was hearing, Cam pushed past her. Turning, she said as calmly as she could, "If you don't leave, I will call the police." She watched the look of incomprehension slowly cross Jessica's face. "I don't have time for this Jessica, there are far more important things going on, ok? So please, just go home. Go back to the UK and live your life."

Walking through the door, she kicked it shut behind her and was greeted by two overly excited children screaming about the snow and Santa and presents. Michelle's niece Dylan and her nephew Zac reminded Cam of her own childhood Christmases when she would wake her older sister Caroline and the two of them would creep down the stairs only to be overwhelmed with excitement once the tree came into view and all of the presents that had arrived overnight sat proudly waiting for them. In that moment, Cam forgot all about Jessica as the snow machine she had hired continued to pump out white fluff all over the house and beach. Her thoughts were pulled back to the present as the kids ran off back towards the stairs screaming for Michelle.

"Aunty Shell, Aunty Shell, come on, get up," they shouted in unison as they tore off, running up the stairs with as much speed as their tiny legs could give them. "Granma, Grampa, it's snowing, look..."

One by one, the adults of the house woke and staggered, stretching and yawning, from their rooms to see what all the noise was about. Looking out toward the beach, they all gasped at the newly laid 'snow'.

"Oh my God, Cam what did you do?" Michelle said, laughing and jumping around with the children. She hadn't seen snow in years, unless you counted the times she had gone away to ski, which hadn't been that often.

"Me? Nothing to do with me, Santa must have caused it." Cam laughed as the kids' eyes went wide. They ran from one window to the other, shrieking in that way that only kids can.

"Santa brought lots of presents Aunty Shell," Dylan said, the R sounding more like a W. The four-year-old tugged on the sleeve of Michelle's dressing gown to get her attention.

"He did?" she said, looking over at the tree. "Wow, well, we better go see then, huh?" she replied as she bent down to pick the youngster up and carried her on her hip.

The children and Michelle sat by the tree, passing out presents to Martha, Bob, and her brother's wife, Jennifer.

Robbie came to stand next to his sister's girlfriend. They were similar in height, but where Cam was lean, he was stockier. Where she was blonde, he was dark like his sister. He had Michelle's eyes though, and when he smiled it was with that same open and honest face that Cam had fallen in love with, the difference being his had stubble.

"Thank you for all of this, the kids will be talking about it for years." Cam had expected his voice to be as smoky and hoarse as Michelle's but it wasn't; it was smooth and calming instead.

"I'm just glad they're enjoying it," Cam replied as Michelle walked towards to them with presents in hand.

"One for you," she said, passing a small box to Robbie, "and one for you too." She smiled and leaned in to kiss both of them on the cheek. "Merry Christmas."

"Thank you," they both replied in unison. Robbie unwrapped a beautiful gold watch and Cam unwrapped a new iPhone.

"You might wanna check out the photo album in private," Michelle whispered before turning and walking away. Cam blushed a little, but made plans to take a private moment and do just that as soon as it was polite to do so.

Sitting tucked into the tree was another present with Michelle's name on it. She pulled it out and smiled over at Cam. It was sweet of her to hide a little extra present in the tree. She would save it for later though, just in case it wasn't *child-friendly*. She giggled to herself and tucked the small parcel in her dressing gown pocket.

When all the gifts had been unwrapped and the paper cleared away, Martha served breakfast, with Dylan and Jennifer's help. Maria was not allowed to work Christmas, New Year, or her birthday regardless of how much she insisted she wanted to. However, she was invited as a guest at the party tomorrow, and Cam would then give her the gift she had been planning.

Everybody sat around the large table talking animatedly with each other. The children were still too excited, but managing to eat something under the watchful eye of their grandmother.

"So Robbie," Michelle said. "Cam and I have one more gift for you and Jennifer, if you would like it?" She grinned at her brother.

"Intriguing, please go on younger sister of mine." He laughed and took his wife's hand in his. Michelle turned to Cam and nodded.

"Well, when Michelle mentioned that your wedding anniversary was next week, we thought maybe you might like to enjoy a second honeymoon, she said you hadn't been able to get much time away together by yourselves since the kids were born and so we thought maybe you would like to spend a week or two in Paris, and we would be happy to have the kids stay with us," Cam explained to a shocked Robbie and Jen.

"Are you serious?" Jen asked.

"Yes, I have an apartment in Paris, and we can arrange flights to get you there, unless you would prefer a different destination. I have a villa in Greece and property in Italy, the UK, and Spain, so you can take your pick," Cam suggested.

"And you want to voluntarily take the children while we're gone?" Robbie laughed, his teasing smile growing by the second.

"You bet!" Michelle said. Grabbing Dylan in a bear hug, she kissed her head, making the four-year-old giggle.

"So what do you think?" Cam asked them both. "I'd love the opportunity to get to know them better." Jen looked at Robbie and smiled. There wasn't much to think about other than how long they could go for. It was the holidays, and Michelle had already discovered that Robbie had taken a few extra days so they could fly out here and enjoy their time at the beach. She was pretty sure they would say yes.

"I think we say yes, thank you," Robbie answered for them both.

~Next~

That night, once everybody had finally gone to bed, Cam took Michelle's hand and led her to their bedroom.

"I have spent all day thinking about you and I'm not waiting a minute longer so, I have done everything you asked of me today. I created the perfect Christmas for your niece and nephew. I helped cook a perfect dinner *and* I didn't complain when I had to wash up either! Nor did I whine when your father decided to have a night cap. So, I think it's only fair that I get my real present now!" Cam finished speaking and sat on the edge of the bed, waiting.

"I see, and what exactly do you think your real present might be?" Michelle teased. "Was the iPhone not enough?" She winked, climbing onto Cam's lap to straddle her thighs. Once settled, she leant forward slowly and began to kiss the long neck of her lover.

"Oh the phone was great. I especially enjoyed the photo of you wearing the black lace...I am rather hopeful it will require unwrapping sometime soon." Cam sighed gently as Michelle continued with the tender brushing of lips against skin.

The actress sat up, fixing her lover with her eyes; there was no need for words when they got like this. It was as though they could read each other's minds; one glance, a raise of an eyebrow, the shift of a hip, every subtle nuance was read by the other and acted upon. Cam glanced down at the buttons on Michelle's shirt, and Michelle unfastened them. Cam licked her lips in anticipation. As the shirt fell open, she leant forward. Kissing Michelle's throat, she slid her hands under the shirt, easing it from her shoulders to reveal the very same black lace.

Michelle rocked her hips almost imperceptibly, but Cam felt it and lifted her so she could turn them and place Michelle on her back on the bed, tugging jeans down her toned legs. Michelle sat up and rid the blonde of her trousers. She then encouraged her to her knees and yanked her top free and up, off over her head.

Both of them were left with nothing more than their underwear. Black lacy underwear, Cam grinned before glancing at Michelle's chest and observing the bra come off. Another raised brow and Cam was topless too. A small smile from both and they stood together. Cam dragged Michelle's underwear down to the floor, then stood and waited for Michelle to reciprocate.

She took Michelle by the hand again and climbed onto the bed, Michelle following her wherever she would lead. Falling onto her back, Cam pulled Michelle to straddle her again. Holding her by the hips, she encouraged her to start moving, her slick folds sliding back and forth over Cam's tight abs. They moved together in sync, each pulling the other further along the path of ecstasy until the route was mapped. The jolt of collision brought a shuddering halt as bodies crumpled into a heap.

Chapter Twenty-Two

"Morning," Michelle rasped, her voice thick with sleep. She lay prone on her stomach, satisfied and relaxed. Her long raven hair fanned out across the pillow as Cam ran her fingers through it.

"Hello gorgeous, I was wondering if you might like to join me for breakfast?"

"Of course, where is everyone? It's very quiet," she said, sitting up and leaning against the pillows. The cover fell across her lap, leaving her bare-breasted and a sight for Cam's sore eyes.

"I think they went out. It's a beautiful day on the beach."

Michelle considered her answer, a sly grin appearing on her face. "I say we forgo breakfast and then stay here." Her hand reached up to wrap behind Cam's neck and tug her closer. Odours of sweat and sex hung in the air, baiting her into forgoing her plans and clambering right back under the sheets to claim her lover's body once more, but there was too much riding on this breakfast.

"Well, on any other day I would jump at that offer, however, I have plans for you already." She kissed her briefly. A moment longer and she really would give in and climb back into bed with her.

"You are full of surprises this morning."

"Yes, yes I am, and hopefully a few more, now shift it Dimples. I need you up, dressed, and ready to go in 30 minutes."

"30 minutes? You are joking? That's never going to happen babe!" Michelle sat upright, her knees brought up to her chest under the sheet as she chuckled at Cam's retreating form.

"29 minutes!" Cam called over her shoulder, grinning as she left the room.

Thirty-five minutes later and Michelle swanned into the kitchen, expecting to find Cam cooking breakfast. Instead, what she found was Cam in a beautiful yellow dress, her hair hanging loosely around her shoulders. Holding a bouquet of roses, she stood at the door waiting for her.

"Well, this is a surprise." Michelle smiled. Her eyes danced and sparkled as she took in the sight in front of her. If she recalled correctly, she hadn't ever seen Camryn in a dress before now. "You look beautiful, darling."

"I thought I'd make an effort!" she remarked, looking down at herself before claiming those brown eyes all for herself once more. "Are you ready to go?"

"We're not eating here?"

"Nope, I like to think I can arrange something a little more romantic than the usual cornflakes and toast at the breakfast bar." Cam smiled that smile, and Michelle felt she would follow her into the ocean if she had to.

And that's almost what she did do.

"Wow Cam, this is magical," Michelle gushed. On the beach waiting for them were a table and two chairs, the artificial snow now evaporated. The table sat beneath a cabana and reminded Michelle of the four-poster bed that Cam had had installed on the deck of the yacht.

Taking their seats, Cam poured champagne and orange juice into two glasses. It was a glorious day for this time of year. The sun was high in the sky, warm, and shimmered brightly on the waves as though they sparkled with fairy dust. "Beautiful," Michelle whispered as she looked out to sea.

"Yes, you are," Cam whispered back. Michelle smiled at her, the moment burning into her memory. From nowhere, Maria appeared, placing two plates down on the table: poached eggs with smoked salmon on an English muffin with hollandaise sauce. She smiled at them both and then, with a small nod of her head, she backed away and left Camryn to finish the plan.

They ate in relative silence. Words were not always needed at times like this, when just being together meant more than anything. Once they were finished, Cam placed the plates neatly on top of one another and moved them to one side before taking Michelle's hand in her own.

"When I moved here I thought all my dreams had come true. I looked out onto the beach and I could see the ocean; it was magical, and everything I'd ever wanted in life...until I found you."

"Aw, Camryn."

Cam smiled, but raised her hand. "I'm not done." Michelle laughed and tilted her head as Cam continued. "I look at you and I see everything I want in life. I can buy houses, cars and things, but...*you*, you're priceless, and I can't buy what we have, no matter how much money I have." A solitary tear trickled its way down Michelle's cheek and Cam swiped it away gently with her thumb and a smile. "Even in such a short space of time, I know that what we have is perfect, and there is only one thing I want to do to change it." Michelle remained motionless, waiting for Cam to say the words she hoped she was planning to say.

Cam reached for a small shell that had been placed on the table as part of the decoration. Michelle watched as she lifted it up and uncovered a ring. A platinum ring, with a diamond set in the centre so big that it caught the sunlight, with sapphires and rubies alternately surrounding it.

"I have spent my entire life waiting for you. I need you, I need your love for me. I want you with every cell of my being and there isn't a day goes by that I don't think of this moment. There is so much love inside of me, and it's only there because of you, because of the love you have for me. So, I'm not going to go down on one knee in this dress," she chuckled, "but I am going to ask you to marry me." She grinned hopefully.

With happy tears now streaming uncontrollably down her face, Michelle nodded and laughed and smiled. "Yes, always yes," she said, as she threw her arms around Cam's neck and kissed her. Cam took her finger and slid the ring on. The world stopped turning for a few moments. The breeze no longer blew; the tide no longer turned; all that mattered was them and this moment in time. Cam felt like all her dreams had come true. If she didn't have a penny to her name tomorrow, then it wouldn't matter because she had Michelle, and that made her the richest woman on the planet.

Back at the house, Martha and Bob, along with Robbie, Jen, and the kids, stood watching the scene with smiles and whoops. Maria clasped her hands together and sent a small prayer skywards. Her girls were happy.

When they looked up, it was to a sea of happy, smiling faces all wanting to kiss and hug them. Congratulations were sung and shouted as everyone celebrated together.

"You were all in on this?" Michelle asked, laughing.

"Afraid so honey, Cam told me last night over a nightcap." Her father smiled, delighted to see his daughter so happy.

"You asked my dad?" Michelle chuckled.

"Well, I told him my plan, I didn't quite ask." Cam joined in with the giggling. There was happiness all around as they sipped on champagne.

"So, what other plans have you made for us?" Michelle asked Cam with a wink.

"We are having a party! Everyone will be here later to celebrate with us."

"And if I'd said no?"

"Firstly, you told me it would always be yes, and secondly, I only invited people over for post-Christmas drinks."

The celebrations began there and then. Maria was in her element, organising the kitchen and everyone else into helping set up the buffet tables.

"Before everyone arrives, do I get to spend a little time with my fiancée?" Michelle whispered into Cam's ear, enjoying the fact that she could now call her girlfriend, her fiancée.

"I think we can find a few minutes to give you what you want!" she replied back seductively.

Chapter Twenty-Three

Naked but for her engagement ring, Michelle lay on the bed, panting and sated alongside an equally out of breath and sweating Camryn.

"Jesus that was good." Cam exhaled a breath and rolled over to face Michelle. "I want to spend every day making you smile like that."

"Oh trust me lover, you already do." Wrapped in Cam's arms, Michelle spoke quietly. "I love my ring. I will buy one for you too." Her fingers danced down Cam's tummy, stroking her skin lightly.

"I had it made in the colours of both of our flags: red, white and blue."

"It's beautiful! I want you to feel the way I do when you wear the one I buy you." She held her hand in the air to study her ring finger. "I can't wait to be Mrs Thomas," she grinned, before considering the other option. "Or will you become Mrs Hamilton?"

"I think I like Mrs Hamilton-Thomas." Cam smiled. "But I like *wife* much better."

Lying together, wrapped up in each other like this, was how Michelle envisaged their life would be. Always so close, partners in everything; there was nothing she wouldn't do for her, and nothing she couldn't ask of her. It was bliss.

~Next~

Copious amounts of champagne had been consumed and all of Maria's food had been eaten by the time the last of the guests finally left. The celebrations had been well and truly enjoyed. Much to Cam's amusement, nobody was surprised at the proposal at all; in fact, most were surprised it had taken this long.

Cam collapsed fully clothed onto the bed, exhausted. Michelle lay tucked up next to her, one leg hooked over that of her lover, her arm laying across Cam's chest. She could feel Cam's fingers playing with her hair. The intimacy of just being able to lay together like this was something Michelle loved more than anything. They were both a little drunk, on alcohol and love.

"Oh, I *forgot,"* Michelle said, suddenly jumping up and moving quickly to the other side of the room. She opened a drawer. "I hid this up here in case it was something a little bit naugh-ty." She practically sang the last part as she waved the box at Cam.

Cam looked at her and then the box inquisitively. "What is it?"

"My present, the one you hid in the tree."

"I didn't hide anything in the tree babe, maybe it's not for you."

"It has my name on it," she said, bringing it back to the bed to show Cam. "It's probably a joke from Robbie then." She laughed when she wobbled and almost fell on top of Cam. It was only a small box. She opened it carefully, expecting something to jump out and frighten her. What was in it didn't jump out, but it did frighten her.

The box held a tiny doll. Each of its eyes had been gouged out and it had been decapitated. Tossing it to the floor, she screamed. The word 'Whore' was written across its bare torso.

"Jesus." Cam sobered in an instant, scurrying off the bed and picking it up to look at it more closely. "What the hell? You found this in the tree?"

"Cam, I'm scared," she said, nodding as she grabbed a hold of her lover and held her tight, needing the haven that she was in order to feel safe again.

"Some fucker came into our home!?" Cam was livid that someone had the audacity to enter their home, their sanctuary, and for what? Because they couldn't see past their bigoted and narrow-minded ideas? It was ok to harass someone and frighten them?

"Oh God, we can't stay here, not while we have the children with us," Michelle cried. "Should we cancel? Robbie will understand."

"No! We are not letting this arsehole change our plans, but I think we need to tell them so they can decide if they want to leave their kids with us still."

"Why are they doing this? I know we expected some backlash against us, but this isn't what I was thinking." Michelle sat against the pillows, as far away from the box as she could get, arms wrapped tightly around her knees.

"We need to tell Detective Gomes. I'm going to call him, ok?" she said, pulling her phone from her pocket.

"Please Cam, can we do it tomorrow? We're celebrating our engagement. I don't want this day ruined by a crazy person." Even so, she knew she would have trouble sleeping peacefully tonight.

Cam thought about it, and though she was worried, she had to agree that with all the people around them tonight, it was highly unlikely anyone would try anything. So she agreed to call the police tomorrow. They put the doll back in the box and, picking up all the wrapping paper, they placed the whole thing in a different box to give to the police the following day and placed it out of sight into the closet.

Chapter Twenty-Four

The following morning couldn't come fast enough for Cam. It was still dark when she got up. The cold air of morning felt throughout the house was no different to the dark chill that ran through Cam's veins just thinking about how close a maniac had come to getting to Michelle. She had barely slept a wink, unable to relax. She wasn't going to allow anyone to hurt her fiancée; she would die before she let that happen.

After explaining everything to her parents and then to Robbie and Jen, it was decided that Bob and Martha would stay on with them and help keep an eye on the kids and Michelle. The police had been concerned but also made it clear there wasn't much they could do about it unless there was some evidence leading them to a potential assailant.

Cam had spoken directly with Detective Gomes. He interviewed everyone who had access to the property. Cam hated that; she trusted every single person who had been invited to their home, and to have them all questioned like criminals was just appalling to her. But Gomes was insistent, and he wanted access to the studio also; this was now no longer just someone sending malicious mail. Twice now, Shelly Hamlin's home had been invaded, and he was livid that it wasn't being taken more seriously by the officers that had attended the house.

"I don't know if it makes any difference," Cam told him, "but as you're speaking with everyone that's been here, I just remembered that two of my ex-girlfriends have been here recently. I doubt either has anything to do with it; in fact, I don't think Amanda was even in the state when this started, but maybe if you have a word with Jessica – she was here Christmas morning, trying to give me a gift."

"Ok, Jessica is causing a problem?" He pulled out his notepad and scribbled her name down.

"Well, yes, no..." She tried to smile, but it was nauseating thinking about Jess when there were much more serious issues to deal with. "She came here thinking she could win me back, we broke up under... difficult circumstances and now, well she thinks an apology will solve it and we will be in love again. Like I say, it's me she's infatuated with. She's harmless; just annoying."

"I see, well let me have a word with her. What is her full name?" Cam gave him her details and he promised to have a word and maybe encourage the young woman that it was best for her to go back home.

In the meantime, Gavin was instructed to beef up security around the house. Wherever Michelle went, he went. It terrified Cam every second of the day that she didn't have Michelle in her sight, but she knew she had to deal with it. She trusted Gavin, and she was trying hard not to put any more pressure on Michelle, but it was a struggle.

~Next~

Two days later and Robbie and Jen headed off to Paris for a week of romance. They were adamant that everything would be fine and their children would both be safe. They had both spoken with Gavin, and he had assured them that Cam had given the green light to use whatever means necessary, and as such he would put a body on both of the children if they wanted him to. They didn't want that if it could be avoided; the kids needed to feel safe and not be followed around everywhere they went. They would ask questions and be frightened for Michelle. Everybody was of the opinion that with the police taking it seriously and the security around Michelle being improved, whoever it was that was doing this would soon realise it was futile to continue or they would be arrested. Plus, the kids would mainly be at home or with Camryn if they went out. That way they could avoid anything untoward happening if the worst occurred.

~Next~

They spent a lot of time those first couple of days just chilling out on the beach. Zac and Dylan were both good swimmers and loved being by the ocean. Cam chased them up and down on the sand to the point that Michelle was never sure which of them was the most worn out when it came to bedtime.

Martha and Bob had taken the opportunity to go to Beverly Hills and enjoy lunch and some shopping. Cam felt guilty that they had had to stay behind and help when it should have been time they spent doing whatever they wanted to. Bob assured her though that they would be more than happy to spend time with their daughter, and Cam accepted that it was probably best that they were here to help, especially if the anonymous lunatic tried anything else.

Gavin took up position with his newest recruit, Jorge, close enough to see anyone approaching, but otherwise they looked like a couple of guys sunbathing.

"Maria, Maria!" shouted Dylan as she dashed screaming into the house with her sun-kissed blonde curls flowing behind her. The other blonde chased her with a bucket of water.

"Oh my goodness Camryn, what are you doing now?" she laughed as Dylan hid behind her, clinging to her legs.

"There was a dragon on the beach Maria, breathing fire, and I've got to throw water on it to stop it burning all the sandcastles down," Cam explained with playful eyes as she chased the little girl into the kitchen.

"A dragon you say? Oh my, then I should help you catch it?" she said, turning quickly and grabbing a squealing Dylan. She lifted her into the air and ran outside with her.

"Quick Maria, put the dragon down and I'll douse its flames." As soon as Maria put Dylan on the ground, she was back off down the beach to where Michelle sat laughing with Zac.

"Oh my God Maria, that kid's going to wear me out," Cam laughed. "Come join us on the beach."

"Ah, you love it." She smiled and turned to walk back in the house "If I get time, I'll come and sit with you later."

It wasn't the warmest day, but it was sunny, and even in their wetsuits the kids were not about to ignore the ocean. They ran in and out of the water, splashing each other under Cam and Michelle's watchful gaze. It was easy to relax when she knew Gavin and the others were dotted around the house and the beach keeping a watchful gaze on them all. It hadn't taken much more than a telephone call from Gavin before he had a team of old Army pals willing to work for Cam.

By late afternoon, Cam was kicking a football back and forth with Zac, while Dylan slept peacefully curled up in Michelle's lap. Sucking on her thumb, she had curled up against Michelle's chest, peacefully dreaming. Cam smiled at the sight. The actress had pulled a blanket up over them both and was gently rocking, her lips moving, and although Cam couldn't hear from the distance, she was sure that she was singing a lullaby. For one brief moment, she imagined their own kids, something she had never considered before.

~Next~

"I think tomorrow I'll take Zac and Dyl to the park while you're out with your parents. I can get them to push me on the swings," Cam said with a smile as she trailed fingertips up and down Michelle's arm.

"Oh, I'm sure they would love that," Michelle said, snuggling up close and wrapping her arms around her soon-to-be wife. "Just remember that you don't have all day, the munchkins will be required to return and you'll have to find some other form of child labour!" she giggled

"Damn, I had such plans too." Cam smiled. She was looking

forward to it; it had been ages since she had gone to the park herself, and getting to know the kids some more was what this week was all about.

Chapter Twenty-Five

"So, shall we take a picnic?" Cam asked, as two sun-tanned and smiling faces grinned up at her from their seats at the breakfast bar. Each of them had spoons in hand, shovelling cereal in like it was running out. Michelle and her parents had just left, heading into Beverly Hills for shopping and lunch. Cam had booked them a table at Rafael's, and Martha was beside herself with excitement. Cam got the impression that Bob would've preferred the park, but he didn't get that option as Martha marshalled him out of the door speaking ten to the dozen on what they would be doing all morning.

"Yeah!" two little voices shouted together.

"Where are we going?" asked Zac, the elder of the two. He looked just like his dad. Dark and brooding, he was gonna be a looker when he was older. He had been blonder when younger, so everyone assumed Dylan would follow suit at some point.

"Well, I thought you might like to go to the park today," Cam replied. "How does that sound?" she asked as she pulled together a quick picnic. She had never spent much time with children, but somehow they seemed to work well together, probably because at heart Cam still felt like a kid. She loved running around chasing them and playing all the silly games they enjoyed. Even playing dolls with Dylan was fun, although the kid preferred Michelle to play with because apparently she did voices.

"And then when we get back, Maria said we can help her make cookies and a cake," Cam continued. She had packed sandwiches and fruit, a bag of potato chips, and waters. They didn't need much because they wouldn't be gone all day; she planned to have them back just after lunch because Michelle would be home by then and they all planned to go to the movies in the evening, where she was pretty sure they would munch their way through popcorn and candy too.

"Yes!!" said Zac with both arms raised above his head. He was a sweet kid, very much a big brother that was always looking out for his little sister.

~Next~

It was a glorious day. The sun was warm and high in the sky. Trees lined the pathway down to the swing park, the branches arching over, creating a tunnel of greenery. It was kind of magical, and Cam noted that unlike back home where the trees would be bare by now, it was still warm and vibrant as they walked the pathways. Cam wore a simple sweater with linen trousers, but even that, she was beginning to think, was too much.

Dylan ran off in front of them, laughing and giggling as she chased leaves and butterflies. That kid was always happy, Cam thought to herself. Zac was much more serious and stuck by Cam's side, wanting to know everything she knew about European football. Soccer they called it here, and it grated on Cam. She couldn't understand how they called a game where you threw a ball to each other football! Europe had it right, the rest of the world had it right. Football was played with your feet, and she was ecstatic that Zac loved the game. Now she just had to convert him to supporting her favourite team.

When Cam looked up, she could see Dylan was speaking to someone. She called out to the youngster, but clearly the child couldn't hear her from this distance. The figure didn't look like anyone to worry about, a woman most likely, judging on size and stature.

"Zac, wait here with the bag, okay? I'm just going to go and get Dylan." She spoke calmly, but she was anxious. The last thing she wanted was for anything to happen to someone else's kids while in her care.

She placed the bag down by the young boy's feet and smiled at him before turning and walking briskly towards the other youngster in her care.

As she drew closer she could see the stranger was definitely a woman. Her back was to Cam, but she seemed familiar in her stance. Cam grabbed a hold of Dylan's hand and gently pulled her to one side. When she looked up, she realised it wasn't a stranger; it was Jessica. Bending down, she spoke to the little girl. "Hey, Dylan. Can you go and wait with Zac, just up there?" She pointed towards where Zac stood watching. Dylan looked between Cam and the lady that was talking to her, and then nodded and headed back towards her brother. Cam watched her go.

"What the fuck do you think you are doing?" Cam seethed now that Dylan was out of earshot. "How dare you keep doing this?"

"Camryn, I keep telling you, but you just won't listen! I listen, I listen to everything." Jessica smiled, looking tired. No, worse than that, she looked drained, and Cam briefly wondered how she had managed to afford to be here this long.

"I'm not doing this with you, Jessica! Enough is enough, I won't have you following me everywhere like this, it's weird. How the hell did you even know I was going to be here?"

"And I keep telling you, she should have ended things with you by now, but she doesn't listen either," Jessica pleaded, her green eyes watering. "Please Camryn, just come home."

It took a moment, but her words kept playing over in Cam's mind. 'She should have ended things with you by now,' and 'She doesn't listen either'.

"Oh my God, it was you," Cam said, incredulous as she put two and two together, annoyed with herself that she hadn't worked it out sooner. But Jess hadn't been obsessed with Michelle, had she? It was Cam that Jess was following like a lost puppy. She had never guessed it was Jessica who was stalking Michelle. "You sent that box and the doll; all the photographs! And what do you mean you listen!!? You bugged my home?"

"You gave me no choice! I gave you my heart, and you continue to keep that whore hanging around. Just tell her that you love me and we're back together—"

"Whore?! You foolish, stupid woman. Just listen to yourself, you're pathetic." Cam was shouting now, angered by this continued madness. "Listen to me. If you were the last living creature on this planet, I would choose to live alone!" she fumed. "I don't love you. I have never loved you, I realise that now. What we had was lust at the very best. You have to be the most delusional person alive if you think you stand any chance again." Her words were barely more than a hiss.

Jessica's face clouded with fury. Anger erupted through her as she listened to Cam tell her such horrible lies. She felt her hand fist and before she could stop herself, she punched Cam in the side; once, twice, three times, she lost count. When her anger finally began to subside, the realisation of what she had done hit her hard. Her line of sight was drawn to the area of Cam's torso that she had been hitting. Blood. Green eyes filled with terror as they scrambled back and forth before finally settling on the stunned blue eyes in front of her, eyes that had yet to register the enormity of the situation. She watched as the recognition of what she held in her hand suddenly became clear to Camryn. A knife.

And then she ran.

The world around Cam fell silent. Like an old black and white movie, she watched as Jessica turned and ran, and then like thunder, the roar of sound erupted once more as she took a deep breath. It hurt. Everything hurt. One second she had been venting her anger at her ex, and then the next she was being punched. But it wasn't a punch; she was bleeding, and she had the kids. *Shit, where are the kids?* She looked around and saw Zac a couple of hundred feet away with his arm around his little sister. Steadying herself, she began walking towards them, pulling the keys to the car from her pocket as she did so and keeping her injured side away from their view.

"Hey kids, we need to go back to the car for a second, okay?" Cam said, as calmly as she could. Her lungs burned, and the pain was ratcheting upwards with every breath and movement. She knew she was in trouble, knew that this was serious, but she had no choice but to keep going. She had to get the kids safe because she had no idea what Jessica would do now.

"Are you ok Cam? That lady hit you," Zac asked, a look of concern on his small face.

"Yeah Kiddo, I'm ok." She winced. "Let's get back to the car, eh?"

"What about the picnic?" Dylan asked innocently.

"We are going to have it in the car!" Cam smiled. She could feel the warm trickle of blood dripping down her torso. Her sweater was clinging to her, and it wouldn't be long before one of the kids would notice. She lifted the bag up her arm and winced, but used it to cover the area where she was wounded.

They moved as fast as Cam could. Each step was becoming more difficult, her breathing erratic, but the thought of keeping these kids safe from Jessica was all that consumed her. Reaching a distance that the car could be opened by the key fob, Cam instructed the kids to get in and not to open the door.

"I don't care who asks you to, you say no and you wait for Auntie Shell, ok?" She looked at them both and watched as they each nodded. Her breathing was ragged.

"Ok, what about you Auntie Cam?" Dylan asked her. Cam's heart strings tugged hearing the little girl call her Auntie for the first time.

"I am going to wait right here for Auntie Shell, ok? She won't be long, take the picnic and if you get hungry then eat something. Now hurry, get in and don't open the door!" She was trying to stay calm, but panic was beginning to creep in. She could see that the children were concerned, but she also knew she didn't have much longer to get help. She was losing a lot of blood and her heart was racing. Breathing was agonizing and with each lungful of air, it became more laboured.

Both of them climbed inside the vehicle with Zac dragging the picnic bag in behind him, and Cam hit the lock button on the fob. She made her way round to the back of the car and fell against it, the smear of her own blood caking the paintwork. Pulling herself over to the next car, she found a spot where she could see the car, but the kids would have difficulty seeing her. She didn't want them to be frightened if anything more serious happened. She was frightened, she knew she needed help, but first she needed Michelle to come and get the kids.

She left a voice message for Michelle. It was urgent: drop everything and come to the park.

Then she made the call to the emergency services.

"911, what's the nature of your emergency?" asked the operator.

"Ambulance," Cam gasped, her breath coming fast and short. "I'm in Tongva Park." She took another short breath. Her lungs were not working. She couldn't get enough air.

"What's the problem ma'am?"

"I...I've been stabbed," she spat out as a jolt of pain shot through her and she almost passed out. "On my side, there...there is a lot of blood and I...I can't breathe."

"Ok Ma'am, stay on the line with me please. Can you press against the wound for me? I need you to try and stem the bleeding. I have paramedics on route to you now. They won't be long, ok?" Cam could hear the woman tapping away on a keyboard as she spoke to her. All other sound had disappeared as she tried to focus on this one thing.

"Ok, I have…I've got…kids with me. I've locked them…in the car…and my…fiancée is coming…She's coming…to collect them." Every word she uttered was torture. Her chest hurt everywhere. Her eyelids were heavy as she gasped for breath. She could see a fine red mist on her hand after she coughed. Blood.

"Ok Ma'am, I'll pass that information on, I have police officers headed to your location too."

"I feel…so tired."

"Ma'am, can you tell me your name?"

"Cam…Camryn Thomas." She struggled to say it, the pain increasing with every moment that passed.

"That's great Cam, you're doing just great, just keep talking to me honey. The paramedics are almost there now. Is the assailant still there Cam?"

"Ok, no, I don't…think so." Her breathing was becoming ragged and her eyes wanted to close no matter how much she struggled to keep them open. She needed to see the kids, that they were safe. "So…hard to…breathe and stay awake, I…Tell Michelle I tried."

"Honey? Cam? Come on now, talk to me baby. Don't you want to tell Michelle yourself?"

Silence.

"Camryn, can you hear me? I need you to speak to me honey, come on now. Open your eyes, Cam."

Cam could hear someone talking to her, her voice was calm

and nice to listen to. She could make out the words, but they made no sense. *I am awake, aren't I? Open your eyes, she said. Open them!*

"I'm here." Barely a whisper, but the operator heard it.

"Thank God. Can you hear the siren yet, Cam? The paramedics are in the park. They are just looking for you now. What car are you in?"

"Audi...Black, Q7," Cam forced out through the pain of breathing and then collapsed.

Chapter Twenty-Six

When Michelle got Cam's message telling her to come to the park right away, she knew it was something awful. She could hear the panic in Cam's words, and now she too was panicking. They had literally just gotten to the first store when her phone beeped. Grinning when she saw the name Camryn pop up on her screen, she wasted no time in flicking the screen across and listened to what she thought was going to be a loving message saying how much she missed her. Instead, it had been a rambling plea to come right now.

She rushed out of the store, her parents encouraging her to go, that they would get a cab home.

"Get in the car now!" she screamed at Gavin, who didn't need to be told twice. He caught up with her, shouting instructions into a phone handset. They sped through the streets that led to Tongva Park while Michelle played the message she had just received. Gavin, serious most of the time, now looked deathly as they manoeuvred between traffic. The drive was a blur, and Michelle's only thought was getting to Cam.

The journey wasn't that far, but it felt like hours until they pulled into the parking area. From there they could see police and paramedic vehicles surrounding a car next to Cam's, the blues and reds of flashing lights bouncing off the windows and paintwork of the other vehicles in the area. A small gathering of people was crowded around as close as they could get in order to see what the commotion was. Michelle scanned the area and studied every face, but she didn't see Camryn.

Jumping out of the car she ran towards Cam's vehicle, almost making it before a police officer grabbed a hold of her and stopped her in her tracks.

"Ma'am, you can't go there," the burly cop with gentle brown eyes said calmly to her, his arm still out, preventing her from moving any further forward.

"I have to. My fiancée called me and said I had to come now to get the kids, where are they? Where is Cam?" she cried as her eyes raked back and forth, still searching for any sign of Camryn.

"Camryn Thomas?"

"Yes! Where is she?" Michelle said urgently, her movements stopping to look directly at him.

"Ma'am, can you follow me please?" He led them around a series of vehicles until they were away from the scene. "Ma'am, can you confirm your name for me please?"

"Michelle, Michelle Hamilton," she replied. "What is happening?"

"Ma'am, the children have been instructed not to open the car to anyone but 'Aunty Shell,' is that you?" Concern in his voice rattled her for a second. Why would the kids be locked in the car? Where the hell was Camryn?

"Yes, yes it's me! What is going on? I don't understand. Where is Camryn? I need to find Camryn."

"Ma'am, Ms Thomas was involved in an incident with an as-yet-unknown assailant. She has been wounded, and the paramedics are working on her as we speak," he explained as gently as he could.

"What?" Michelle couldn't comprehend what she was hearing. "Wounded how?"

"She has been stabbed," he said calmly and then added, "Multiple times, Ma'am."

"No!! No! This can't be happening; you've got the wrong person." She was trembling now. Her legs buckled as Gavin wrapped his arms around her and pulled her into his body tight.

"Ma'am, please, if we can deal with the children first," the officer pleaded, knowing how difficult this must be for her.

Michelle looked at the officer and nodded. Reaching the other side of Cam's car, she stepped forward and tapped gently on the window. Dylan's blonde head twisted around and her little tear-stained face lifted from its place, nestled in the crook of her brother's arm. Zac's gaze raised up too and he scrambled to the door, unlocking it in an instant.

"Auntie Shell, a lady hurt Cam, where is she?" Zac asked worriedly as Dylan clung to Michelle's neck. Gavin picked up Zac and then tried to take Dylan from her, but the youngster was having none of it and just clung harder, screaming.

"I don't know sweetheart, but we are going to find out as soon as we can," she said to Zac as she shushed and cradled Dylan.

Moments later, there was a flurry of activity, and the group of onlookers that had so far hidden the paramedics from view began to move and create a pathway. She could see the paramedics surrounding someone, Cam, on the floor behind a car. She could see what they were doing and she wasn't sure she wanted to look, but she needed to see Cam, needed to know she was going to be ok.

Without warning the paramedics all stood; shouting instructions to one another, they lifted the gurney. Quickly and effectively, they moved towards the ambulance. There was a paramedic sitting on top of Camryn, straddling her hips and lower torso and continuing chest compressions, while another moved speedily alongside, holding a mask against her face as he squeezed rhythmically. They shouted more instructions to each other as they moved together. It was like watching a dance routine; they all knew their steps and moved accordingly as they piled into the back of the waiting ambulance. With the doors slammed shut, the vehicle sped off, lights and sirens blaring. Michelle didn't even feel the tears drowning her face. She barely felt Gavin tugging her arm as he moved them all towards the car.

"What's happening?" Michelle cried out to nobody in particular. Dylan clung tighter.

"Where are they taking her?" Gavin asked the officer, who spoke into his radio and then came back with the name of the relevant hospital. "Can you escort us there?" he said, taking charge. He got everyone into the car, safely buckling both children into seatbelts. He followed the police cruiser out of the park, another behind him. Both cruisers had their sirens blaring, and Gavin was able to keep up as they were assisted through the traffic.

~Next~

Fairmont Medical Center was just a few minutes away, and they arrived just after the paramedics rushed Cam straight through the ER to a bay, where a team of doctors were waiting prepped and ready. The entire scene was surreal; every day Michelle walked onto sets just like this. She smiled to herself as an image of Camryn floated into her head. She always made jokes about Michelle's character on *Medical Diaries,* how she was known on social media as *Dr McSexypants.* What she would give now to hear one of those silly jokes.

They were taken through to a waiting area until someone could update them on what was happening. It was a sterile and overly-sanitised space with hard plastic chairs and a coffee table covered in weeks-old magazines, as well as a couple of polystyrene cups from other families that had sat and warmed these same seats not that long ago, as they too waited for information regarding a loved one. Time stopped for Michelle. It was a never-ending cycle of waiting.

~Next~

"Zac? Can you tell me what happened?" she gently coaxed the

boy. He was upset, rightfully, but he nodded.

"We just got to the park and I was walking with Cam but Dyl – Dylan had run ahead and some lady was speaking to her so Cam said for me to wait." He gulped, trying his best not to cry. "Then she sent Dylan back to me and she argued with the lady, then the lady punched her a lot of times before she ran off." Michelle was glad that he didn't seem to understand that punching meant stabbing. "Then we went back to the car and Cam made us get in and wait for you. She said, if we got hungry to eat the picnic, but we didn't eat it." Michelle nodded and pulled him into her chest, holding him. She made a mental note to get them both something to eat.

Gavin had called Erin and filled her in on what had happened. He didn't really know what to do with himself. Cam had had him looking out for Michelle, but it wasn't her who had needed him, and he wasn't there, he hadn't been there to protect his friend. As he looked around the room at Michelle on the phone to her parents, Zac sitting quietly on the chair, and little Dylan curled up on the bench, he understood what he had to do. Be there for them. That's what Cam would need from him.

When Erin and Angie turned up, they found Gavin guarding the door to the waiting room like a sentry. He seemed lost as they both hugged him and asked after Cam and Michelle.

"It's not good," he declared, solemnly.

Chapter Twenty-Seven

Michelle still hadn't heard anything from the doctors about Cam's condition. She was trying to remain as calm as possible so as not to worry the children any more than they already were, but it was a struggle not to scream and start demanding answers. It had been hours, at least that's what it felt like, each passing minute dragging on and on until they all blurred into one and she completely lost track of time altogether.

Thankfully Dylan had cried herself to sleep and was lying peacefully on a small couch under Gavin's jacket, her little tear stained face looking peaceful at last. Zac, though, was wide awake, and although playing games on Gavin's phone, he was very aware of what was going on around him and constantly looking up to see what the adults were doing.

"Michelle?" Erin gently addressed her; Michelle hadn't even heard the woman enter the room. "We brought coffee, here." She passed one over to her. Michelle took it gratefully, but didn't drink it. Instead, she placed it on the table and sat staring at it. "Gavin said there is still no news on Cam," Erin pressed, looking to Angie when there was still no response from Michelle. She just couldn't find any words that would make any sense. This whole thing made no sense. "It might be a long night, would you like me to take the children home for you and stay with them?" she said, trying again with something that maybe Michelle could talk about.

Finally the actress looked up, her warm brown eyes filled with terror and tears as she focused on the women in front of her who had become her friends over the last few months. Her gaze fell away and onto the children. They didn't need to stay here and be put through this torturous wait, and what if the news was bad? She didn't want them here to listen as doctors explained that.

"Would you mind? It might be easier for them in a more familiar environment," Michelle finally said, her eyes settling back on the coffee.

"Sure, I'll take them back to your place and stay as long as you need me to, ok?"

"Hey Zac, come say hi to my friends Erin and Angie, they're going to take you guys back home for me, and if you're really good they're going to order up some pizza and ice cream and let you watch some TV until I get home, ok?" Michelle explained to him.

"Ok Aunty Shell. Is Cam going to be ok?" Zac asked, concerned, while Dylan started to stir and move around.

"I am sure she is doing everything she can to make sure she will be," Michelle said, swallowing down the lump that had taken up permanent residence in her throat, not wanting to make any promises she wasn't sure she could keep, but desperately not wanting to believe anything could get any worse.

"I'll take care of them, don't worry, and give Cam our love when you see her," Erin said as she picked up Dylan and Angie took hold of Zac's hand. "She will pull through, I know her. She's too stubborn for anything else."

~Next~

The following few hours seemed to drag on for a lifetime. Her parents had arrived with Maria; they were all in shock themselves. Everything had been great when they had left the house earlier this morning. Cam and Michelle were as happy as happy could be. The kids were so excited to be staying with their aunts. What the hell had happened? It was Michelle who had been the target of a lunatic, not Cam.

It was another hour before there was a light knock on the door. Michelle stood up as a woman in her fifties wearing the same surgical scrubs that she wore on set entered. Only these scrubs were real, this was a real hospital, and Cam was a real patient. She introduced herself as Dr Laura Cartwright.

"I am the head surgeon dealing with Ms Thomas. I understand that you're her next of kin?" she asked kindly, clearly a woman used to dealing with relatives.

"Yes, Michelle Hamilton, I'm Camryn's fiancée," she said shakily, wrapping her arms around her torso. She had spent the last hour or so preparing herself for this, for someone to tell them what was happening, and she still wasn't prepared. Her mother appeared on one side, with Maria the other, both placing a comforting arm around her.

"Ok, well what I can tell you right now is that we have Ms Thomas stabilised. However, I do need to explain quite a lot to you, shall we sit down?" A small flutter of relief mingled with the anxiety as Michelle understood that Cam was, at least, alive. They took seats along a wall, Michelle perched on the very edge as Dr Cartwright began to explain. "Camryn presented to us with several puncture wounds to the left side of her chest and upper abdomen, three of which have caused further issues to her kidney, liver, and lung." She took a moment to allow the women listening intently to process that much before continuing on. "At the scene, Camryn's heart stopped. Thankfully the paramedics were able to resuscitate her quite quickly. She has what we call a hemopneumothorax. This happens when the chest cavity becomes filled with blood and air." She tried to explain things as simply as she could; it was frightening enough for the family being here already without bombarding them with medical terms they wouldn't understand. "When she arrived, we very quickly inserted chest tubes to drain the problem. She was then taken into surgery, where we performed an exploratory laparotomy. That's an incision we make in the abdomen that allowed us to fix the kidney and liver problems; however her heart stopped once more and we had no option but to perform an open thoracotomy." Michelle's eyes widened as she understood the term; she had picked up a lot of medical jargon in her time on *Medical Diaries*. Cracking someone's chest open on a medical drama show was always a points-winner with the viewing public.

"Oh my God," Michelle cried out, her hand covering her mouth, barely able to comprehend everything she was being told. Nothing made any sense; they were just going to the park to play on the swings.

"Like I said, we have her stabilised and I am fairly sure we have fixed the problems with her lung; however, she isn't out of the woods just yet. The next 24 hours are critical. It's my belief that any damage to her kidney and liver is not serious, but will obviously have some bearing on her recovery time span and will need to be monitored. She is currently sedated and will remain so for quite a while so that we can monitor her and give her body time to repair itself. Do you have any questions?"

Michelle nodded, she had thousands, but the only one that mattered right now was, "Yes, when can I see her?"

Dr. Cartwright smiled and replied softly to the actress, "I will speak to the staff taking care of her and make sure somebody comes and gets you the moment you can see her. I will also make sure that you are given the privacy you need at this time," she added kindly. Of course the hospital was well aware of who Camryn Thomas was involved with and the interest this was going to bring from the media. There would be a frenzy of paparazzi here the moment the news was released and this poor woman, who only wanted to know if her partner was alive, was going to be harassed and bombarded with questions and photographers. The hospital would have to do all it could to keep that at bay.

"Thank you, thank you so much. I can't ever repay you for everything you've done." Michelle spoke with genuine gratitude.

"We are just doing what we are trained for, but you're very welcome."

When Dr. Cartwright left the room, Michelle collapsed back into her chair and sobbed tears of relief.

Chapter Twenty- Eight

A quiet knock a few moments later was followed by a nurse popping her head around the door to inform Michelle she could now come through and see Camryn.

Michelle was up and following her along the corridor immediately. Her parents and Maria took the opportunity to take a seat once more. It was going to be a long night. Gavin followed Michelle; wherever she went, he went, even more so now. He had already organised for Jorge to come in and take over from him at the hospital. He was aware that Michelle wasn't going to leave, but at some point he would need to sleep. Until then he would become her shadow. It was the least he could do.

~Next~

She was in a room by herself. A huge glass window and a sliding door gave the medical staff the ability to keep a watchful eye on her from their station. Monitors beeped and whirred, tubes and lines linking them all to Cam as they registered every movement of her fragile body. She had a breathing tube down her throat, and her right arm had an IV attached to it. She looked gaunt, her face pale and her eyes closed. Her chest rose and fell with each breath the ventilator took for her. It was a scene from anybody's nightmare.

Michelle stood still by the door for a moment, taking it all in. She needed to accept it as real and process what she needed to do for Cam. She took a deep breath and then took the first tentative step forward. One by one her steps took her closer. Picking up a chair and bringing it to the side of Cam's bed, she sat down and really considered her lover lying there prostrate. She took her hand in her own; it was warm. Kissing her palm, she leant forward and placed her forehead against Cam's arm. Michelle sat that way for what felt like a long time and then, once she had composed herself, she sat up and began to speak.

"Hey Baby, I'm right here, ok? Don't you go getting any more ideas about leaving me, you hear?" she whispered as the tears slithered silently down her already tearstained cheeks. Her eyes stung from the constant saltiness and the rubbing of them. She was tired too, mentally drained; exhaustion wasn't too far away.

She stroked her hand along Cam's arm over and over, needing to touch her and feel the warmth of her.

"Zac and Dylan are both ok, you did such a great job looking out for them like you did, they think you're a hero." She laughed softly. "I told them that you were and you would show them your superpowers when you get home."

A few minutes later there was a knock on the glass and Martha and Bob slipped inside, along with Maria, to see how Cam was. They were visibly shocked to see their future daughter-in-law looking so ill. It was almost too much for Martha, who burst into tears and sobbed into her husband's chest.

"Oh Michelle, oh God, who would do this?"

Speaking very fast in Spanish, Maria rattled off what Michelle could only assume was a prayer as she crossed herself over and over. The woman looked rattled; she was watching one of her own lying in a hospital bed, and it was clearly taking its toll on the pseudo-mother.

Bob wrapped his arms around his wife and led her to a chair next to Michelle. "I'm going to go and get some coffee for us all, do any of you want anything else?" he asked, pulling up another chair for Maria.

"No Dad, I'm fine, coffee would be great though." She smiled wearily at her father and took her mother's hand. "She is going to be ok Mom, she can't be anything else!" Michelle said, her eyes never leaving Cam.

"She's a tough one, and so are you, we will get through this darling. Together, as a family, like we always do."

"That girl will not give up," Maria said, wiping her tears and taking the chair that Michelle insisted she bring closer.

The three women sat together in silence until Bob returned with coffee and sandwiches. They drank the coffee, but the sandwiches remained untouched while they chit-chatted about all the things that Cam had done, stories shared as they bonded over the one woman who linked them all.

When the clock struck midnight, Bob suggested they all go home and get some sleep, but as he knew she would, Michelle refused to leave.

"I'm not leaving her Daddy."

"Ok, we will get going then and let Erin go home, the kids will be fine," Bob said as he leant in to give Michelle a hug.

"Dad?"

"Yeah, baby?"

"Someone needs to collect Cam's car from the park, and I need her phone, someone should tell her family in the UK."

"I'll see to it," he said, resting his big, comforting hand on her shoulder. She reached her own hand up and gently patted his.

"Thank you."

When they left, Michelle got settled in the chair next to Cam's bed and tried to sleep. It was cold and uncomfortable, but she would suck up any amount of discomfort to be sitting here with Camryn. She awoke sometime later, unsure how long she had been asleep for, to find a nurse checking Cam's vitals.

"Is everything ok?" she asked the nurse, whose name badge read Rita. She was short and skinny with mocha-coloured skin and her hair cut close-cropped to her head. She looked to be about the same age as Michelle's mom and she had a kind face, with a warm smile that calmed Michelle in an instant.

"As good as she should be, she's a fighter this one," Rita calmly said as she moved about the room. She had seen a lot of people come through these doors. Many had had injuries like those that Camryn Thomas had and they hadn't gotten this far.

Michelle smiled at the woman, watching her as she went about her job. "Yes, she is." She wrapped her arms around herself and shivered a little.

"You must be cold. Here," Rita said, as she reached inside a cupboard and brought out another blanket, "put this around you. You're no good to her if you get ill, and she is going to need you."

"Thank you," she whispered, thinking about just how hard things were going to be for Cam in the next few weeks and months. But then she reminded herself that *difficult* was a whole lot better than *dead*.

Chapter Twenty-Nine

For three days, there was no change. They wanted to leave Cam under sedation for as long as they could to give her body the best chance of healing, but leaving her too long brought other complications, so the discussion as to when she would be brought out of it went on a little longer than Michelle cared for.

Medical Diaries was shut down for the holidays, but the network had made it clear that Michelle wouldn't be required on set until she was ready to return. Erin had organised the club as usual, Angie and Fran had been in to visit with Cam, and Gavin had not left her side except to sleep (and when he did, Jorge was in place). When her father brought her Cam's phone, she went through it searching for Cam's family. There was nobody listed as Mom, or Dad; however, there was a Caroline Thomas. She was pretty sure that was Camryn's sister's name, and so she took a chance and called the number. It went to a very impersonal answerphone and she left a message.

Maria had been popping in during the mornings with breakfast for Michelle and then again in the evening with dinner. Mostly it went uneaten, but still she brought it, along with clean clothes and anything else that she felt Michelle or Camryn would need.

"You no good to her if you don't eat," she said on the third morning. "You think she will be happy when she wakes up and find you too skinny?" So she ate the food and thanked Maria.

"Who did this to her?" Michelle asked as Maria pulled out another Tupperware container and placed it in front of Michelle.

"Only she can tell us, if she knows." Maria took hold of the hand that Michelle wasn't holding and brought Cam's fingers to her lips.

"What if it's because of me?" the actress asked, her gaze never leaving Cam's face. "What if I am the reason she is…" Maria didn't allow her to finish before she moved around the bed and grasped her by the shoulders, forcing her to look at her.

"You listen to me good. Whoever do this, is cos they crazy. You understand me?" She waited for Michelle to acknowledge that she did. "Camryn, she loves you and nobody, not a crazy person or a mugger or anyone is going to change that. So, you eat! And when she wake up, you love her. No more wasting time worrying who do this, that's the job for the police." When Michelle burst into tears, the little Mexican woman wrapped her in an embrace and sang to her.

~Next~

When Michelle finally slept, she would dream of Camryn, dream of her hands touching her again, her mouth on hers, smiling into kisses and whispering words she couldn't quite hear. She could see her up ahead, illuminated with sunshine, and she would run after her, never seeming to catch her before a huge shadow rose up and engulfed her, snatching her away before Michelle could reach her.

Her parents were back and forth, either keeping an eye on the children or taking turns staying with Michelle at the hospital. It was while Martha was with Michelle that the doctors finally decided it was time to try and wake Cam up from her sedation.

Dr Cartwright warned them that she would be groggy and most likely have no idea where she was or what had happened; she would probably talk nonsense for a few hours too, until the sedatives had completely left her system. It could take a few hours for her to start to come around, but Michelle didn't care about any of that; she just wanted to see Camryn's eyes open again, hear her complain and babble and waffle. It didn't matter what noises she made, so long as she was awake to make them.

Chapter Thirty

Four hours later, Cam's eyes began to open. She felt like she had been hit by a truck, her eyelids had been concreted over, and her voice box had been left in the Gobi Desert. She was pretty sure the last thing she remembered was feeling just like this, only this time it was worse. Much, much worse.

The pain in her chest was exponentially more than before, and different. It was more physical, like someone had ripped her open and moved all her innards around before slamming them all back in and stitching her up with red hot pokers.

She wanted to move her head, but it hurt; she wanted to squeeze the hand that was holding hers, but it hurt; she wanted to call for Michelle, but there was something blocking her throat. Someone was talking to her though, but she didn't recognise the voice. She had heard Michelle talking to her; she didn't know when that was though.

"Camryn, can you open your eyes for me?" asked the voice. She began to struggle, trying to understand where she was, who was talking to her. Everything was weird and woozy.

"Try not to panic Camryn, you are in the hospital and on a ventilator, it is helping you breathe, so don't fight it, ok?" said the voice she didn't recognise. She squeezed the hand that held hers and heard the voice as it continued talking to her, but she was tired, so tired.

Cam tried hard to focus just on her eyes, trying to force them to open. *Why is it so hard!? Just open!*

Bit by bit they flickered. It was bright, too bright, but she kept forcing them to open. She needed to see where she was and to find

Michelle. *Where is Michelle?* She could now see a face looking at her. She didn't recognise the face though. She looked nice, kind eyes, Cam thought as her own closed again.

The voice kept asking questions and Cam was sure that she was answering them. In her mind, the answers made perfect sense. Unfortunately, what came out was mainly grunts and moans and gibberish as expected, but for Michelle it was the greatest sound she had heard in the last three days.

When the doctors left the room, Michelle moved back to her spot by the side of the bed. She picked up Cam's hand in her own and felt Cam squeeze. It was barely perceptible, but it was there. Tears sprang to her eyes.

"Oh, thank God. Cam? Camryn? Baby, can you hear me?" For the first time in days, she looked into those beautiful blue eyes. They couldn't focus or hold her gaze, but it didn't matter. Cam was awake.

~Next~

Cam spent three more hours sleeping off the sedatives before she finally started to come around properly. Martha had left to get the children to bed and give them all the good news, but Michelle hadn't moved from her chair, her hand glued to Camryn's.

The doctors returned and did more tests on Cam. They spoke to each other and then to Michelle to explain what they were going to do next and to advise that she leave the room as it wasn't going to be pleasant to watch, but that Cam was perfectly safe and ok. She didn't want to leave her, not now, not when she was finally awake, but the doctor insisted that it was best all around if she wait outside. All too often the patient's families could become overwhelmed with the patient's distress, often becoming more of a problem than the patient themselves when it came to removing the ventilator, and the patient could become more distressed because of the family member's reactions, so it was best for everyone if Michelle just popped outside for a few minutes.

"Ok, Camryn can you hear me ok?" Doctor Cartwright asked gently and received a small nod from Cam. "Good, good. Ok, we are going to remove the ventilator so you can try to breathe for yourself."

It was one of the most unpleasant things Cam had ever experienced, but the relief at being able to finally breathe for herself was one of the best. The doctors did more tests, wanting to make sure her lungs were working by themselves. They seemed pleased enough.

"Now, Camryn, it is going to be quite difficult for you to talk. Your throat will be sore for a little while, ok? It is all completely normal, so try not to worry," Doctor Cartwright said softly to her patient. "I'm going to go and get Michelle now, ok?"

~Next~

"Shell?" her hoarse voice whispered when she heard the door open. The sweet scent of Michelle's perfume wafted across the room, and Cam breathed her in. It still hurt to breathe, but not like before; this was a different kind of pain. It wasn't because she couldn't breathe. It was because she did.

Michelle moved across the room in an instant, unable to stop the emotions that played out; she felt everything from euphoria to absolute agony. She was angry, not with Camryn, but with whoever did this.

"Hey, you," she said, smiling down at Cam, who was now fully awake and focused.

"Hey," she croaked. "Water?"

"Oh, of course, hang on," she said, grabbing a jug of fresh water and pouring a little into a plastic cup. She placed something that looked like a sponge on a stick into the water and held it to Cam's lips.

"You have to suck on this for now, sweetheart," she said, watching as Cam did just as she was told. It was like nectar.

"More, please." The whisper was so quiet, but for Michelle it was everything. When she had arrived in the park that awful day and watched as they worked to keep Cam's heart beating, she imagined the worst, that she would never hear her voice again, never see her eyes look at her the way they did. And she knew it wasn't something she could live with.

"I thought I was going to lose you," Michelle admitted.

"No, never babe," Cam croaked. The pain rocketed through her, an immense and fatigue brimming pain. "Why do I hurt so much?"

"Cam, you were attacked, someone stabbed you and..." she broke off, catching the lump that appeared in her throat and swallowing it down. "When they got you to the hospital, your heart, it...it—"

"Tell me." Cam wheezed, her eyes pleading for understanding.

"Cam, your heart stopped...twice and so, you've had major surgery sweetheart, to fix everything." Now it made sense, why her whole body felt like one gigantic bruise. She took a breath and, relieved she could actually breathe by herself again, she let her mind wander back to the park. Back to where it happened, to when...

"Jessica." Her voice was gruff, but louder as she tried to move, trying in vain to sit up before the pain ratcheted up a notch.

"What? You want Jessica!?" Michelle couldn't deny she was hurt by the outburst, but Cam was shaking her head and trying desperately to move. "Camryn, stop. You're going to hurt yourself." She placed a hand on Cam's arm and tried to calm her.

"Gavin...get...I need...Gavin." Her breath was laboured now.

The exertion she had spent on trying to move was draining her of every ounce of energy that she had.

"Cam no, stay still, you can't get up like that. Gavin is outside, and he hasn't left me or you once." Michelle was urgent in her belief that Cam shouldn't move, gently pressing her shoulders until Cam relaxed and settled back against her pillows.

"Don't...let...her in," she huffed. A monitor began to bleep loudly. "Jess...ica...Don't...she did." And then she passed out. A nurse rushed into the room and began to move around the bed, checking her vitals and the equipment. Michelle remembered the nurse from the previous day, Kelly. Like Rita, Kelly had helped to keep Michelle up to date with Cam's treatments, but right now, she was ushering her out of the room while she dealt with Cam.

"Jessica did this," Michelle whispered to herself as she was pushed from the room to the other side of the glass doorway.

"What?" Gavin asked, assuming she was speaking to him.

"Jessica, it was Jessica...at least that's what I think Cam was trying to say."

Chapter Thirty-One

She was asleep for a couple of hours, her pain medication increased. Detective Gomes was desperately wanting to speak to her now that she was awake. Michelle had called him and explained the conversation she had had with Cam and her suspicions that the assailant was Jessica, and so he was waiting, coffee cup in hand, for her to come around again.

~Next~

"Detective Gomes wants to speak to you, are you up for that?" Michelle asked, the moment Cam was awake and cognisant again.

Cam nodded as much as she could. "Yes, I wanna...I need him to know." Michelle placed a finger to her lips.

"Save your strength, I'll go get him." She was back within minutes, Detective Gomes following behind her, his bulky frame unmissable in his dark brown suit jacket.

"She was the one...sent the box...the doll," Cam explained. "It's all Jessica." Gomes took notes, writing everything Cam told him down in his tiny notepad. "She...I thought she punched me, but...and then, she ran and I had the kids..." She could feel the tears brimming. The pain was less, much more bearable now, but still there, lingering in the background.

"It's ok Camryn, take your time." There was nothing but gentleness in his voice. It was a shocking turn of events, and he was impressed by this woman's ability to endure what she had been through. "Did she say anything to you?"

"We argued about her following me and she started talking about Michelle. How she didn't listen and she should have ended things by now."

"This was because of me?" Michelle interrupted. Unable to look Camryn in the eye, she stared at the wall.

"No, this was because she got angry with me. I dunno what is wrong with her, but she's not right in the head, something's...I dunno, off, but, whatever the reason she is doing this...it's not because of you." She reached up and tentatively touched Michelle's cheek, bringing her eyes in line with her own. "It's because of me." And with that, her eyes closed and she drifted off to sleep again.

It was like that for the next 48 hours. Cam would wake and talk for a few minutes, but it would exhaust her and she would sleep for an hour. The doctors had been back and forth performing test after test. They removed the drain on her lung and checked her wounds, redressed them, and checked the staples and stitches. It was a continuous in and out of white coats and nurses' uniforms.

The detective had been in to interview her again, gradually filling in the gaps as he worked with her to regain all of her memories of that day. It had taken a lot of effort on Cam's part to tell them what had happened, but she needed to do it so that Michelle would be safe. The faster they picked up Jessica, the better.

~Next~

On the sixth day of her stay in hospital, she was feeling much better. She had been moved out of ICU and into her own room, somewhere a little more private. She was able to sit up a little and could move about a little more easily. The painkilling drugs they had her on were a godsend. As the evening wore on, she noticed how tired Michelle looked; she was virtually falling asleep in her chair. When she thought about it, Michelle was always there. Anytime Cam woke, be it morning or night, Michelle was sitting right next to her or walking back into the room moments later.

"Babe, when was the last time you went home?" Cam asked, reaching out with her hand to take Michelle's.

"I haven't," she admitted.

"You haven't? You've been here this whole time?"

"Yes, I couldn't leave you," Michelle said, squeezing Cam's hand. "I told you in Greece, I will never leave you."

"You look tired, why don't you go home tonight and get some sleep. I'll be fine," Cam suggested. She felt guilty that her girlfriend was so absolutely exhausted.

She shook her head and smiled at her fiancée. "I won't sleep without you there anyway. I'm better off here where I can keep my eye on you," she said softly, finally able to relax and tease a little now that Cam was fully awake and on the mend.

"Then you had better get up here with me, cos sleeping in that chair isn't going to do you any good," Cam said. She slowly and very gently tried shifting over in the bed enough to make room.

"Cam, I can't sleep in your bed with you!"

"Why not? I am paying for this treatment, right? I am paying for this room and this bed, so if I want to share it with my lover, then I will. If they don't like it, they can throw me out." She smirked defiantly, knowing full well they never would.

"I don't want to hurt you," Michelle argued, though she had to admit that she wanted nothing more than to throw herself into that bed and wrap herself like a limpet around Camryn. She would cling on and never let go again.

"You won't, my stitches are good," she said, holding her chest, "and they don't really hurt too badly now. Got good pain meds. Come on, get in, I need to feel you too ya know. Just get in on this side." She indicated the right side of the bed, well away from her wounds.

Michelle considered the idea. It was ridiculous, she could cause all manner of problems, but no matter how many sensible reasons she came up with for saying no, there was one overriding one that told her yes. She needed to be in her arms, to hold her.

Cam giggled as she watched Michelle attempt to climb into the bed without touching her.

"I'm not going to break. Get in here," Cam encouraged, lifting the cover higher for Michelle to scoot under.

"Ok, but if you so much as wince, I am out of here!" Michelle said seriously. She wriggled her way into the bed and got closer to Cam. Cam drew a deep breath and Michelle jumped back immediately.

"Wait. I'm not in pain…I'm relieved." She paused to look at Michelle and waited for her to snuggle back in. "I thought I'd never get to do this again. I thought I was going to die in that park, that I'd never kiss you or touch you, make love to you again. And if I had survived and couldn't do this anymore, then that would kill me anyway. So, scoot over and help me feel alive again."

For the first time since Cam was brought in, Michelle slept soundly.

~Next~

Maria bustled into the room the following morning speaking rapidly in Spanish to her God in thanks or prayer, Cam wasn't quite sure, but she was crossing herself and weeping as she gained on the bed.

"Oh my goodness Camryn, you scare the shit out of me!" she exclaimed, and Cam couldn't help but laugh at the use of the expletive. It just sounded hilarious the way she pronounced it more like *sheet.* Whenever Maria had been in to visit so far, Cam had been asleep. The relief of seeing her friend awake and laughing brought much happiness to the older woman, though she wouldn't show it right away. It was always much more fun to let the blonde think she was upset.

"I am sorry, I will try not to do that again," she said, reaching out to take Maria's hand. "Thank you."

"Why you thanking me? I do nothing, this one she here every day and night; no eat, no sleep," she said, pointing to the still-sleeping Michelle.

"Yeah, and I'm sure you let that continue for more than 24 hours, right?" Cam said knowingly.

"I tell her she need to eat otherwise no boobies," Maria laughed. "She too skinny as it is."

"I *am* here," said Michelle sleepily from the crook of Cam's arm. Her voice was still heavy with sleep, making it deeper than usual; raspier was how Cam would describe it, and it was sexy as hell.

Maria stayed for the morning, allowing Michelle to use the bathroom for a shower and a change of clothes. She took the time to talk with Camryn. She cried tears of relief, something Cam was getting used to seeing from most of the people who came to visit her.

The rest of the day was filled with poking and prodding from various medical staff. It was tiresome for Cam; she didn't like people poking and prodding her at the best of times, but just as she was about to complain, she saw the look Michelle was giving her. It was the 'you won't get any sex if you open your mouth and give these nice people trying to help you any lip' look. So, she thought better of it and closed her mouth, narrowing her eyes at Michelle in a returned look that said, 'you might win this round, but I will pay you back.' Michelle sniggered and Cam smirked. The doctor wasn't quite sure what he had said or done to warrant either, but carried on regardless.

~Next~

"I missed this so much," Michelle wept in Cam's arms later that night. "I'm sorry, I shouldn't be crying when it's you that's going through this."

"Don't be silly, this has been hard on you too. I can't imagine how I would have dealt with this if it hadn't been you; in fact, I know I wouldn't have been able to deal with it. You've been amazing, I can't thank you enough."

Michelle reached her hand up and pushed the tendrils of hair off her face. Cam gently kissed the corner of her mouth. "You're so beautiful." She snuggled against her and they lay together silently for a while.

"Hey, we missed New Year's Eve?" Cam complained.

"I am afraid we did. Erin had everything running smoothly at the club though, so don't worry."

"I wasn't worried about that; I just had plans."

"For New Year's Eve? We will just celebrate twice as hard next year," she said, looking at Cam.

"Yes, you're right. It's just a shame, I was looking forward to seeing the New Year in with you, and I had a lot of *plans*!" She smiled and emphasised the 'plans' part again.

"Now, why am I not surprised at that Camryn?" She couldn't stop looking into those beautiful blue eyes. Those eyes that she had seen in her dreams for days now were finally fully focused just on her again. "I missed your eyes," she whispered.

"I'll never close them again," Cam said seriously. "They are all yours."

"Good, and I want them looking at me at all times Camryn," Michelle replied just as seriously before breaking out into a huge grin.

Cam felt so much better already and she had only been awake for a couple of days. She still had pain and was grateful for the meds they were pumping through her to counter it, but her brain was clearer now, her throat wasn't as sore, and she had a bit of energy that she had been lacking the day before.

"Ya know, nobody has ever called me Camryn the way you do?"

Michelle frowned. "I just say it. It is your name after all."

"I know, I like it, the way you use it and say it."

"Well, once you're better, *Camryn,* I can say it in a lot of different ways that I think you will find equally satisfying."

"Jesus, you're killing me here." She laughed out loud and then grabbed her side in pain. "Yowser." Strangely, she felt more pain from the smaller injuries than the biggest one of all, the one that started at her collarbone and headed south to her sternum.

"Shit, sorry, are you ok?" Michelle said, bolting upright. She looked decidedly concerned, but at the same time, she was stifling a laugh.

"Yes, I am fine thank you, Ms-I-laugh-at-others-in-pain." She laughed too but added, "I promise, but I will also promise you this, when I get out of here and get rid of these stitches and staples, I am going to take you away and spend as many days as I'm stuck in here, adoring every inch of your body until I am unable to move another muscle, okay?"

"If you say so, Lover," she replied with a wink. "And I am glad to hear that you still have the urge! However, you will need all your strength to fight me off from adoring every inch of your body that I am being forced to ignore right now!"

"Maybe we can fool around a bit and see just how much strength I have?" Cam winked playfully.

"As tempting as that is, and believe me, I am truly tempted to test you, I am going to be the better person and say no, even though right now I would give anything to have you touch me," Michelle admitted with a sigh. *God, how I wish I could touch her.* It was a strange sensation to be so turned on in this situation. She figured it was probably down to stress and relief all mixed up and causing havoc with her hormones.

"Have I told you today how much I love you?"

"You have not." Michelle smirked, waiting for the answer.

"Oh, how remiss of me." She leant a little to her right and kissed her chin. "I love you."

Chapter Thirty-Two

After two long weeks in the hospital, Cam was finally on her way home. It was on the condition that she take complete rest and attend physiotherapy and her numerous other appointments with doctors and specialists, but she didn't care; she agreed to it all. She just wanted to go home.

Her staples and stiches had been removed, all her wounds were thankfully healing well, and there had been no infections. Alone in her room while Michelle dealt with paperwork and having her photograph taken with all the staff, Cam removed her hospital gown and prepared to get dressed. Naked, she caught sight of herself in the mirror. It was the first time she had really looked at her new body. Gone was the flawless tanned skin she had flaunted on the beach and by the pool in Greece. In its place was a pale and thin copy marked by the various scars. There were eight from the attack, all the same size but at different angles and areas from her left breast, under her armpit, and down the length of her torso, between her ribs. She touched them one by one, shrinking back each time at the raised skin. Bright pink and raw, they all stood out.

There was a more rounded mark further around to her back, just below her shoulder blade. From the chest drain. This scar was more like a small dent than a raised and puckered piece of skin. Her abdomen was next, scalpel clean straight line just about her navel. This one had been held together with staples, just like the one that she had been trying to ignore the most. From collarbone to sternum was a long straight line that looked like a zipper. Tiny marks either side and all the way down where the staples had held meant that it stood out even more so. Which was ridiculous, she thought, because you couldn't ever miss it. It was a thick, bright red line straight down her centre. It felt numb, the entire area where the nerves had been damaged. And she hated it.

~Next~

Michelle arrived back in the room, smiling, just as Cam was slipping on her shoes. The effort of dressing had tired her, and she was wheezing a little. She hadn't felt this unfit in years. She was wheeled out of her room in a chair, much to her disgust, but once again she was given a glare by Michelle and so she shut up and let them get on with it. She said her thanks and left gifts of flowers and expensive European chocolates. She wouldn't miss this place, but she couldn't have asked for better people to have taken care of her.

She was wheeled through corridors and into elevators that took them down to the hospital entrance. She expected there to be journalists and photographers outside. Michelle had warned her they were there. They had been camped out there the entire time as they tried to get pictures of Michelle coming and going. They hadn't gotten much though, seeing as Michelle hadn't left for the first week or more. It had only been in the last few days that she had gone home to make sure all was ready for Camryn's return.

"Put these on," Michelle said to Camryn as they reached the front doors. Cam did as she was told and pushed the sunglasses up her nose. "There is a ton of cameras out there." She was concerned that the constant flash flickering would hurt her eyes. "I've got the car right outside. You just have to keep moving and we will be out of here." She smiled and kissed her mouth, grateful that she could do that once more.

Bob had taken all of their baggage earlier in the day, so all Camryn had to do was get herself into that car and she would be on her way home. Nothing was going to stop her.

~Next~

Being at home with nothing to do was just as frustrating for Cam as it was being stuck in a hospital bed. For the first few days she was fine with it; she really didn't feel up to doing much anyway, and if she was honest, she enjoyed the attention. But now she was getting itchy feet, and boredom was setting in. Michelle was at home, and between herself and Maria, they wouldn't let her lift a finger, and it was pissing her off.

She wanted to go for a walk, just a stroll, on her own along the beach. Getting her stuff together and finding a windbreaker, she was halfway out of the door when Michelle caught her escape.

"Cam, where are you going?" Her voice was gentle, but laced with concern. Walking towards her, she placed the cup she was carrying down on the nearest surface and studied her lover.

"For a walk, I just need some fresh air." She took a deep breath and rolled her eyes, trying to keep her annoyance at bay. *She just cares; she loves you, don't be an arsehole.*

"You can get some fresh air on the deck," Michelle countered, moving herself closer to the blonde.

"Yes, that's correct. However, I want to go for a walk." Barely able to suppress her annoyance, she left no room for an argument.

"What if she's out there?" Terror etched itself on Michelle's face, and Cam felt guilty for putting her through this, but it was driving her mad just sitting indoors.

"I'll be fine." She softened.

"Ok, well hold on and I'll get my coat." Cam stopped and turned quickly to face her girlfriend. Her temper got the better of her, and she was going to be an arsehole.

"*No!* I want to go for a walk by myself." Turning to leave once more, she was stopped by Michelle's soft hand on her arm.

"Camryn, please, just hold up and—" But she shrugged her off. "Let me come with you."

"Michelle, will you please just stop. I don't want you to come with me. I'm not a child, okay! Just let me be for one fucking minute,

I'm so sick of these four walls and what *she* might do. Hasn't she done enough?" she screamed before storming out of the door onto the beach. Gavin's newest recruit, Carrie, took up position 15 feet behind her, and Michelle burst into tears as she watched her walk away.

Maria had witnessed the altercation from the kitchen and after saying a quick prayer, crossing herself several times over, she wandered over to where the forlorn figure of Michelle stood, looking for all the world as though she would fall apart at any moment.

"She just needs time, everything's changed for her." She spoke softly, motherly, and Michelle appreciated her words and touch.

"I know, I just wish I could do something to help her."

"You are, loving her is helping her," Maria said. "She knows that too. The doctors warned about depression, don't take to heart honey."

Michelle turned her head to look at Maria. "She is still out there Maria. Jessica is still...what if she tries again?" Maria said nothing, her grip on Michelle's arm tightening.

~Next~

She walked like a woman possessed for all of three minutes before her lungs made it clear they just were not ready for that kind of energetic action yet. Huffing and puffing, she flopped down onto the sand and watched out of the periphery of her sight as Carrie came to a halt, just a few feet away.

Was this what her life had become now? Not allowed to leave the house without somebody else's permission? Being followed everywhere she went! She hated it, hated it all. Jessica had ruined everything. Her gaze fell on the ocean and she watched as the tide ebbed and flowed. Got her breathing back under control.

Anger had never really been an emotion that Camryn had ever had to deal with before. There had been times when she was pissed off, but that generally didn't last very long before she bounced back. This, though, was different. This was something she had no idea how to fix.

She had shouted at Michelle, that had made her angry too. She had no right to be angry with Michelle. Beautiful, kind Michelle who had done nothing but love her and be there for her, whose only concern was for Camryn's welfare, and what had she done to repay that? Shouted at her. Been mean and horrible when all Michelle was doing was trying to care. She shook her head because it was worse than that. The anger was being fuelled by frustration, and it wasn't just because she couldn't go for a walk. Sex. It was about sex, more than that; intimacy and the lack of it.

She had never been a vain person. Now, though, she found herself wondering how Michelle would ever want to look at her again, and it meant that she had distanced herself, pulled away and held back; shrugged her lover off and made excuses because she didn't want pity.

~Next~

She had no idea how long she had been sitting there. It was only when Michelle flopped down beside her that she realised it had gotten darker. Silence between them lingered uncomfortably, each woman unsure how to approach the other. Eventually, unable to stand it any longer, it was Camryn who spoke first.

"I'm sorry." Her voice was quiet, reverential. "For shouting at you."

Michelle nodded in acknowledgement. The silence dragged on a little longer, until it was her turn to break it.

"I'm sorry that you feel so smothered by me. That was never my intention, I just..." She spoke with her gaze firmly placed on the sand between her feet. She hated that Cam could feel so upset with her.

"I know, you're scared about Jessica and you just want to help me. You are. I'm just frustrated, and I took it out on you." She reached out and took Michelle's hand in her own, warm and tender, the connection back in a heartbeat.

"Do you want to talk about it?" Michelle asked hopefully.

Cam rubbed her left hand over her face and looked up to the sky for some kind of celestial guidance, just like she always did. It had been so long since she had been so insular, since she had held herself so guarded, and she didn't like it. She didn't want it like that, not with Michelle.

"I need for you, and everyone else too, to let me start doing things. I know what my limitations are. I don't want to do anything that means I end up back in hospital, but there are things I can do, and I need you to let me do them. Please."

Michelle nodded. "Okay, you're right, I guess I have been overprotective of you. It's only been 3 weeks, Camryn. It scares me how close I came to losing you."

"I am alive, Michelle." She pulled her hand toward her heart and held it there. "Can you feel that? My heart beat is strong and I'm not going to go anywhere. The doctor is happy with my progress."

"I know that, in my head, I know that. But, I can't stop thinking about how close I came to losing you and it terrifies me Camryn," Michelle confessed honestly.

"I promise you I won't do anything I can't manage but, I can't just sit around anymore doing nothing, it's driving me insane babe."

Michelle turned to her properly now, needing to see her, to watch for any sign that she wasn't ready, but also to let her see that she was ready, to let go just a tiny bit.

"So, what is it that you want to do?"

"I can go to the club, do some paperwork for Erin, sit and chat with my friends. I can go to the shops, and I can definitely cook for us. I want to start seeing my trainer again."

"I think that sounds reasonable," Michelle agreed. "I will try to be less of a helicopter around you."

"Thank you," she said, leaning against her shoulder.

"Do you want to stay here a bit longer or come back with me to the house?" Michelle asked, concerned it was getting a little chilly for Cam to be out.

"I want to come home with you." She smiled and got up, brushing the sand off her trousers as she stood. She held her hand out for Michelle to take. Michelle hesitated for a second, not wanting to put any strain on Cam at all, but she trusted Cam to do what she said, so she took her hand and allowed her to help pull her to her feet. Whatever happened from now on, they were in this together.

Chapter Thirty-Three

It was the first day of February. The beach was cold and quiet, but that hadn't stopped Cam from taking her evening stroll. Five weeks had passed since she had been injured, and she was beginning to feel stronger, physically. Slowly she had begun to rebuild her muscles. Physiotherapy wasn't as bad as she had expected it to be. It was strenuous and painful at times, but it meant progress. Now, she was about to start back at the gym and really test her cardiovascular system.

Her doctors had been impressed and had given the go ahead for her to now start to enjoy life again, and that meant she was able to enjoy physical intimacy too, something that both worried her and excited her. The idea of being able to touch Michelle once again, to love her in the most intimate of ways, was something she couldn't wait for, but at the same time she dreaded it. In the five weeks since she was attacked by Jessica, Michelle had not seen her naked. While she was in hospital it hadn't even occurred to her; she was injured and getting well enough to go home. It was once she was home, however, that she began to hide herself. Not even realising she was doing it at first, she would get dressed and undressed only when Michelle had left the room.

Entering their bedroom, Cam wandered about, absently picking up her T-shirt and shorts. "Just gonna get changed," she muttered, not daring to make eye contact with Michelle as she moved swiftly toward the bathroom.

"Cam? Can I come in?" Michelle asked, knocking lightly on the door. She could hear the water running and a gentle splashing. Cam had never once locked the door before.

"I'll be right out, two minutes," Cam replied quickly, her

words slightly distorted with the toothbrush in her mouth. Michelle was aware of her behaviour; she had worked it out a few days earlier, waiting for the right moment to broach the subject.

Inside the bathroom, Cam stood in front of the mirror looking at the scar that ran through the center of her chest, her toothbrush placed down on the countertop as she investigated the scar, still raised and pink. It itched, and still felt somewhat numb when she scratched it. She ran her fingers over it and tried to imagine what she looked like before it, but she couldn't conjure the image. She moved her fingers around to her side and counted the different welts one more time. Still the same, still eight. Twisting to stare at them properly in the mirror, she hated it and pulled her T-shirt back over her head to hide them. She wanted to throw something at the mirror, to obliterate what she looked like now.

"Camryn? Are you ok?" Michelle asked, concerned.

The unexpected knock on the door made her jump. "Yes, I'm fine, just coming," she said before she finally unlocked the door. Passing Michelle, she jumped into bed and pulled the covers up to her chin. She closed her eyes and tried desperately not to see the hurt on Michelle's face. She failed.

Michelle entered the bathroom, leant her palms on the edge of the sink, and took a shaky breath. Swallowing down the lump in her throat, she closed her eyes, fighting off the tears pricking at her eyeballs. She exhaled and brought her own gaze up to the mirror. She had thought once Cam came home that things would be back to how they were previously, but that wasn't how it was. Something was very wrong, and she wasn't sure how to fix it. Their talk on the beach previously had alleviated one problem, but Michelle could feel the need for another kind of talk very soon.

Climbing into bed next to Camryn, she couldn't ignore the huge gulf between them, both in terms of space and emotion. It had been like this since they had first come home from the hospital. At first Michelle assumed it was because Cam was worried about hurting herself in her sleep, but the longer it went on, the more she worried about it. It didn't make sense to her. They had been so close and even in the hospital, Cam had insisted on sleeping together in her bed. Now, Michelle might as well be in a different room.

She lifted the covers and scooted over to Cam's side of the bed. As she got closer she could feel Cam stiffen at her presence. It hurt. Her heart ached to feel her lover emotionally, and now physically, withdraw from her.

"Camryn, will you please talk to me?" she whispered into the darkened room.

Cam stiffened some more, but remained silent. The air around them stifled her. Michelle waited a moment, but getting no response, she was at a loss as to what to do next. The doctors had told her that once Camryn was home, then things would be different. There would be times when she would be angry and lash out, Michelle understood that, and they had dealt with it when it happened. They never said that she would withdraw and completely disengage herself from her emotionally. She changed tact.

"Cam?" She let her finger dance up her lover's arm, back and forth in a slow tease. "I was thinking ... maybe we could fool around, what do you think?" Her fingers stopped their movement as she edged closer.

"Ok." Cam spoke quietly, but didn't move. Her eyes closed in the darkness as she willed herself to respond. Because she wanted to, she wanted nothing more than to fool around with Michelle, she just didn't want Michelle to touch her, to have her fingers feel the roughness of the mess that was now her body.

"So, I was thinking it's been a while." Cam could tell she was smiling, could hear it in her words even if she couldn't see her. "What if we just kissed, would that be ok?" Her lips ghosted across Cam's ear, close enough to send a shiver of anticipation and fear racing through her. Cam nodded. "I can't hear you." She moved, bringing herself up onto her palms to hover just above Camryn, their lips almost, but not quite, touching.

"Yes." Cam's voice was barely a whisper as Michelle closed the distance and pressed her lips against those below her. Moving slowly, she gently encouraged Camryn to join her. Unhurriedly, she continued, softly manipulating Camryn's lips until they moved with ease. When she silently requested entrance, it was given.

"Touch me," Michelle pleaded. Slowly she lowered herself, desperate to feel the warmth of her lover's body against her own. Cam's hands flew to her side and held her, stopping her movement, keeping the inch gap between them. "What's wrong?" Michelle asked. Straddling her thighs, she sat up.

"Nothing, it's fine." Cam smiled, at least that what she tried to do. Michelle squinted at her, sizing up the situation. Camryn's gaze shifted, slowly moving down from her face to her chest, then lower to the apex of where they joined. She reached out her palms tentatively, placing them on Michelle's thighs. "Take it off," she said, looking up once more to lock eyes with Michelle.

"I will if you will," Michelle countered. It was dark in the room, but she could see the panic that etched itself across Cam's face.

"I…I'm not…can I just…"

"Can you just…take off your shirt?" Michelle inquired. "I want to make love Camryn." She reached for the hem of her own shirt and lifted. In one fell swoop it was off and over her head. She was braless, her breasts visible in the moonlight. "Take it off Camryn." Her words were firmer now, willing to push her buttons a little. When Cam failed to move, she made a decision and reached forward, grabbing the hem of Cam's shirt in her fists.

"No, don't," Cam said abruptly. She grabbed Michelle's hands in her own. "Don't." She felt Michelle release her grip, but her hands remained where they were.

"Why not?" she asked, her words soft and compassionate.

"Just, I don't..."

"Camryn?" She waited until the blonde stopped rambling and she had her attention. "Camryn, I want us to make love. I want to touch you."

"I know."

The silence grew louder before Michelle asked, "Why are you marrying me?"

"What do you mean?" Cam asked, her eyes instantly searching Michelle's face.

"Exactly what I said, why are you marrying me Camryn?" She pulled their joint hands towards her own thighs, pressing Cam's palms back against her naked skin.

"You know why."

"Yes, I know why, but I want to hear it from you, Camryn."

"Because I love you." She kept her eyes locked on Michelle. "I love you, you know that."

Michelle nodded, a sad smile adorned her face. "And yet, you don't trust me or believe that I love you." Cam sat up in an instant, balanced on her elbows.

"Don't be ridiculous, why would you think that?"

"Why? What should I think? You won't touch me, let me touch you. You hide from me." Cam tried to interrupt her but she was stopped by a firm finger against her lips. "You're hiding from me, Camryn, and I don't like it, I don't like it one bit." She moved from her position on Cam's lap and grabbed for her shirt, pulling it back on as she left the room.

Chapter Thirty-Four

She found Michelle sitting by herself on the couch in the lounge, her legs tucked up underneath her as she rested her head in her palm. Michelle heard the movement, the footsteps on the stairs as Camryn made her way down. She didn't move; instead she waited.

"It's not you, I love you, I just..."

"Just what Camryn? What has changed so much that we can't even talk to each other anymore?" she implored as she turned to face her. She didn't want to cry, but she could feel the prickling sensation, the watery sting of salty tears threatening to overspill. She blinked them away.

"I...I don't know how you can bear to touch me," Cam finally admitted, relief and fear washing over her in an instant.

"What?" Michelle could barely believe what she had just heard. "Tell me you didn't just say that? Why Cam, why?" she asked. "Why would you ever think that?" The silence lingered between them before Michelle finally got it. Sitting forward, her feet now planted flat on the floor as she whispered, "Oh my God, you think I am so shallow that I won't be attracted to you anymore because of your scar? Is that what you think?" She was incredulous, outraged even that Cam would think that about her, about them. Hadn't they been through enough that proved just how much she was in love with her? Of course she was attracted to her physically, who wouldn't be? Camryn Thomas was gorgeous.

"*Scars*, plural, I...I can't...How can...? You haven't even seen them! It, it's horrific," she cried out, wrapping her arms around herself. She flopped to the floor and sat cross legged in front of her.

"You won't let me see them," Michelle cried out in frustration.

This was the crux of it! This was what it all came down to.

"I don't want you to see them!" she whispered back, her voice small and childlike.

"Oh Camryn, baby how can you think that sweetheart." Her heart melted at the sight of her lover in such distress. She dropped to her knees in front of Camryn but held back from touching her. If she wasn't ready, she wouldn't push her.

"I hate it! Why? Why would she do this?" She sobbed and fell into Michelle's waiting arms. She was so angry, so confused and desperate to feel normal again, but her biggest fear was that she never would, that Jessica had finally won and ruined everything.

"I don't know, I can't give you the answer beautiful girl, other than she is crazy." She let Cam cry, let her sob her heart out and exhaust herself. It hurt her to watch. Her strong, beautiful fiancée was falling apart, but she relished the fact that she was touching her, that she was allowed to hold her and soothe her. It was all she could do not to fall apart herself.

~Next~

She had no recollection of how she got into bed or of falling asleep wrapped safely in Michelle's arms, but she had. She woke just once in the night from a nightmare. Covered in sweat, she had forced her eyes open just as Jessica raised her hand. Her breath quickened, but she felt the calmness enter her soul. Michelle's palm lay flat against her chest, right over her heart, only the thin material of her shirt between them. Between her and the scar.

"It's just a dream," her lover had mumbled. Sleepily she moved her palm, slowly stroking unknowingly up and down the scar, and Cam allowed it.

When she woke up again she found the bed empty. Stretching out leisurely, she listened. There was the sound of water running in the bathroom. Michelle was in the shower. Naked. God, she missed that body.

The bathroom door was pulled shut but not locked. She padded across the room and gently pushed at it until it swung open enough to walk through. Her heart thumped in her chest, palms sweating as she considered what she was about to do, if she could do it. Steam billowed out from the cubicle as the water cascaded down over Michelle's head. Cam watched it bouncing off her shoulders before running down the contours of her back until her eyes were staring at the sexiest glutes she had ever laid eyes on. Her olive skin tone glistened, inviting.

"Are you coming in?" Michelle called out. She kept her back to Cam, allowing her the privacy to undress. Cam smiled as she understood the sensitive way Michelle was dealing with her. She sucked in a deep breath, dropping her shorts to the floor. *Just take it off,* she told herself. Before she could change her mind, she grabbed the hem of her shirt and lifted. Holding the shirt in her hands against her chest, she exhaled the long-held breath and took a step forward. She was ready to cover herself the moment she chickened out, but she didn't; she just kept moving. She kept herself focused on the naked body in the shower, the body that loved her.

The cubicle door opened, and Michelle felt the draft of cooler air wrap her body before it was closed again and the warmth of Camryn radiated behind her. She held her breath, her eyes closed as she waited, giving Cam the time she needed to adjust to this.

And then she felt it, the hesitant touch of fingertips on her right shoulder. The desire to just turn around and kiss her, take her, be taken by her was huge and yet, she kept still. Waited. Fingertips on her left hip. Michelle exhaled, her breathing slow and steady until she felt the warmth of skin on skin. She couldn't help the soft groan that escaped from her when Cam's hands moved around her to cup her breasts. Or when one moved lower and dipped between the folds of her sex, teasing in all the ways she knew worked. Michelle let herself fall back, relaxing into the touch, letting Camryn explore her in any way she needed to. She lost herself in the feelings Cam brought her until the moment she peaked and crested and fell gloriously over the edge of climax.

"I love you, so much," she whispered, hoping that Cam heard her. "Do you remember when you told me that you loved me for all of me?" She felt Cam's head nod from its position pressed against her back. "Why would you think that it would be any different for me?" She felt her head lift, felt Cam's breath against her skin, but she didn't speak. Michelle closed her eyes, the water washing over her face as she slowly turned around until she was facing Camryn. "Can I open my eyes?" she asked.

Camryn was so far out of her comfort zone that she couldn't think straight. She wanted to run, wanted to turn and hide and get out of there because she couldn't deal with it if Michelle opened her eyes and, seeing the horror of it all, looked away or worse, pitied her. Not that she would blame her if she looked away, ran in horror, because it was what Cam wanted to do. And then she heard it. Heard herself say the word. "Yes."

It took a second before Michelle opened her eyes, to find Cam with hers closed. Reaching out, she touched Cam's cheek. Cupping her face, she rubbed her thumb back and forth until Cam opened her eyes. "I'm going to look, okay?" She smiled and Cam nodded, her face impassive, staring at the ceiling. Michelle's eyes slid slowly from Cam's, past her lips, her throat, and down. Her fingers followed, down her cheek and neck before finding the long pink line that divided her chest. "Does it hurt?" she asked, as her palm flattened once more over her heart.

"No, not really," Cam whispered shakily. "It's...it feels numb really." Michelle nodded. She looked up briefly and smiled before her eyes darted back to Cam's chest and the eight different little lines that marred her breast and ribcage.

"I love you Camryn, every little part of you. This changes nothing. If anything, it just proves how right I was to fall in love with you." She saw the hesitance, the lack of understanding in Cam's expression, the frown that creased her brow. "You're the strongest person I know. Everything you have been through and you just keep getting back up and carrying on, and that's why I know that marrying you will be the best thing I ever do in life."

"But—"

"No, no buts, I love you. Nothing has changed just because you have these." She moved her palms up and swept them over Cam's shoulders, locking her arms behind her neck and pulling her body in tight against her own. "Let me love you. Let me love you the way we used to, no barriers, no crazy ex-girlfriends between us. Just me and you, can you do that, can you let me love you?"

There was no hesitation this time. She nodded. She wanted this, wanted her. She was still angry, angry with Jessica for doing this and angry with her for coming between them. She wouldn't allow that to happen anymore. She couldn't let it happen. She had scars; she would live with them.

She was broken from her thoughts by warm lips pressing against her neck, lips that moved sensually, covering the expanse of flesh available. Michelle moved lower, grazing across Cam's collarbone; in seconds she would find the scar. Cam began to relax, letting her head fall to the side as her lover's hands joined her mouth. She felt her skin begin to tingle, her heart begin to race as the sensations started to have an effect. Michelle moved from one scar to the other. Up and down her torso she moved, slowly peppering her breast, her ribcage. She took Cam's arm and raised it, bringing her fingers to her mouth, kissing each one. One long swipe of a tongue slid down her arm. Cam giggled. The ticklish effect made her squirm a little, but it was all good. The water and Michelle helped to wash away her fears.

Chapter Thirty-Five

"I was thinking," Cam said to Michelle as they lay in bed together the following morning.

"Hmm?" Michelle was drawing patterns on Cam's stomach with her finger, her skin erupting in tiny goosebumps with each stroke, and Cam would shiver faintly at the sensation. Her abdominal muscles would tense ever so slightly. It made Michelle smile to see the visible impact her touch had.

"I was thinking two things actually," she replied, trying to focus.

"Which are?"

"Hmm?" she said, focusing on the feeling's Michelle's fingertips were causing.

"What were you thinking, darling?"

"Oh. Yes, I was thinking." She lost track of her thoughts again. "God, I really love your fingers!"

"Yes," Michelle chuckled, "but what were you thinking, baby?" she asked as her fingers dipped lower, teasing her lover even more now she had the knowledge that it was affecting Camryn.

"Uh, yes, I was thinking I might buy a gym," she said quickly before she lost her train of thought again. Wonderful feelings were beginning to wash over her.

"A gym? Where did that idea come from?" Michelle stilled her fingers and sat up so they could discuss this seriously. The blonde groaned at the sudden halt.

"Gavin mentioned that the gym we used to use was closing, it's running at a loss and the owners can't keep it going."

"And do you think you can turn it around?"

"I think that I have the money to try. It's quite a big space, and it's in an area of town that doesn't have much going for it; take the gym away and a lot of kids are out on the streets with nothing to do. I was thinking of redesigning it. Get some classes in there, maybe set up a personal trainer training programme and get some better equipment. Maybe put in a small café. I mean, it would all take time and money, but I think it's doable and it keeps people employ—" She was cut off by the brunette as she brought her lips to Cam's and kissed her soundly. Soft skin slid against her own as the actress moved to straddle her.

"You are such a wonderful person. I love you."

"So, you think it's a good idea then?"

"I think it's a wonderful idea." Her smile was infectious.

"Great, I will organise it then," she said, lying back and pulling Michelle with her. They lay like that for a while, enjoying the intimacy.

"What was the other thing?" Michelle asked, sitting back on her heels once more.

"Hmm?"

"You said you had two things you were thinking about?"

"Oh, yes I did, well. I thought maybe we should buy a house… together. Somewhere up in the hills maybe, a bit more secure and more in keeping with a Hollywood star and her extremely rich wife!"

Michelle reached out her hand, cupping Cam's cheek and turning her face slightly so they were looking at each other.

"You love this house, why would you want to move."

"It's just a house, and it's my house, I want *our* house." Her words were mumbled and barely audible.

"I don't think so, what's going on in that head of yours?"

"Nothing, I just thought that—"

"Camryn, you have never 'just thought' anything in your life, everything you say and do is because that's what you want to say or do, it's never just a thought you had. You wouldn't mention something to me unless you had it all figured out like you did with the gym pitch!"

"No, I…okay, well yes…I have thought it all through that's true…and it would need your say-so of course."

"Oh of course." She smiled, letting her know she wasn't angry or upset.

"So, what do you think?"

"I think I still want to know why you want to move."

Cam sat up and bashed the pillows behind her until they were comfortable to lie against once more. "Why do you think there is any other reason than what I have already said?" She wasn't annoyed, but she felt somewhat under pressure, a feeling she hadn't expected to feel. Wasn't it obvious why she wanted to move?

Michelle moved, tightened the grip on her thighs, shifted so that they were eye to eye.

"Because my darling, I know you and I can see it all over your face that there is something going on in here," she said, tapping Cam's head gently with a long finger, "and I want you to tell me what it is."

There was a puff of air as Cam blew out a breath and

contemplated what to say next. Once she had the answer, she looked up into molten chocolate and reminded herself that there wasn't anything she couldn't say to this woman. So, she opened her mouth and let the words that had haunted her go free.

"Do you feel safe here?" She could feel her heart rate speeding up, her skin flushing.

"Don't you?"

Cam shook her head gently back and forth. "No, not anymore."

"Oh baby, why didn't you say something?" Michelle kissed her face, her cheeks, and her lips before pulling her against her body to hold her.

"I thought it was normal and that after some time I would settle and be okay again, but..."

"But it's not?" Michelle was concerned, and she couldn't believe she hadn't spotted it. She had been so watchful of Camryn over the last weeks, but in the past few days she had begun to think they had turned a corner. Now, she realised how little she really understood Cam's pain.

"No, it's not," Cam admitted. "She was here, in our home...how did she just walk in here? Place that box in the tree for you to find?" She shook her head at the thought of Jessica leaving a decapitated doll wrapped like a present for Michelle to find.

"I don't know, but we've changed all the locks and had the security updated," Michelle reassured her.

"Yes, and I feel a lot better about it, but I don't know." She dragged her fingers through her hair. "She was in here 'Chelle, touching our things. What if she comes back?"

Chapter Thirty-Six

Work. It wasn't something that Michelle had thought much about lately. With all that had happened recently, all she wanted was to be with Camryn. She understood, however, that that wasn't what Camryn wanted, or needed. Cam was going to start back at the club, working mostly in the office, but occasionally working the bar on quieter shifts. So, Michelle needed something to do.

Janice had a few offers on the table that they needed to go over. While *Medical Diaries* was about to start reshooting its new season in April, Michelle's part had been significantly reduced for a while, in order for her to care for Camryn. Now that Cam was back up and about, her part as Dr. Ashton Corrigan would gradually be introduced back into the storylines along with an added storyline of her own, but right now, she had the opportunity to take on other work to showcase herself. And it didn't hurt that she would be paid ridiculous sums of money for her time and name to do it.

"So, we got an offer for a part in the next spy thriller with Nix Jackson. Its 8 days filming in Canada, not the biggest part you've played, but it's certainly going to be a high-profile film with Nix taking the lead," Janice said, taking a sip of her green tea and leaning back into her extremely expensive and comfortable leather chair, a satisfied smile on her face as she congratulated herself on having one of her clients lined up for such a movie.

"What else?" Michelle asked, uninterested as she picked at imaginary dirt from under her nail. Janice placed her cup down on the desk, a little surprised at the reaction.

"Well…there is a small independent filmmaker asking for you to take the lead part. It's about a small-town mom fighting for her husband's release as a hostage in Baghdad, but there isn't anything exciting about it."

"Where is it being filmed?" Michelle took a sip of her coffee.

"In LA, mostly, some of it will be out in the dessert, Arizona probably, Nevada? But mainly local."

"How long are they planning to take to shoot it?"

"They are looking at a 14-day shoot for the part they want you to play. They are quite keen to have you and are prepared to work around you."

"Okay, send me the script, if I like it then I'll do it. I don't want to leave Cam right now, I know she appears to be okay but she isn't, and although she doesn't want me under her feet every second of the day I know she needs me nearby."

"Okay, I'll organise it." At any other time Janice would have argued against taking this and pushed her towards the blockbuster Nix Jackson film, but right now, she knew there was no point fighting her on it. Michelle wasn't leaving Camryn and that was that.

"Great, I am going to head over to the club and tell Cam, unless there is anything else?" Michelle grabbed her coat from the back of her chair and shrugged into it.

"Nope, we're good, enjoy the next few days off. I'll get the script over to you by the morning."

"Thanks, and I will." She smirked and left the room with a tiny spring in her step.

~Next~

Since the attack on Camryn by Jessica, Michelle hadn't gone anywhere without a bodyguard. Today it was Henry by her side, as usual, and she was at least grateful for the way in which he stepped back and allowed her a certain amount of freedom.

Inside the building she had been fine. They had their own security. Now as she was readying to exit the building, she sent a quick text to Henry informing him she was leaving. She could see him standing by the vehicle, his eyes scanning the area before he gave the signal that she was to walk, as quickly as possible, to the car.

He gave the signal and she opened the door and walked out onto the sidewalk. It was barely 30 feet from the door to the car and she was focused. So focused that she didn't notice the woman reading a map until it was too late and they collided. Henry was off and running, reaching her within seconds.

"Oh, I am so sorry." The woman said from under her sunhat. "I was looking at the map and I just didn't see you there, are you okay?"

"Yes, I'm fine, it's no problem, really," Michelle smiled at the poor woman. "Are you okay?"

"Oh yeah, I'm fine, I'm just an old clumsy klutz." She laughed and shook her head at her own clumsiness. "I'll let you be on your way."

"Okay, well you take care now," Michelle said as Henry turned her and gently pushed her towards the car once again. In an instant the door was held open for her and she climbed inside, ready to begin the short journey to the club, to Camryn.

On the seat next to her was an envelope.

Chapter Thirty-Seven

Henry pulled into the parking lot at Out and before the engine had even been shut off, Michelle was climbing out of the Audi and moving with speed to get inside.

"Hey Erin, have you seen Gavin?" she asked urgently. The manager of OUT looked up from behind the bar to see the actress close to tears. Henry stood nearby, just as agitated.

"Yeah, he is in the staff room taking a break, everything ok? You look upset." She put the bottles she was holding down on the bar and waited for Michelle to answer.

"I'll get him," Henry said, before heading behind the bar and out to where the staff room was located.

"Where's Cam?" she asked instead of answering the question.

"In her office." Erin was a tad worried at Michelle's demeanour; usually Michelle was upbeat and Ms Smiley face whenever she came to the club. "Michelle, what's going on?"

"Is she on her own? Has anyone else been here?" Michelle's words were urgent now. She was looking around the space, her eyes searching for something, Erin didn't know what.

"Anyone else? We aren't open yet so, no, it's just staff. Michelle, what's going on?" she insisted. Michelle finally let herself breathe. Her left hand raised slowly and Erin watched as she placed a plain brown envelope on the countertop. Just as slowly, she slid the contents from inside of it, out on the bar. She raised her eyes and looked at Erin, and they held each other's gaze until Erin finally looked down at the photograph that now lay by itself. She took a step forwards to look at it before a sharp intake of breath forced her away.

"Where did you get that?" she stammered.

"It was on the backseat in the car after I left Janice," she said, her voice shaking a little now.

"It's a joke, right? Someone is playing a sick joke?"

"Only if it is someone we know, the photo details where never released to the press."

"Have you called the police?"

"Not yet, I wanted to speak to Gavin first. If this is her, I don't want Cam to know about it."

"Michelle, you can't not tell her." Erin spoke quietly but clearly. "She needs to know!"

"No, what she needs is to feel safe," Michelle replied immediately. "She is already terrified about the prospect of her returning." She placed the photo back in the envelope and then went around the bar and poured herself a Coke.

Every time Cam took a step forward, there seemed to be something else that would knock her back again. It had only been a few weeks, and Cam was already dealing with her scars, physically as well as mentally.

Michelle tensed as she felt warm hands around her waist as warmer arms followed and then relaxed into them when she felt knowing lips on her skin.

"Hey gorgeous, I didn't know you was coming over today," Cam said as she continued to kiss her neck and shoulder.

"Hey sweetheart." Her voice faltered slightly, but Cam didn't pick up on it. "I thought I'd come over and see how you are doing and tell you about my next project." Erin looked away and went back to counting the stock.

"Cool. Let's go upstairs then and you can tell me all about it." She was pulling on Michelle's hand when Gavin and Henry both appeared behind her. "Hey guys, excuse me while I drag my beautiful fiancée upstairs." She winked as Gavin blushed in an instant. Since opening up to Michelle, her heart had lightened. Finally there was a light at the end of her tunnel.

"Okay, I'll meet you up there then, I just need to go powder my nose as they say." Michelle said, turning in Cam's arms to kiss the corner of her mouth. "Will you take my drink with you?"

"Sure, no problem."

With Cam out of the way, Michelle pulled the envelope out of her bag again and laid it on the bar for Gavin to see.

"How did this get delivered?" he asked, his face serious and unmoving.

"It was on the backseat in the car."

"Where was Henry?" he asked her, not once looking towards Henry.

"He was there the whole time, it's not his fault."

"Then how did she get this into the car?" he asked, finally turning to Henry. The young bodyguard looked as if he wished the ground would open up and swallow him. He shrugged at first, but a raise of a brow from Gavin brought forth a report of the incident.

"I parked outside the building, escorted Ms Hamilton inside and then took up position by the car. Nobody approached. Approximately 25 minutes later Ms Hamilton appeared at the door, I gave her the all clear signal and she proceeded to move towards the car. It was all clear. The only incident was a tourist bumping into Ms Hamilton while she was reading her map. She didn't see her and—"

Gavin held his hand up for him to stop speaking.

"So, it was a set-up? The tourist knocks into you, causing Henry to take his eyes off of the car while he made sure you were safe, giving her enough time to slip this inside and be gone before you even know she was there." He was calm and controlled as he spoke, but if you looked close enough you could see an anger simmering underneath.

"I guess so, I hadn't thought of that," Henry replied honestly. He was good at what he did, but he still had a lot to learn.

"We have to take this to the police, there is no question about it," Gavin said quietly.

"Ok," Michelle agreed. She noticed Erin nodding in agreement.

"Take what to the police?" They all spun around at the sound of the Cam's voice. She had gotten upstairs only to realise she had forgotten what she had originally gone down for: her own drink.

"Cam, baby let's go upstairs and—" Michelle had moved away from the photograph and toward Camryn.

"Take *what* to the police, Michelle?" Cam repeated, this time with more insistence. She walked towards them and watched as each one looked away or fidgeted uncomfortably. All except Gavin. He stood stoically, ready to deal with whatever needed dealing with.

"Cam, you don't need to worry, we will deal with it, okay?" Michelle wanted so desperately to spare her from this.

"Deal with what? What has happened?" She was getting more agitated the longer they kept whatever it was they were hiding from her. They all looked from one to the other, except Gavin, who stared at Michelle.

"I found this," Michelle finally said, the glare from Gavin

speaking volumes. Maybe she couldn't protect Cam from this, but she would keep trying.

Cam took a step forward and saw an image of Michelle. She was walking between her mother and Jen along the beach. The image was grainy, taken with a bad quality camera. Michelle's face was scratched out with red ink. The blonde staggered backwards, her breath trapped in her lungs as her throat constricted and the ability to simply breathe became more difficult. Michelle moved quickly. Wrapping her arms around her, she took her weight and supported her physically and emotionally.

"Breathe Camryn, just breathe baby. It's ok. Please, just look at me baby." She lowered them both to the floor and took Cam's face in her palms, face to face as Cam gasped for air. "Look at me Camryn, now breathe. Slow it down sweetheart. Deep breath in...and now out." Cam's eyes locked on with hers. Terror filled the blue as tears formed, but she followed Michelle's instructions and tried to slow her breathing. It took time, but eventually she had it back under control again.

"Where?" she panted, catching her breath steadily. "Where did you find it?"

"On the backseat of the car," Gavin replied hesitantly. He could see how fragile Cam was and didn't want a repeat of the anxiety attack she had just had, but she needed to know. That much he understood. "She organised a diversion tactic to draw Henry away from the car, giving her enough time to slip the photo inside the car."

"When were you going to tell me?" Cam asked, becoming more agitated again. They all stood silently looking at one another again before looking back at Cam. "You wasn't going to tell me?" she said quietly, almost to herself. "You wasn't going to tell me!" she repeated *again, her* anger rising, rage building. "What was you going to do?" She asked coldly, looking directly at Michelle.

"I, I wanted to speak to Gavin, see what he thought about it,"

Michelle said quickly.

"Why?"

"Because, I—"

"Because *you*? This is about me." Her voice was breaking. She knew tears were not far off and yet she was so angry. Angry with Michelle for treating her like a child again. Angry with all of them for conspiring. But mainly, she was angry with Jessica.

"Can we talk about this upstairs?" Michelle asked pleadingly.

"No, why do we need to do that? You was quite happily discussing it here before I arrived." Coldness enveloped her now, protecting her from the fear she felt, cutting off her sense of fairness and allowing her to speak freely to them all. Because they all needed to hear this.

"Camryn please, don't do this," Michelle begged once more to no avail.

"You're right. Let's not do this, let's not keep treating Camryn like she's a fucking child!" she bellowed. Erin and Gavin slowly backed away and tried to leave them with some privacy, but Cam was having none of it. "Where do you think you're going?" she said, turning to launch her tirade in their direction for a moment. "If either of you value your job right now I suggest you stay where you fucking are." It was rare for Cam to lose her temper, rarer still for her to swear. Other than Michelle and Erin, nobody had ever really seen her lose her shit before, and it was unnerving to say the least. "*I* am not a child and you will *all* desist from treating me as such. Am I clear on that?" She looked at each of them and waited. They each nodded their heads as they looked anywhere but at her. "It's your job to protect me physically, nothing else. I pay you to make sure she," she pointed at Michelle, "is safe," she said to Gavin. Michelle swung around to look at Cam.

"Wait, it's you she attacked, not me!" Michelle argued back.

"Yes that's right, I was the one stabbed over and over and over." She screamed and yanked her top off, leaving her standing in just her bra, her scars on full display to them all. She heard Erin gasp, but was too far gone down this path of rage to be bothered by it. "I'm the one that has to live with these!" she said, pointing to the largest scar on her chest. "But, it isn't my face crossed off in these pictures, is it?" she screamed at Michelle. "So YOU!" She swung back around to face Gavin. "You fix whatever issue allowed that maniac to get within 20 feet of her, I don't care if you have to surround her with ten men. You keep her safe!" She pointed again at Michelle. "Go!" Gavin turned to leave, followed by Henry, and Erin went to go with him.

"Not you!" Cam said to Erin, who stopped mid-step and winced. Turning back around slowly, she forced a smile in the hope of diffusing Cam's ire at her. Cam pulled her top back on before speaking again. "It's your job to run this bar, it is not your job to protect me, that's why we have security!"

"Oh fuck off Cam, not my place? You sound like you're the only one allowed to care about anyone around here. I thought we were friends. Yes, you are my boss, but I thought we were better than that and as a friend I'm allowed to give a shit about you," Erin fired back, seemingly the only one prepared to put up a fight. "But hey, if you just want me to run the bar so be it!" And with that, she turned and walked away.

Cam spun around, marching back upstairs to her office. Michelle stood there for a moment and contemplated what to do next. She could just leave and allow Cam to simmer down, she could follow her upstairs and just have this out. Or she could just sit at the bar and get drunk, that was sounding like a great plan, but instead she went with option two and walked towards the office like a prisoner on death row walking towards the electric chair, slow and fearful!

~Next~

She didn't bother with knocking. Instead she opened the door and walked in calmly to find Cam sitting on the small couch, elbows on her knees and her head in her hands, sobbing.

"Cam? Camryn." Her heart broke for her lover as she dashed across the room and dropped to her knees in front of her. Without further thought, she wrapped her arms around Cam's shoulders and held her tightly as she wept more loudly. "I am so sorry baby, I'm so sorry."

"I love you so much," Cam stuttered. "If she hurt you I would kill her," she admitted before adding with venom, "With my bare hands. I would rip her throat out."

"She won't, she won't hurt me baby. I will call Detective Gomes and ask him to come over so we can work out what to do next." Cam nodded her agreement. "She isn't going to win, Cam, and I am sorry, I am sorry I tried to shield you and you should know that Erin… Erin told me to tell you."

"I'll apologise to her," she said, wiping her face of tears. "And I'm sorry I shouted at you too."

"You don't need to apologise, you're right, I was treating you like a child, but…" She paused and raised a finger. "You are very wrong to think this is just about you. You want to protect me? Well I want the same for you, and I won't apologise for that. I went about it the wrong way, but my intentions were good so…let's just have make up sex and forget it, okay?" She smiled and hoped Cam would let some of the anxiousness within her dissipate with some humour.

"Call the cops, and then I'll consider make up sex." Cam smiled back.

"Can I at least kiss you first?" Michelle asked with a slight tilt of her head.

Nodding, she drew a finger down Michelle's cheek and stopped only when she reached her chin. "I would never deny you anything, especially a kiss," she said, leaning in.

Chapter Thirty-Eight

Erin was downstairs sitting at the bar by herself with some paperwork when Camryn came down to find her. She didn't look up or acknowledge Cam's presence at all. Instead her pink-haired head bowed down over her work.

"Erin, I want to apologise. I…well, I'm not dealing with things too well right now, and this kinda threw me for a loop." Erin was yet to acknowledge her, but her head had raised and she was listening, even if she did have her back to her still. "We are friends and you have every right to care, and I also know that you were the one in my corner and I shouldn't have jumped to conclusions," Cam said, speaking quickly in case Erin decided to get up and walk away.

Erin turned slowly. She didn't hold any grudges. She understood that this must be the most horrific of things to go through and that Cam was doing pretty well all things considered. But she appreciated the apology too; it meant a lot that Cam saw her as more than just an employee.

"Thank you, I appreciate it," Erin said with a smile. "Are you okay?"

"I don't know," Cam answered honestly.

"We all care about you Camryn, everyone here does, and nobody wants to see this bitch get away with it."

"I know, I am grateful."

"You don't need to be grateful Cam, you treat people with respect and they love you for it, don't push us away when you need us, okay?"

"I will try," she said with a smile. Erin returned to her

paperwork as Michelle joined them at the bar and sat next to Cam.

"Cam? Detective Gomes is here." She spoke gently. Cam looked up at the sound of her name to find Michelle standing next to the tall dark-skinned man who had been hunting Jessica on Cam's behalf.

"Hello Camryn, how are you doing?" he asked. His deep baritone voice had a calming effect on most people he spoke to, and that didn't exclude Cam.

"I was doing okay," she muttered. "Until today." She stood up quickly and walked around the bar to pour herself a drink. She offered one to Gomes, but he declined with a raised a hand and a small shake of the head.

"Of course. Michelle tells me we have had another visit from Ms Montgomery."

"I don't know, Michelle found a photograph in her car," Cam explained and looked to Michelle to continue the story and produce the photo.

Gomes took the picture from her and studied it, noting the red ink. He began jotting down notes on where, when, and how it was delivered. "I am going to go and take a look, see if we can use any local CCTV. Hopefully we can find our *friend* and follow her."

"You'll let me know as soon as you find anything, right?" Cam asked with an urgency to her voice that couldn't hide just how scared she was.

"You know I will. In the meantime, might I suggest that you keep a very close eye out; don't go anywhere alone. You have the means Cam, so use it," He insisted, knowing full well she could provide an army of paid soldiers to defend her if need be. "Don't take any risks."

Chapter Thirty-Nine

The last thing Michelle expected to find when she opened their bedroom door that night was a very naked Camryn sitting crossed legged on the floor, meditating to trickling water and bird call.

Moving quietly into the room so as not to disturb her, Michelle quickly removed her own clothing and took a seat on the floor opposite. She wasn't going to meditate though, she was too wired to even consider it, and so she just watched Cam.

"I can feel you staring," Cam said, barely moving her lips.

Michelle smiled, but said nothing as Cam took in a deep breath and slowly released it, in through the nose and out through her mouth, a calmness settled over her features that hadn't been there a few hours ago when they had gotten home. She had spent over an hour searching the house for any sign that Jessica had gotten inside, double checking every lock on every door and window, before searching the house for a second time. Michelle had let her do it, knowing she needed to have peace of mind if they were ever to get any sleep later.

Gavin had made sure that every possible access point to the house was covered. He had staff posted on every door, others patrolling the beach, and still more parked along the road at specific points of interest in order to keep a look out for anyone who could potentially be a danger to Camryn or Michelle. Nobody was getting past them tonight.

"You're still staring."

"I'm not staring. I'm observing, there is a difference," Michelle whispered into the quiet night. Her eyes scanned the torso of her lover, enjoying the dips and curves of her.

"Uh huh and what are you seeing?" Cam asked, interrupting her thoughts. Still with her eyes closed, she hadn't moved an inch from her pose: legs crossed, palms balanced on her knees facing up, each of her thumbs touching the pads of her middle fingers. Meditation was something that Dr Swanson had encouraged. She enjoyed it and found a little bit of inner peace every time she tried to do it.

"You, and how beautiful you look naked," Michelle replied back, noticing a slight scrunching of Cam's nose at the idea she was beautiful naked. "I saw that," Michelle reproached.

"Saw what?"

"I saw you make that face at the thought of my thinking you're beautiful naked. Don't make me disturb your meditation by proving it to you."

Cam couldn't help but laugh. She opened her eyes to see an equally naked body in front of her, one she was intrinsically turned on by.

"I did not pull a face," she laughed some more.

"Oh, yes you did, you did this." Michelle pulled the same face, but with an exaggeration and made Cam laugh again. It was good to hear, to see that she could still find humour no matter what Jessica tried to do.

"No I did not, you are such a drama queen," she said, giggling.

"I'm a drama queen? Moi?" Michelle pointed to her own chest, drawing Cam's eyes to her breasts unintentionally. "Uh, who was it that spent an hour last week ranting about the fact that they couldn't get a ticket to some soccer game?"

"Football match! It's not called soccer, it's football," she complained very seriously. She would never tire of trying to educate America on football.

"My point proven!" Michelle laughed too as she made to move closer to Cam. On all fours she crawled over to her and kissed the corner of her mouth. "Can we have make up sex yet?"

"I don't know, can we?" Cam flirted. Michelle continued to kiss her mouth, tugging lightly on her bottom lip.

"Pretty sure we can, I mean, we are dressed for it." Michelle gasped as she felt knowing fingertips drag lightly up her left side.

"That is true, it would be a shame to waste such an opportunity."

"Hmm mm. So, wanna fuck?" Michelle asked unashamedly and with a little sparkle in her eye.

She didn't get a verbal answer. Instead, two strong hands took hold of her face and pulled her into a searing kiss that sent shockwaves through them both. Michelle crawled into her lap, her knees sliding on either side of her lover's hips as she pressed herself tightly against Cam and let their arms tangle around one another. She rocked gently and found purchase against the smooth abdominal muscles encased beneath her lover's skin.

"We need to go shopping," she announced mid-kiss.

"Uh huh, what kind of shopping?" Cam asked, chasing the kiss. Her hands moved deftly to cradle Michelle's butt, guiding her movements.

"The kind that involves...you having two hands on me at all times." She ground harder to emphasise the point.

"I've got two hands on… oh!" Cam finally understood. "Oh you want me to…" Michelle nodded.

"I think it would be fun, don't you?" Her rhythm changed up a gear, increasing the tempo. "But, for now…" She grabbed a hold of Cam's right hand and brought it down between them. "For now, I am more than happy to…" Cam's fingers instantly hit all the right spots. Michelle's head flung back in a moment of pure delirious pleasure, leaving her neck wide open for Camryn's advance. "…ride you in any way I can." The utterance of guttural moans mixed easily with encouraging words as she bore down and rose up. Cam tried not to think of the image that had been conjured up; her lover astride her lap bearing down onto the silicone appendage. It sent her own arousal into overdrive.

"Huh, what?" she had barely realised that Michelle was still talking, so wrapped up in the fantasy was she.

"I said…have you ever…used one…before." Her words were interspersed with the need to breathe or just enjoy. Soft grunts and groans accompanied the sounds of flesh slapping gently against flesh. Heavy breathing mingled intimately with short gasps of air.

"No…" Cam shook her head, trying to remember. She was sure she would have remembered, but her brains were turned to mush right now as Michelle once more claimed her lips in a kiss that took her breath away.

"I want one," she said quickly, her body tensing and retracting before relaxing and releasing. "You…wear, I want…to feel you…inside me. Deep inside me." She barely finished her sentence before she cried out and collapsed against her lover. Cam could feel her smiling against her neck.

"So, what other things are you fantasizing about?"

Chapter Forty

"I want to go back to the park," Cam stated very matter-of-factly the next morning as they were showering. The water washed over her and calmed her in ways she didn't often feel lately.

"The park? As in *the* park?" Michelle asked. She was in the bathroom drying off from their joint shower. One she had enjoyed rather a lot.

Cam nodded. "I think it's something I need to do. To go back, to go and see where it happened and put things straight in my head. I don't really remember much of what happened there."

"Okay, I can tell you if it would help," Michelle said, stilling her movements. She stood naked, towel in hand. She wasn't sure if she was more concerned for Camryn's well-being or her own, in revisiting the place where Cam almost died.

"It might, but I still think I want to go and see it, do you mind?" The blonde stepped out of the shower and into a towel that she had hung nearby. Michelle stepped forward, closing the gap instantly to wrap herself around her.

"What? No! I, whatever you need to do is what we will do." She felt herself cling harder to Cam and pull herself against her chest, subconsciously protecting her from anything the world might have left to hurt her.

"Can we go now?" Cam asked. She felt Michelle stiffen a little in her arms.

"Right now? You, you want to go now?"

"Yes, do you mind? I mean I can take Gavin if you—"

"Stop." She held up her hand, "Stop babe, of course I will go with you. You're sure you want this?"

"I think so yes, I can always turn around and come back if I change my mind, but I think I'd like to try, and if I don't do it now I might never do it!"

"Ok, let's do it."

~Next~

The park was just a short drive away. Michelle drove and pulled the Audi into a space a little way away from where Camryn had parked on that awful day. She couldn't park in *that* exact spot; just looking at it brought her back to that terrifying moment when the police officer had informed her that Cam had been stabbed. And if she felt sick about it then, she could only imagine how Cam was feeling right now.

"You don't have to do this," Michelle said, her voice calm and quiet. Cam turned in her seat and smiled at her.

"Yeah I do." She opened the door and stepped out. Her feet hit the ground and in an instant, she was transported back. She could see Dylan running off and heard the car door close as Zac climbed out.

"Are you okay?" Michelle was asking, taking her hand and pulling her back to the present. Grounding her.

Cam shook herself, shook the thoughts from her head and took a deep breath. She squeezed Michelle's hand in her own and looked up. "Yes, I'm okay." She looked around her, half looking to see if she remembered things, and half looking to see if Jessica was anywhere around. It was a different day, a different time of year. The leaves were greener now, and flowers were starting to show through the foliage, but it was still very much the same path she had trodden before.

"She isn't here baby, you're okay," Michelle calmly told her as she pulled her into a hug, mind reading now. "It's just me and you here, okay?"

Cam nodded. She could feel her muscles were tensed. Her heart rate was elevated and there was a little nausea deep down in the pit of her stomach, but all she needed to feel it all disperse was to stare into those chocolate orbs that were giving her their full attention.

So, she took a step, and then another, and another, and then they were walking. Slowly, but walking towards where Cam had parked the car. They bypassed the area for now and took the path that led down to where Jessica had been waiting.

Cam remembered talking with Zac about soccer, or football as she was explaining to him. When she looked up, Dylan was talking to someone. It had panicked Camryn, because she was being given the responsibility of looking after someone else's children, and here she was on their first trip out together and already dealing with stranger danger!

"I saw her," she said quietly, barely audible. "She was talking to Dylan, but I didn't know it was *her*." She looked around her again. Checking, always checking before she continued, "I told Zac to wait here," she said, stopping in her tracks. "I said he had to wait here and not move or talk to anyone."

"That was the right thing to do, and he did as you told him, didn't he?" Michelle confirmed. Her palm stroked lovingly up and down Cam's arm.

"Yes, he is a good kid." Cam looked away again, her eyeline drawn to further down the path. "I ran, fast as I could, and I shouted for Dylan to come to me. I saw the person put their hand out towards Dylan and I thought they were going to try and grab her so I shouted again, louder this time, and the person pulled their arm back." Cam could feel the prickle on the back of her neck as she talked. Her skin felt clammy and she was breathing harder, she knew that. Her heartbeat was racing, and she gripped Michelle's hand harder in her own.

"It's okay baby, we can go anytime you want to," Michelle soothed, trailing her hand up and down Cam's back now. She could feel the tensing of Camryn's muscles. She could sense that it was becoming difficult, and she wanted nothing more than to just turn around and take her lover home where she could wrap her in cotton wool and keep her safe. "Take a deep breath or two."

Further along the pathway, Michelle noticed Camryn slow up in her stride. "It was all so fast, I sent Dylan back to Zac and watched her run all the way back to him and then I turned to Jessica." She swivelled and Michelle realised that they were standing in the exact spot that it happened. She looked down at their feet, expecting to see the droplets of blood that must have been there. "I don't remember what I said, but I know I shouted at her and she was…I don't know what she said, but then she said something and I knew it was her, it was her that was threatening you, and I saw red…and I screamed at her that I'd never loved her and then…" She sobbed as she remembered it. She felt the physical pain then too and gripped her sides. "Then she was punching me, at least I thought she was punching me and I didn't want to hit her, I really didn't want to get into a fight with the children watching so…so, I let her hit me and then…" She paused and took a deep breath. Michelle wrapped her arms around her, wanting to shield her from all the pain. "And then," she spoke into Michelle's ear, her voice a chilled whisper, "then I saw it," and Michelle knew she meant the knife. She withdrew from the embrace. "I saw it and I couldn't process why she had it, she was punching me, but she had a knife and my brain couldn't put the two together until I felt the pain. Just like that…one minute I felt okay and then there was this pain." She reached her own arms around her torso again and held herself tight. "And blood, *so much* blood."

Michelle felt the tears rolling down her face. This was almost as bad as the day it had happened, and the memories for her too forced their way back into her mind.

"She ran then. Just turned and ran, left me to…" She couldn't finish the sentence, but Michelle knew the word she couldn't say was *die* and she was right, that was what Jessica did. She stabbed her and left her with two kids in her care, to die in a park, scared and in pain and desperately trying to protect those children from seeing anything that would scar them in future.

Cam turned then and started walking back up the path, her arm linked with Michelle. "I walked back towards the kids and tried to hide my side from them. I had a jumper tied around my waist so, I moved it up and around. Zac was worried, he had seen Jessica hitting me and was concerned so…had to assure him I was fine."

They were nearing the area where the car was parked. "I unlocked the car and told them to get inside, don't open the door! For anyone, stay in the car until Aunty Shelly arrives." Cam said the last part as if she was actually talking to the children there and then.

She turned now and walked over to where she ended up sitting, sitting alone and out of sight of the kids, although she could see them through the car windows.

"That's where they found you," Michelle said softly, unable to look at the ground where Cam had lain, bleeding and unconscious. "They wouldn't let me come to you, but I saw you."

"I didn't know that, I'm sorry you had to go through that baby," Cam said sincerely. She really did wish she could take those memories away from Michelle.

"I wanted to hold you, but they were working on you. You had so many wires attached already, and I didn't know what was happening. I was so scared Camryn." She fell against her chest, felt Cam's arms wrap around her.

"I'm sorry," Cam whispered against her head, kissing her hairline.

"Don't you dare apologise, this wasn't on you." Their eyes met. "This was all Jessica's doing, not yours." She sniffed as they held each other close.

"I thought I was going to die...I said goodbye to you." She closed her eyes, unable to look into tearful brown eyes.

"Oh god Camryn, don't please. I can't even think about how close that came to being true."

"I'm sorry, I am so sorry you had to go through any of this." They both cried together.

"I wish neither of us had had to go through that, but we did and we made it, we got through the other side together and you are alive," she said, holding Cam's face in her hands. "You are alive and I love you." She kissed her, she poured everything she had into kissing her, trying to convey just how much she loved her.

"Can we go home now please?" Cam asked as they broke the kiss.

"Yes, let's go home baby."

Chapter Forty-One

The days and weeks since Cam had come out of hospital had been a rollercoaster. Emotionally she was up and down. She could laugh and make love and not think about Jessica for hours, if not longer, but some days she thought she was doing great and then she would catch a glimpse of herself in the mirror and it would all come crashing down again. Other days she would wake up drenched in sweat. Nightmares swamped her dreams, and she would toss and turn before waking up screaming. Michelle had become an expert at calming her and helping her get back to sleep. Dr Swanson said all of it was normal and over time would work itself out; time and sessions with her talking about it.

On days like that, days like today, she would find herself yearning to just see Michelle. The actress had started working on her new film the previous day. But, she made sure that Camryn had access to the studio and all location sites. She would be able to come and go as she wanted; if she wanted.

It was almost lunchtime as Cam rolled up in the Audi. Gavin drove, Jorge riding shotgun, and Carrie sat in the back seat with Camryn. The Brit felt ridiculous about it and yet, she was so grateful for these people.

They were filming in a studio. The set was designed to replicate a house, a living room. Huge cameras on tracks slid back and forth capturing the scene as the players acted out the script. Cam sat in a director's chair, quietly watching while Gavin and his team took a break and caught up with Michelle's team. Henry had now been bolstered with Ava and Kalu since the media began printing details of the film. Websites listed location details, and Janice had had no option but to allow information to be filtered out. The film company were paying for an A-list star after all, and that meant they expected a certain level of publicising.

"Cut, well done everybody. Let's all take a quick break." The director of this film, Anja Kowalski, shouted to the actors before turning around to the crew and directing them on how she wanted the next scene filmed.

Michelle walked across the set and laid eyes on Camryn. Her face lit up in an instant. "Hey you, when did you sneak in?"

"I just got here. You were great."

"Really? I'm not sure I am feeling this character yet." She grimaced. Normally she could read a script and fall a little bit in love with who her character was and be able to become them almost instantly when she shed her own clothes and put herself in the hands of the costumer.

"Well, I am no expert I will admit, and I guess I am also biased seeing as I am head over heels in love with you." She grinned as Michelle blushed. "But, I thought you was brilliant."

"Thank you sweetheart. I think I needed that." She took hold of Cam's hand. "So, what has brought you all the way down here?"

"I just wanted to see you," she admitted. They were trying to be honest with each other and not keep things to themselves when something bothered them. Especially Jessica-related somethings.

"Everything ok?" The concern in her eyes was evident immediately.

"Yes, I…I'm fine, I just felt a little anxious I guess."

Michelle smiled and nodded. "Why don't we go sit down, I've got a few minutes before they need me again." She guided Cam by the elbow to a quieter corner and pulled two chairs closer together so they could sit down.

~Next~

Michelle poured two glasses of mineral water and passed one across to Cam before adding ice to her own and taking a seat opposite her lover.

Cam remained pensive and rocked back and forth gently on the edge of her chair.

"So, what's up, Cam?" Michelle asked the question gently, never taking her eyes from her. When Cam looked up at her there was a sadness in her eyes; more than that, fear.

"I think I'm just...I have this gut feeling since we went to the park. I just...she is still out there, and I worry ya know, that she's going to come back and get to you."

There was the quiet jingle as a drinks trolley was wheeled past them towards the set. One room was being transformed into another for filming the next scene. Michelle smiled at the guy as he passed before turning her attention back to Cam.

"I think that's perfectly rational. We both know she's out there, and she's making it clear she isn't finished, but I feel safe, Cam. Gavin and the team, they're doing everything that can to make sure she doesn't get anywhere near either of us again." Cam nodded and tried to smile. Knowing Michelle was right was one thing, believing it was something completely different. There was a bell that rang out and a whole lot of shouting as actors and crew were called to set. Michelle looked around and then back to Cam. "I need to get back, but you can stay here if you want?"

Cam shook her head. "I'm fine, honestly I'll be fine."

"Ok, so I'll see you at home tonight?" They both stood and embraced, Cam's grip just a little tighter than usual.

Chapter Forty-Two

Cam was busy working on getting the Gym re-opened now that her purchase of it had been confirmed. With Gavin and Dan hovering nearby, she tried her best to ignore the fact that she needed them. She had a meeting organised with the construction team that were tasked with making the changes Cam had envisaged, so they kept out of the way, but Cam still knew they were there and why.

The plan was simple; have the Gym re-opened within ten days. During that time she would be holding interviews to staff the new Café area, more cleaning staff, and organising a manager, as well as personal trainers. It was going to be hectic, but after that was all done, Michelle would be finished filming and they were getting married.

For 4 days they were like ships passing in the night. Michelle didn't get home until almost 10 pm, and Cam was out the door by 6 am. Saturday morning was the first time they got to just lie in bed together.

Cam awoke to find arms and legs limpet-style around her. She chuckled to herself and attempted to move, but gave up when those same arms and legs squeezed their hold on her.

"Don't even think about leaving this bed," Michelle mumbled against her neck where her face was currently embedded.

"Okay, but do you think maybe I can at least breathe?" Cam chuckled as she felt Michelle relax her hold just a tiny bit.

"God I have missed you," Michelle whispered as she kissed the skin in front of her lips.

"It feels like forever since we just did nothing," Cam agreed, enjoying the attention.

"I know."

"How much longer do you have on this film?"

"Another week, maybe 10 days," she replied, kissing a collarbone, her lips gently touching the skin they met.

"And then we're going to get married, right?" Cam stated.

"Yes, and then you're stuck with me." She giggled and rolled herself to hover above Cam.

Cam studied her face, reminded of all the times she had looked into someone's eyes and had seen nothing much staring *back,* and yet when she looked into Michelle's eyes she saw the future, her future, their future. She saw light and love and lust, a lot of lust!

"I want to make love to you," Cam said quietly as she gazed at her.

"You never need to ask to love me." They rolled again as this time Camryn took her turn to look down into her lover's eyes.

"I want to make love to you every day for the rest of my life." The blonde used her strong biceps to support herself as she lowered to kiss the plump lips beneath her.

Michelle smiled into the kiss. "I have absolutely no objections to that either."

Cam's fingers had a life of their own. She didn't need to think; she just did. Her mouth moved slowly from her lips, along the strong jawline before she found her favourite place: her neck. Her lips drew gasps and quiet murmurs from her girlfriend as she sucked gently on her pulse point.

"Did you go shopping yet?" Michelle stuttered, her heart rate rising.

"No, not yet, but..." Her mouth moved lower as her palms settled in the hollows of her hips. "It's on my to-do list."

"Good, not that I am complaining, but I like you watching me." Cam's eyes opened in an instant, locking on with Michelle's as she trailed open-mouthed kisses down her stomach. "Just like that, don't take your eyes off of me."

The brunette's lips parted in a silent gasp as she felt the warmth of her lover's mouth encompass her. It took everything she had not to close her own eyes, but she managed it, exhaling slowly. She held those blue orbs in place with her own gaze as Cam's mouth and tongue worked to bring her to the edge.

"Fuck..." There were times when, just at the point of no return, she could swear that Camryn had some magical knowledge of her, because it was impossible that any other person could know so innately just when to push her over the edge. Right now, she was floating along the rim, skating the edges and just waiting, waiting for the moment that Camryn would... "Oh, God yes!" she cried out as the moment surpassed anything previously known to her. A torrent of profanity left her lips as she stared deeply into Cam's eyes and felt herself gliding again, higher, higher still.

Chapter Forty-Three

The office was quiet as Cam set about finishing off paperwork. Erin was busy downstairs organising the staff meeting. It was something she had instigated the moment she had taken over as manager, and it was working well. It had been a busy few days for everyone.

Michelle was on the brink of finishing her movie, and Cam had been shopping. It was amazing all the different styles there were to choose from, but she had managed it. She just hoped Michelle liked her choice.

Her phone chirped from its place on the desk. The screen lit up with Detective Gomes' name. She grabbed it up in an instant.

"Detective, I hope you are calling me with good news." She spoke into the mouthpiece of the mobile device as she searched a drawer for the file she was looking for.

"As it happens," he said, his tone stopping her in her tracks, "I am."

"Seriously, have you got her?" Her heart raced in anticipation. It had been a couple of months now since the attack, and weeks since she had reappeared with the new photograph. They were living a life dictated to by Jessica.

"No," he replied. Her heart sank. "I don't have her but," she could hear the lightness in his voice, "the Mexicans think they do."

"Think?" Her heart raced again. She swore she was going to have a fucking heart attack at this rate, but she took some deep breaths, tried to calm herself, and listened.

"Yeah, we tracked down the CCTV after she left the photo in

Ms Hamlin's car, and we picked her up as she made her way to a car parked on a side street. That car was detected entering Mexico the next day. Its occupants were two Hispanic males and a white female matching Montgomery's description," he explained. "They hadn't received details of the car at that point, so nobody stopped it. However, a very smart police officer in a town fifty miles further south had received the details and noticed it parked in a small hotel."

"Okay, so..."

"So, he went inside and asked a few questions about the people travelling in it and was given a different name than Montgomery, but the assistant did confirm the woman was British," he explained further. "He then liaised with us, and we have requested that they arrest and hold her until I can get down there to verify it's her. The photo from the border crossing isn't perfect, but it does look like it's her."

"Thank god, I can't believe it's finally over." She blew out the breath she didn't realise she had been holding.

"It sure does look that way, I'm flying down there this evening and will hopefully be arresting her in the morning and bringing her back here to face justice."

~Next~

Hardly a day passed when one or the other of them wouldn't be counting the hours till this damn film was done. Michelle had expected it to last a further 2 or 3 days max and then she was out of there. They had been filming on the beach all day. It was sunny and looked warm for the cameras, and her outfit was skimpy enough to have the viewer believe that it was the height of summer, but in reality she was freezing her ass off. The only good thing about it was that she was going to be getting home early.

Henry escorted her to the door, just like he did every night. Stepping inside, she found a slightly tipsy Camryn dancing to a song she didn't recognise about being free. She leant against the door jam and watched her sing along as she jumped around holding a bottle of champagne in one hand and a glass in the other. She was cute.

She chuckled to herself as Cam swung around and caught sight of her. Which made her jump out of her skin and lose her footing. She ended up on her back on the couch laughing.

"I didn't spill a drop," she slurred triumphantly as she held the bottle and glass aloft still.

"So I see." Michelle snickered at her antics as she tried to right herself and almost did a somersault in the process. "So, what are we celebrating?"

"Gomes called," Cam said, as if this should be an adequate explanation. Finally she was sitting on the edge of the couch. She placed her glass down on the coffee table and poured another glass of champagne. Michelle's eyes widened questioningly, and Cam tried not to giggle. "He got her!" she said, holding out the crystal flute for Michelle to take.

"Say that again," Michelle said, coming to a halt. Joy began to rush through her system, only to be held back by the fear of mishearing Cam's slurring words.

Cam grinned and repeated her words more slowly. "I said, he got her!"

~Next~

"Guess what I got today!" Cam said with glee as she jumped up from her spot on the couch where they had been cuddling and kissing; celebrating. She leapt from the couch to the floor and bounded across the room, stumbling once or twice as the effects of the champagne lingered.

"What did you get?" Michelle giggled. She really was fun when she was drunk.

"Just wait and see, I'll be right back."

She was gone for less than a minute before she bounded back into the room and fell, sprawling out on the couch laughing with a plain white bag in her hand. She grinned as wordlessly she handed it across to her.

Michelle narrowed her eyes at her with a slight tilt of her head that Cam found very sexy. "What did you buy now?"

"Open it and see." Cam moved onto her knees, bouncing like a kid at Christmas as Michelle opened the bag and peered inside. She gasped in surprise, but her eyes lit up as she raised them back up from the contents of the bag to look at Cam.

"When did you?" She reached a hand inside and pulled out the package.

"This morning. Gavin will never forgive me." Cam laughed out loudly as she recalled the look on his face when they pulled up outside Eve's Playground. She watched as Michelle unwrapped the purple appendage. She held it in her hand and examined it, just the same way that Cam had done earlier as the young woman in the store gave her all the information she needed, and then some.

"So, how does it work?" There was a hunger in her eye as she gazed up from the phallic-shaped object and looked straight into Cam's eyes.

"Well, basically, this bit goes… and that bit…ya know?" she said before reaching for it. "Oh, just give it here, hang on." She got up and disappeared out of the room again. When she returned a few minutes later empty-handed, but strutting proudly, Michelle was intrigued.

"So…" Cam placed a finger against her lips, ending any further small talk, and held her hand out for Michelle to take. "Dance with me," she said, the cockiness that Michelle loved on full display.

Michelle let herself be pulled to her feet. There was no music, but that didn't seem to matter as they moved together. When Cam kissed her, she responded with just as much gusto. It was heady as she lost all sense of where she was. She needed air, and as she broke the kiss to take a breath, she realised she was against the wall. Her back pressed against the firm support as Cam continued to kiss her. Her fingers were inching Michelle's dress higher, lifting the fabric until it was bunched hastily around her waist. Her underwear was next, slowly tugged down smooth thighs until loose enough to fall to the floor unaided.

"Unbuckle me," Cam whispered against the shell of her ear, causing a shiver of delight to quiver its way down her spine. Anticipation.

She wasted no time, her fingers deftly sliding Cam's belt out of its buckle, the buttons on her jeans popping easily. She didn't need any instructions now as she yanked and revealed just where the toy was hiding.

Cam smirked as she lifted her, her palms holding the back of her thighs, the wall doing its part.

"Ok, now I just need to..." She wiggled her hips.

"Ow, that's not..." Michelle's fingers gripped her shoulders more tightly as the pair of them tried to adjust and get the toy on target.

"Sorry," Cam mumbled, the tip of her tongue touching the bow of her lips as she concentrated. "This is more difficult than it looks." She had to readjust her position, hoisting Michelle higher as her biceps began to burn. "Ok, this isn't working."

"Why don't we try it with me on top?" Michelle suggested, her back scraping against the wall for the 4th time.

"I guess so." Cam loosened her grip and put Michelle back on her feet. The brunette took the opportunity and lifted her dress the rest of the way and pulled it off. She moved quickly toward the couch. When she turned to see what was taking Cam so long, she couldn't stifle the giggle that erupted. Her lover, still tipsy from her earlier celebration, was standing with her trousers around her ankles, but proudly erect, until she started to stumble forwards, the toy wobbling back and forth.

"Oh sweetheart, take your trousers off." The blonde looked down, realising the problem she was having. She too laughed and kicked off the offending apparel. "And that shirt can go too."

Once naked, bar the floppy toy that continued to keep them both giggling, Cam felt much more able and covered the short distance across the room. Flopping down onto the couch, she groaned as the movement caused a sensation she wasn't expecting.

"Can you feel everything?" Michelle asked Cam, moving closer, her lips connecting with Michelle's bare neck. Cam bit her lip and nodded. Michelle smirked and wrapped her palm around the appendage. "You feel that?" Again Cam nodded. "Words darling. I wanna hear you," she husked, her voice deep and smoky as she held her gaze. "Eyes and words, baby."

"Fuck, yes, yes I...feel it." Her hips reared upwards. She couldn't help but glance down. Her lover was taking her time, slowly and torturously. "I thought...you wanted—"

"All in good time. This is fun." She had a devilish look on her face as she grinned.

Chapter Forty-Four

Michelle had spent the morning re-shooting the same scene over and over, mainly due to the fact that the other actor in the scene with her couldn't get his lines right. It wasn't a difficult line, but for some reason he just couldn't articulate it. At first it was comical and they all enjoyed the laughter, but as time went on it became frustrating. He was apologetic and she got it, it happened to everyone at some point, but still, she was tired. Mentally she was exhausted already. When they were finally done she decided a quick lie down in her trailer would help alleviate the headache that was just starting to pinch at the back of her head.

As she opened the door and walked inside, she noticed how it was the first time she had just entered a room without Henry going first and checking it out. Life was feeling back to normal.

Her trailer wasn't big, just an area with a small table and seating for two, a tiny kitchenette and a day bed with a small closet toilet and shower to the side. She bent low to open the miniature fridge and grabbed a soda, sighing deeply as she stretched, readying herself for a nap.

~Next~

When Cam's phone rang in her pocket for the first time, she ignored it. She was in the middle of a discussion with her design team that had been put off twice already, so she needed to have this conversation. However, the insistent ringing and buzzing continued. Someone wasn't giving up.

"Yes!" she said rather loudly, somewhat irate at the caller on the other end of the line.

"Cam, it's Gomes, listen it's not her." His usual silky baritone voice was now urgent in its delivery.

"What?" She turned away from her employees and walked to a quieter spot.

"It's not her! Jessica, it's not her!" he reiterated. "She used a decoy, this woman was paid to take a vacation."

"Then where the hell is she?" Cam shouted in fear, looking around to see where Gavin was and checking to make sure Jessica was nowhere near.

"In LA still. Gaynor Hansen is the woman down here, she said they met in a bar and Jessica said she needed to be in LA, but was supposed to be in Mexico and if her boss found out then she would be in big trouble, the woman isn't the brightest," he said. "Anyway, Montgomery asked her if she would like a vacation, all she had to do was drive her car across the border and spend a few nights in some hotel."

"Wait, so you're telling me that Jessica planned this." Her fingers tugged at her hair. "Shit, I need to find Michelle."

"She has Henry with her, right? She will be ok"

"No! No she doesn't, she wanted to drive herself, and we thought it was safe for her to do so. Shit!" Cam was panicked now. "I have to go, I need to call her and tell her."

"Ok, look, I'll be back in LA later today. I'll come straight over."

Cam hung up and quickly scrolled through her phone's contact list until she reached Michelle and hit call. It rang just twice.

"Hello Camryn." An ice cold sweat covered Cam in seconds. She froze to the spot. That voice in her ear felt like venom surging through her veins.

"Jessica, where is Michelle?"

"Oh, don't worry sweetheart, she is quite safe, for now." Jessica cackled.

"If you hurt her I swear on every God there is, I will kill you with my bare hands," Cam hissed. Her hands clenched tightly into fists.

"Oh, Camryn don't be so dramatic." She cackled again. "Now, I suggest if you want to see her again that you meet us on your boat in say, 30 minutes?" She sounded calm, and for now that was Cam's only saving grace.

"Alright." Cam was already moving. She thanked God she had rode the motorbike today; it meant she would get to the boat a lot quicker than 30 minutes. If she was lucky then maybe she could surprise Jessica and get the upper hand. Call Gomes and have the police pick her up as she arrived.

"Oh, and Camryn?"

"What?"

"If you do anything stupid like call the police then…well then I'll have to rethink my plans on hurting her, am I clear?"

"Crystal."

Chapter Forty-Five

From her cheap hire car, Jessica hunched down in the driver seat. Parked outside of the studio the Actress was working from, she had gotten lucky as Camryn's car drove up to the large gates and was ushered through.

She had spent the last few days following the Actress, which wasn't an easy task with all these people around her, but she had gotten lucky when it was reported online that she would be filming here as of yesterday.

Now though, as Camryn's car drove out of the studio and headed away from her home, Jess was intrigued. She let them get a little way down the road before she pulled out and followed. They drove south, dropping down to the coast road before turning off for the marina. She had to be careful now, keep her distance and hang back. Keeping them in sight, she pulled over and climbed out. Walking, she was able to keep to the shadows and get as close as she could.

She stayed there, hidden, for hours before another car arrived. The Actress. She watched as Camryn walked back down the gangplank to greet her. She kissed her on both cheeks and then they walked up footway together, Cam's arm around her shoulders. Jessica sneered, bile rising in her throat as she watched the public display. What hold did this woman have on Camryn?

She closed her eyes to it, swallowed down the urgent need to vomit, and considered the positives. There was only one, an important one. Camryn had a boat, or at least access to a boat. They could go anywhere on a boat. All she had to do was find a way to get Camryn to take her out on it.

And she had found a way. The Actress was all she needed for leverage. It was so easy too. She had no clue as to why the bodyguards had suddenly disappeared. She could only hope that her plan had actually worked and that gullible idiot Gaynor had inadvertently led them astray. She didn't care though. All that mattered was that she now had the opportunity to get to Camryn, and nothing was going to stop her this time.

Chapter Forty-Six

She was at the Marina within 20 minutes, her bike hitting 110mph as she flew down the freeway. It was a risk, if she had been pulled over for speeding, but thankfully she avoided the patrols. She reached the yacht and climbed aboard quickly. She tried to think, but her brain was in overdrive until she just stopped. Taking a deep breath, she looked around and tried to find anything that might help. There was nothing. So she paced back and forth until the sound of a vehicle could be heard.

Michelle was driving the car, with Jessica sitting sideways facing her in the passenger seat. She had the knife held low, but it was clearly pointed towards Michelle. She could see Jessica's mouth moving as Michelle twisted in her seat, looking towards her before parking the car right next to the gangplank.

They both climbed out together. Michelle turned to look up at Cam as she closed the door behind her, her hair whipped around her face in the breeze, but it didn't hide the expression of fear. Cam stood tall, her face passive. She would be damned if she gave Jessica the satisfaction of knowing she was terrified too.

Michelle walked ahead of Jess, but they remained in close quarters, the knife pressed against her back as a warning of what could happen.

"Now, isn't this lovely?" Jessica said as they climbed aboard. She glanced quickly around, checking for any surprises while inspecting her new surroundings.

"Just let Michelle go and I'll do whatever you want me to do," Cam pleaded.

"Do you take me for an idiot Camryn?" Jessica said quite

seriously.

"No, of course not, but you don't need her, you have me. I'm what you want, right?"

"Hmm, right now I want to get the hell out of here, and you and this boat are my ticket." She nudged Michelle in the back and pushed her forwards, following up behind with the knife still pressed against her back.

"Where do you want to go?" Cam asked. "I can have the crew here within the hour to take you anywhere." She didn't take her eyes from Michelle.

"That's not going to happen. You can sail us."

"I don't know how to."

"Don't fuck with me, Camryn," she said, pulling Michelle closer to her and closer to the knife she was holding. The sunlight glinted off of it, making it sparkle like a beautiful gemstone, though it was anything but.

"I'm not, I swear," Cam pleaded, finally turning her attention to her ex. "I haven't got a clue how to sail, but I can get the crew, they will do as I ask."

Jessica paced, talking to herself and waving the knife around. Michelle took the opportunity to edge slightly away from her as Cam edged closer to Michelle. Finally she seemed to come to a decision and spun around to face Camryn. Then she moved quickly and before Cam knew it, she was in her face, the knife between them. Her heart rate elevated instantly, and she saw Michelle move to intercept. She couldn't allow that, she couldn't allow Michelle to be between them, so she threw up her palm and stopped her from moving any closer. She stared at Jessica and then down at the knife.

"Fine, get them here, I want to go to Mexico," Jessica said. Cam raised her line of sight back up to Jessica's face. She pulled the phone out of her pocket and made the call to Captain Henderson, ascertaining he could be there within the hour with a skeleton crew and they could be in Mexico within a few hours. Cam told him to just come aboard and get going when he got here, that she was already onboard with guests and they didn't want to be interrupted.

"Ok, it's all arranged, you can put the knife down," Cam suggested to Jessica.

"You are joking, right?" Jessica asked incredulously. "Let's just remember who is in charge right now Cam, now let's go inside, ok."

They moved towards the door that led down to the living quarters. As they reached it, Cam moved aside to allow Michelle to go first, gently placing her palm on the small of her back to guide her, trying to convey she was there physically with her while putting herself between Michelle and her deranged ex-girlfriend. She needed to touch her one last time, if it was to be the last time.

They all sat in silence for a few minutes. Time had slowed and every second felt like an eternity, but she had managed to seat herself next to Michelle, whilst Jessica had taken a chair opposite. Cam reached slowly for Michelle's hand, inching her fingers closer until their pinkies were touching. Cam risked a glance sideways at her. She was looking intently at Jessica with something in her eyes that Camryn never thought she would see: hatred. Michelle was no longer fearful; she was angry and ready to kill this bitch.

"Fine, if we're going to have to sit here then I am at least going to have a drink," Cam said, standing to walk to the bar. She needed to take Michelle's attention away from Jessica.

"Sit back down!" Jessica shouted.

"Or what? You'll stab me again?" Cam said, pulling her top off. "Here, check out your handiwork from last time, well done you!" She spoke calmly and continued walking to the bar, pulling her shirt back on as she went. “I am going to get a drink, then I am going to sit back down and wait this out. I have no interest in getting in your way, the sooner you are where you want to be and away from me, the better.”

Jessica watched her, anger building, but she kept a lid on it this time. It had shocked her to see the scars on Cam. She had never intended for that to happen, but Cam just wouldn’t hear her, and she had to keep doing whatever it took until she finally understood. They were meant to be together.

“Drink?” Cam asked sarcastically as she opened a bottle of wine and poured herself and Michelle a glass. Jessica shook her head. The offer confused her.

When Cam returned to her seat she deliberately sat closer to Michelle as she passed her the glass. Now she could place her hand over Michelle’s more easily, squeezing gently. Michelle squeezed back.

A few minutes later and the engines started up. The crew were aboard and they would be on their way. It couldn’t come soon enough for Cam. Get to Mexico and get rid of Jessica, then call the police and hopefully have her picked up. Her thoughts were interrupted when she heard Jessica speak.

“I didn’t mean to hurt you Camryn, it wasn’t ever my intention.” The apology wasn’t something the blonde had expected to hear, and it rocked her slightly. She had always believed in accepting an apology, that everyone deserved a second chance, but now she wasn’t quite so sure if that rang true anymore.

“Well, if you will play with knives,” Cam shot back cruelly.

“I had the knife purely for protection,” she said. “When you wouldn’t see sense and take me back I had to find a cheaper place to live, it wasn’t very nice, so I got the knife for protection. I didn’t realise I had it in my hand until it was too late.”

“Yes, I can see how one would find it easy to misplace where your knife would be. Drawer, pocket, hand!" Michelle squeezed Cam's hand, trying to get her to stop winding Jessica up, but actually Cam thought she had the upper hand on this. Jessica rarely apologised to anyone, and Cam actually believed she was contrite; she didn't trust her an inch and she certainly wasn't going to forgive her, but she would use it to her advantage if she could.

"It wasn't like that. You made me so angry. I just wanted you to love me, and all you had to say was how awful and pathetic I was." Her eyes clouded over and she wiped at them quickly.

"I did love you, but you threw that away the moment you decided to sleep with Kate." She closed her eyes as the image of Jess and Kate in bed together flooded her memory banks.

"Don't you think I know that?" Jessica shouted, "Don't you think I've lived with that regret every day since?" She stood up and paced the room. "When I lost you, I lost everything. The flat, my friends, my job!"

"And that's all my fault, is it? That's why you thought you would come here and terrorise my fiancée." Jessica stopped pacing and allowed Cam's words to sink in. *What had she just said*? Michelle saw the connection, the way Jessica's brain synapses were firing on all cylinders as Cam's words hit home.

"Fiancée?" she said quietly as she turned to face Cam. Time stood still.

Cam hadn't meant to say that, she didn't want Michelle in the firing line, but she had made a mistake. Slipped up, and now what else could she do? "Yes, we're getting married!" she said.

Suddenly Jessica was gone, the calm was gone. Any aspect of a woman that Camryn once knew and loved, was gone. In its place was the crazed maniac from the park. Green eyes had hardened, her glare rigid and unwavering.

"Why would you say that Camryn? You know that you and I

are getting back together," she said as she slowly walked the few steps across the floor towards Michelle. "I told you to get rid of her, didn't I? But you just don't listen to me."

"I do! I listen to you!" Cam said, trying to appease her in any way she could. "I think we...We should go and get some fresh air, don't you? Just me a-a-and you, watch the sunset together and...talk, without *her* there," she said conspiratorially. She needed Jess to think that she could still be on her side.

Jess was thinking about it. Cam expected her to say no and was ready to fight her if she had to, because she could only see this going one way, and that was going to involve Michelle being hurt. But Jess surprised her. "Okay, just me and you?" she asked coyly, her attention moving away from Michelle. She turned, her arm lowered with the knife as she took a tentative step towards Cam.

"Yeah, like that time we went to Greenwich Park and watched the sunset, remember?" Cam said. "We can...we can do that on deck."

"I do remember." A small smile emerged on Jessica's face at the memory. "Okay, let's go," she said, ushering Cam forward. Turning back to Michelle, she warned, "One move from you and I'll finish the job." She sneered, looking to the knife and then Cam. "Understand?"

Michelle nodded, her beautiful charcoal eyes swimming with tears. Cam winked, trying to convey that she knew what she was doing, but she wasn't sure she did. Cam knew she had to persuade this crazed side of Jessica that she was interested in her, a thought that left her feeling nauseous.

Once they were on the deck and Michelle had been locked in downstairs, Jessica pulled Cam over to the railings to look out at sea. It was still a little too early for the sun setting, but Cam had managed to get Jessica away from Michelle, and that had been her main goal.

"Thank you," Cam said, trying to build some trust.

"What for?" Jess asked, giving her a sideways glance.

"Getting us out of there and up here," Cam said, smiling. "I couldn't say what I wanted to say while *she* was there." Her stomach churned at having to talk this way about the one person she loved with everything she had.

"She makes me sick, so fucking perfect and that fucking fake smile of hers when she looks at you," Jess sneered. "I don't know why you put up with it."

"She's rich and famous I guess." Cam shrugged. "But she isn't what I want."

"And what do you want?" Jessica said, leaning in closer as if she were going to kiss her. Cam swallowed, knowing what she was going to have to do next.

"You, of course," Cam lied and leant the last few inches towards Jessica's waiting mouth, sealing their lips together. Bile threatened to rise in her throat, but she forced herself to continue on. Breaking the kiss she smiled, and Jessica smiled back, but then her face turned to fury as she caught a glimpse of something over Cam's shoulder. Cam turned quickly to find Michelle standing there with Captain Henderson.

Chapter Forty-Seven

Jessica raised her arm, the same arm with the hand that gripped the knife. Terror filled Cam's heart as once again she was forced to confront Jessica's anger. Before Jessica could plunge it down, Cam did the only thing she could think of. She grabbed Jess around the waist and forced them both against the railings, and overboard.

The force of them falling 20 or more feet into the icy cold water expelled all of the air out of Cam's body on impact. She let go of her grip on Jessica and tried to swim away, but Jessica had other ideas and Cam felt herself being pulled back under as her ex grasped a hold of her left leg. She kicked hard, over and over, until she was finally free and able to swim up. Breaking the surface once more, she gasped for air, feeling it fill her lungs. She could hear the shouts from above, Michelle screaming into the night's air. Hands pulled at her again as Jessica also broke the surface and climbed all over her to get air for herself. She was sinking.

It was black and cold, so cold. She fought to rid herself of the weight that held her under. She wanted to tell Michelle she was sorry. Sorry that she couldn't get back to her, but she had tried so hard. Her lungs burned with the need for air. Her legs and arms were numb from the icy water all around her as they tried so desperately to drag her body through the water and up. *Was she going up? She had to be. Down wasn't an option. She wanted, needed to live.*

Michelle and Captain Henderson looked over the railings towards where they fell, but could see nothing. He called for the life raft to be readied and a couple of the crew were put to sea in it to search for Cam and by default, Jessica. It felt as though time slowed; every second seemed to last a minute. There was no sign of them.

Suddenly a voice called out, ‘over there,’ and as they all looked to where the young sailor was pointing: there was a body floating on the water.

Chapter Forty-Eight

With the sun now setting, the small life boat was barely visible as it ploughed through the waves towards the body. Michelle wrapped her arms around herself and prayed. She silently pleaded for it to be Camryn, she begged for her to be alive. That they would get to her in time. And she promised herself that if it was Jessica, she would kill her herself.

She watched as the body was hoisted into the small boat. It rocked gently with the movement and they waited for it to settle before turning and heading back to the yacht.

Michelle ran across the deck and down the side of the boat, following Captain Henderson and the other crew members that were all needed to help bring the body aboard, and then the small boat would need to be hoisted back aboard as well.

"Is it her?" she shouted. The men dealing with whoever it was looked up at her. She was lying on her side. Pink shirt and blue jeans. It was Cam. She was coughing and spluttering as she expelled the water she had swallowed in her fight for survival. "Oh, thank God." Michelle sank to her knees, wrapping herself around Cam's wet shoulders. "We need to get you warmed up, can you walk?" Michelle asked, desperation in her voice. She needed to get Cam to safety as soon as possible.

"I'm okay, I'm okay," Cam said, trembling as she spoke.

"You're shivering baby, we need to get you out of these clothes." She tugged Cam to her feet and tucked herself under her arm to support her. As they straightened, she noted the Captain standing to her left overseeing the crew.

"Get us back to dry land, now," she barked at him. She didn't care if she appeared rude; right now all that mattered was getting Camryn checked out. Her lungs had already been damaged; half drowning in the freezing ocean would not have been good for her.

"What about the other woman?" Henderson asked. Michelle stopped in her tracks and considered Jessica.

"Leave her, just get us back, right now." She scowled and continued to move Camryn into the warmth.

"As you wish, I'll broadcast to the coastguard that a person is in danger."

"Fine, just get Cam back so that I can get her to a hospital."

"I don't need a hospital," Cam said, coughing up some more sea water. Her grip on Michelle was looser, her strength lessoning with each passing minute.

"Do not even start with me, Camryn," Michelle said sternly, "You're going."

"Yes ma'am," answered Cam and Henderson in unison.

~Next~

"Detective Gomes, I am sure you understand where I am coming from when I say this, but what the fuck is going on?" Michelle asked as the tall man stood towering over her. "Have they found her yet?" She was aware that she was pacing. The hospital corridor was the perfect place to just pace.

"Miss Hamilton, as of right now they have not located Montgomery, dead or alive, but they continue to scour the ocean as we speak and I hope to have word sooner rather than later."

"And you will let us know as soon as you do, right?" It wasn't a request in any sense of the word, but a polite demand.

"Absolutely, you cannot know how sorry I am that the

debacle in Mexico played right into her hands as she planned. Everything worked exactly how she wanted it to. How is Camryn?"

Michelle and Gomes were standing outside of Cam's room at the hospital. She had her arms wrapped around herself as she thought about the answer to that question.

"Physically she is fine, a little hypothermic, but nothing that can't be treated. I fear for her mentally though, she was fragile enough as it was after…well you know what she went through. I'm not sure how she is going to deal with this now?"

Gomes nodded his head. He could understand completely. He had been a cop for a long time and had seen a lot of victims who never recovered from their attackers. "I'm sure that with the right help Camryn will work things out; she's a strong woman."

Chapter Forty-Nine

Cam was not impressed at being told she was staying overnight in the hospital. In fact, as soon as the nurse left her room she was up and looking for some clothes, but she didn't have any. The clothes she had been wearing were soaking wet, and all she had was this bloody hospital gown that did very little to cover her modestly. *Where the hell was Michelle?*

"What are you doing?" Michelle said sternly as she entered the room and found her searching a cupboard.

"Looking for something a little less revealing than this," she said, lifting the gown slightly with her fingers.

Michelle couldn't help but snigger at the sight in front of her. Cam's long blonde hair was darker than usual as it was still damp, and the gown she had on was clearly made for someone with much shorter legs than Cam had. In any other circumstance she might have found the entire scene appealing.

"I will go home and get you something more..." She paused and couldn't hold back the grin any longer. "...appropriate for your overnight stay."

"How about, you go home and bring me back some clothes appropriate for my going home in?" Cam said brightly, eyes wide in hope.

"Not a chance lady, get back into that bed and stay there until I get back," Michelle said, leaning up and kissing her lightly on the lips. Lips that thankfully were now warm and pink again.

"Michelle?" Cam's voice croaked as tears welled in her eyes, clouding the blue. "Please take me home. I just want to go home.

Please don't make me stay here," she begged. Camryn had never pleaded or begged for anything in the whole time that Michelle had known her.

"Cam, baby what's wrong?" Her voice now softened with concern. She closed the space between them and held her close.

"I just want to go home, please baby I promise I'll do anything you tell me to, just take me home." She fell onto the edge of the bed sobbing. Michelle flopped down next to her.

"Camryn, I'll go and speak to the doctor and see if your test results are back. If they say you can go home then I'll go get you some clothes, okay?" she said. Kissing the side of her head, she felt her nod. This was what she was worried about. Physically, Cam would heal within hours, but emotionally she was struggling to deal with the impact that was Jessica.

~Next~

When Michelle explained the situation to the doctor and they had spoken to Camryn herself, it was agreed that she would probably be better off resting at home than in the hospital. Thankfully her lung function tests had come back clear and other than a dose of antibiotics to fight off any potential infection, she was given a clean bill of health.

The drive home was virtually silent. Gavin drove as they both sat in the back seat. Camryn stared vacantly out of the window as Michelle gently stroked her thumb across her hand.

"Do you think she's dead?" Cam asked in a hushed voice.

"I don't know, sweetheart," Michelle said. Turning to look at her, she couldn't help but feel useless. "Gomes said he would call as soon as they found her. One way or another."

After another bout of silence Cam spoke again, and it sent a chill up Michelle's spine.

"I think I killed her."

"How can you say that? Camryn you didn't, you didn't." She watched as a single tear dropped down Cam's cheek and puddled in the corner of her mouth.

"When she grabbed me under the water, it wasn't to hurt me," she whispered. "She was trying to live." Another tear rolled down the path already in place. "I kicked her, over and over until she let go."

"You had no choice, Cam," Michelle said as she placed her fingers under Cam's chin and brought her face around to look at her. "You didn't have a choice."

"I kicked her and she sank, it's my fault, I killed her," she said, collapsing against Michelle's chest.

"She would have killed you," Michelle answered. "She was insane"

"But I killed her, what does that make me?" Cam asked sincerely.

"It makes you a survivor, and we don't know that she's dead."

"I know."

~Next~

With the media interest in the story, it wasn't long before Janice was calling. It was now common knowledge that the police were actively seeking the whereabouts of Jessica Montgomery. Not that they had ever stopped looking, but the latest news was that she had returned and once again had gone after Shelly Hamlin and, subsequently, Camryn Thomas had ended up in hospital again.

"Michelle, you can't hide it any longer, the press have got wind of the story. They know about Jessica going after Cam again, and that you are involved makes it a story."

“Damn it.” She moved about the kitchen, agitated. Cam was asleep upstairs, resting as she was supposed to.

“Look, I think I have a way of getting them to back off of Camryn, but well, I’m not sure you’ll like it either.”

“Right now I will do anything to give Cam some space from this. Tell me.” She stopped pacing and leant back against the counter.

“Announce your engagement.”

“What? No. they have no right to that.”

“I said you wouldn’t like it, but if you give them that as the story I think I can get them to back off from Camryn.”

“God, this is so shitty.”

“Look, they want a headline. And they will print one. Right now, all they have is that Cam was almost killed again. So, that’s the one they are going to go with, and you are going to have them camped outside your door until they get the photos and comments that they want. The vultures only care about selling papers.”

“Fine, announce it, but I promise you if any one of them turns up trying to talk to Camryn about this, I will sue their ass off.”

Chapter Fifty

Dr Pamela Swanson was someone that Cam would have liked under other circumstances, but these were not normal circumstances, and Dr Swanson was hitting too many sore points for Cam to want to like her.

For the first two sessions Camryn Thomas just sat there. She had nothing to contribute other than "hello" and "goodbye." That wasn't an issue for Dr Swanson; lots of her clients began their road to recovery the same way. What was an issue was the fact that she had missed this last appointment.

They had initially agreed on 3 sessions a week to start with. Her partner, Michelle, had done most of the talking on the first contact meeting, which was fine. Somebody needed to explain things, and it wasn't going to be Camryn. So, it was Michelle she contacted to see if all was well with Camryn when there was no answer from her.

"I'm sorry Doctor, did you say she didn't attend?" Michelle asked her to clarify once more. She was worried about Cam. She was closing down and keeping things close to her chest again.

"I am afraid so, yes. I know things have been up in the air lately, what with the return of Jessica, but...I didn't want to assume, is she unwell?"

"No, she isn't unwell, in fact she told me that she was on her way." Michelle said. She began to panic. Where was Jessica? They still hadn't found any sign of her. "I'll get a hold of her and reschedule, if that's okay?"

"It's no bother, this is quite normal for a lot of people, Michelle. We will get there in the end." They ended the call and Michelle walked through the house to the kitchen where, Maria was preparing dinner.

"Maria, have you seen Cam today?" Their housekeeper was busy dusting her way around the house.

"Not since breakfast, she say she was going to an appointment."

"Hmm, did she say what appointment?"

"No, she didn't eat her breakfast either, I forever telling her to eat things, but she never listens." Maria stopped what she was doing and took a good look at the newest member of the household. "Everything okay?"

"I hope so, she missed her appointment with Dr Swanson." Michelle was intrigued and worried. What if it was Jessica again? Her heart thumped in her chest as she picked up her cell and called Cam's number. Surprisingly, she answered.

"Hi."

"Cam, where are you?" Michelle tried to ask nonchalantly, but who was she kidding, she was worried and annoyed. Cam should know better than to just wander off like this right now.

"I'm..." She looked around her, "I don't know, on the beach somewhere."

"Which direction did you go when you left the house, baby?" Michelle asked while putting her coat on and grabbing her bag.

"I...turned...right," she answered, taking her time to think about it.

"And how long did you walk for?" Michelle delved, gleaning information as she walked. She had been worried about Camryn.

"Hmm, not sure. What time is it now?"

"It's 11 o'clock."

"Oh. Already? I lost track."

"You missed your appointment with Dr Swanson," she said as she began to walk along the beach as fast as she could. Her feet sinking into the cool sand.

"I'm sorry."

"It's okay though, we can make another one," Michelle said as she kept up the brisk walk towards where she hoped she would find Cam.

"Gomes called this morning," Cam said after a brief silence.

"Really? Why didn't you tell me?"

"I…I needed time to absorb what he said." Her voice was quiet as she spoke.

"Okay, Cam I'm on my way to find you, okay?"

"I figured you would be," she said, smiling at the thought of Michelle coming to her rescue. "She isn't dead."

Michelle stopped in her tracks. Had she heard correctly?

"She isn't? Where is she?"

"Nope, she has more lives than a cat." She chuckled at her own joke.

She spotted Cam up ahead and moved as fast as she could in the sand. "I can see you, so I'm hanging up, okay?"

"Sure."

With that, she put the phone back in her pocket and ran the distance between them. Cam was sitting facing the ocean. She had made a little sandcastle and built an empty moat around it. Gavin, or any of his team, were nowhere to be found.

"Hey," Michelle said, falling down next to her and lacing their fingers together. Cam's fingers were gritty with sand. "You had me worried."

"I'm sorry." She looked so contrite that there was no way Michelle could stay angry with her.

"So, you said she's...she's alive?" Was it never ending? "Please tell me she is under arrest." She watched as Cam nodded slowly.

"Yes, she always was a good swimmer." Cam smirked ironically. "She made it back to the beach, further along with the current and stuff, and then someone took pity on her. She fed them some bullshit story and they took her home, gave her a change of clothing, and she hung out with them for a few days." Michelle listened intently. "Until one of them had a friend visit. He is a big fan of yours." Cam grinned, proud that her soon-to-be wife was so popular. "He called the police, and Gomes arrested her last night."

"Thank God for him then." And for once, she internally thanked the bastard editor who had insisted on going with the story on Cam. Jessica's face had been front page news.

"They also got a report back from Scotland Yard. It turns out that she was sacked from her job with the police two months before she arrived here. Since we split up she lost the flat, her job, and her grandmother died."

"That's all very sad, but..." Michelle was cut off by Cam kissing her.

"She was assaulted, around the same time she lost her job. The police back in the UK think that with the stress of it all she snapped, and when she saw that magazine with my picture in it, her brain took her back to a place when she was happiest, and in her mind that was when she was with me."

"So, what happens now?" She placed her hand in the small of Cam's back. Cam took a deep breath and slowly exhaled. When she turned and looked at Michelle, it was with bright, clear eyes. That look had been missing all week, and Michelle breathed a sigh of relief to see it once more.

"I was thinking that I have wasted enough time on this woman and been totally neglecting the one woman I vowed never to forget."

Michelle smiled and nudged her shoulder. It was starting to feel good having Cam back.

"Have I told you today that I love you?" Cam asked, smiling.

"No, you have not!" Michelle said, smiling back and shaking her head.

"Ah, how very remiss of me!" She leant in and kissed her, hard. "I'm sorry."

"For what, babe? For being human? For caring?"

"For shutting you out." She hung her head "I didn't want to, but I couldn't stop it."

"You just needed time." Michelle said to her as she stood and pulled her to her feet. "And I have all the time in the world for you."

Chapter Fifty-One

It didn't take long for things to go back to normal. With the guarantee that Jessica was now locked away, albeit in a psychiatric hospital for now, Cam was able to scale down the constant shadowing by Gavin and the team.

There had been a meeting. Gomes had been very thorough in his investigation of Michelle's stalker and had put together a comprehensive (and, in Camryn's opinion, too large) file of all the negative comments, as well as any threats, weird groupies, or fan bases that should be kept a close eye on. So, as much as neither of them wanted it, it was agreed that for now they would keep one bodyguard each whenever they went out publicly.

The rest of the team would be kept on to monitor the house, places of work, and social media. Gavin now had an office. Since he'd been promoted to managing the team, Cam felt it was essential that he have somewhere to work from. So, on the ground floor of the house, next door to Cam's home office, Gavin would take up residence. From there he could organise his team to fill the shifts at OUT, as well as around the house.

But, today was different. Today was Valentine's Day, and Camryn had plans.

Michelle was finishing off the last day of filming. With everything that had happened with Jessica, the production company had delayed filming for a week. A costly week, they were after all on a budget, so as a thank you, Michelle waived most of her fee. But, today, regardless of whether it was Valentine's Day or not, she had to finish the final scenes.

Cam had dropped her off. Henry followed behind now, in a separate vehicle along with Carrie. He would stay, and Carrie would follow Cam wherever she wanted to go.

They headed into Beverly Hills, parking in an underground lot just off of Rodeo Drive. Cam used to be able to walk down these streets unnoticed; now, however, she was often the focus of overzealous fans of Michelle's. On the whole she didn't mind. The only person she had ever had to be concerned about was Jessica. Strangers taking her photo, stopping her for an autograph, was still something she found amusing.

Nazori, a high-end jewellery store that was frequented by anybody who was anybody, was expecting her. It was not somewhere Camryn was usually to be found, but it was Valentine's Day, and she had something planned.

~Next~

"Maria!" she shouted as she came through the door. Her diminutive housekeeper strolled slowly out of the kitchen to the hall.

"You yelled?" Her voice was full of mirth even if her face was stern.

"Yes, I did." Cam smiled. "Go home, it's Valentine's day, you should be with your loved ones."

"I will be, soon as I finish what I was doing. Why you interrupting me?" she pulled the dishcloth from her waist belt.

"Oh no, you're not getting me today." Cam laughed, turning tail and running back toward the door and the stairs. "I am going out tonight and I won't be back until tomorrow," she called over her shoulder at an advancing Mexican woman grinning from ear to ear.

"Good, you take that beautiful woman somewhere nice."

Cam reached her room before Maria even made the first step. Laughing to herself, she grabbed a small case from the closet.

Chapter Fifty-Two

The film wrapped and Michelle said her goodbyes. There would be a few people she would keep in touch with, but on the whole, most of them would go their separate ways.

Cam would be picking her up, and she assumed they would go out to dinner, so she had come prepared and was now wearing a beautiful blue satin dress that hugged her figure.

The minute her phone beeped, she grabbed her bag and almost ran outside. What she found took her breath away.

Camryn was wearing a suit. A black, made to measure, fitted suit that made her look even taller. She wore chunky heeled boots and had her hair slicked back. She was almost androgynous, and yet so very feminine. She had her hands in her pockets and her ass perched against the hood on a car, one foot lifted and rested on the chrome bumper.

Michelle took a moment to just take it all in. She almost felt weak at the knees.

"Hey," Cam smirked. She hadn't realised when she got dressed that she would quite have this effect on Michelle, but now armed with the knowledge, she was going to use it to her advantage.

"Hi." She actually blushed. The way that Camryn was looking at her, the way Camryn looked, it was all just overwhelming.

"Wanna go for a ride?" She pushed off from the car and began moving towards Michelle.

Michelle could only nod, much to Cam's amusement.

"Are you okay?" Cam bit her lip and just stood there, looking at her.

"Yes, God yes," Michelle finally answered. Cam wasn't quite sure which question she was saying yes to, but she began walking to the car. "You buy this today?"

"I did," Cam answered, moving quickly to open the door for her. "You look beautiful, by the way."

Michelle stopped halfway into the car and turned. Standing to her full height once more, she kissed Cam. A tender, sweet peck. "Thank you. And you..." She licked her lips as she studied Cam's face more intently. "Let's just say, tonight is your lucky night."

"Oh, after you see what I have planned, that's a given darling." Cam smirked and closed the door before running around the car and jumping into the driver's seat. "Open the glove compartment."

Michelle grinned as she pressed the small button that would release the catch. Inside was a box, neatly wrapped. "What's this?"

"Open it and see." Cam grinned back at her. There was a small sharp intake of breath as the last piece of paper came away, revealing the word Nazori.

"Oh my god, Camryn!" Michelle gasped. "It's beautiful." She held up the gold necklace and examined it more closely.

"Stars and moon," Cam explained. "I wanted to—"

"Remind me of our first night together?"

Cam glanced quickly across at her and smiled, remembering herself the night spent on her yacht under the stars.

"Yes." She drove at a steady speed along the freeway and out towards the airfield. "You like the car?" she inquired as Michelle took a moment to look around at her surroundings.

"I do, it's sexy." She smiled as her eyes fell upon Camryn's face.

"It's yours," Cam stated, keeping her eyes on the road ahead.

"Mine?"

"It's Valentine's Day," Cam reminded her. "Did you forget?"

Michelle laughed, her palm reaching across to settle comfortably on Cam's thigh. "No, sweetheart, I haven't forgotten. However, my plans included removing things rather than giving them."

"My favourite kind of gift." Cam laughed as she turned the car to the right and pulled in. She parked the car and climbed out, grabbing their bags from the trunk. She noted out of the corner of her eye that Gavin and Jorge had pulled into the space three along and were now retrieving their own bags. "Shall we go?" she said.

"Where are we going?" Michelle trotted alongside her. It was just about daylight still. A small chill was beginning to cling to the air, and Michelle shivered a little.

The small plane was up in the air in no time.

~Next~

They landed a couple of hours later. Cam opened one of the cases and pulled out a heavy faux fur-lined coat.

"You're going to need this," she said. She pulled a similar one out for herself as Gavin and Jorge did similarly.

Descending the stairs from the plane, it was obvious they were somewhere much colder than L.A. There were mountains on the horizon, and the dusk was arriving fast. The blue skies of daylight were quickly being pushed aside by the vibrancy of the setting sun. Pinks and oranges were dragged across the sky by the clouds as they covered the world in a marshmallow blanket.

The loud buzzing Michelle could hear was getting louder as they walked around the plane; a helicopter proudly sat on the tarmac, its rotors whirring faster and faster as Cam grabbed her hand, grinning, and pulled her towards it.

~Next~

From the windows of the helicopter, Michelle could see that they were high up and on a mountain somewhere. There was snow on the peaks. They had landed on a helipad, but she had no idea where.

Cam took her hand and led her down some steps and towards a small building. They bypassed the restaurant and headed straight down a long corridor. Their shadows hurried along after them, each of them carrying a bag in both hands. There was a huge sign up with the acronym C.A.R on the wall above the desk. A flamboyant man in a suit that fit him extremely well welcomed them and proceeded to give Camryn the details she needed to complete her booking.

Following a map, Cam led them back outside, and Michelle instinctively pulled her coat more tightly around her. Her breath hung like a cloud in the air as they walked briskly. The night was drawing in, and the sun was setting on another day.

"Ok, you have to put this on," Cam said. Suddenly stopping in her tracks, she pulled a blindfold from her pocket.

"Really Camryn, you want to blindfold me with the boys here?" she teased. They both giggled as Gavin blushed, but she took the strip of material from Cam's fingers. She felt the softness of the silk, and because she trusted Camryn with her life, she held the mask to her eyes and turned for her lover to tie it.

Guided left and then right, she waited patiently until she felt Cam's fingers against her elbow. There was the sound of a door swishing open, and warmth hit her face as they moved, she was sure, inside.

"Just a bit further," Cam whispered against her ear. The feel of her breath sent a shiver of anticipation down her spine. Her coat was undone and slid effortlessly down her arms.

Soft furnishings hit the back of her calves as she stumbled backward and found herself being lowered. "Just go with it," Cam said, smiling as she took in their surroundings.

Michelle was on a bed; that much she could work out. She felt the dip as Cam climbed on top and moved into the space between them until she was lying next to her; close enough that she could remove the covering.

There was an audible gasp as she opened her eyes and for the first time saw for herself where they were. She was right, they were on a bed, a bed covered in fur-like blankets, but above them, where a ceiling should be, was a glass dome. Hexagon-shaped frames held large pieces of glass, and through it was the night sky. Blackness surrounded them. There was only the twinkling of the stars, appearing and disappearing as she tried to focus on them.

"Camryn." Her voice was barely a whisper. "Where are we?"

"Colorado. At the Canter Arctic Resort."

"It's beautiful." Michelle was wide-eyed. The room was in darkness, allowing for the full effect of the night's sky. The resort was in the middle of nowhere and on top of a mountain, with no light pollution to ruin the view. Guests where given torches to get around with once the sun had set.

"So, beautiful," Cam whispered in agreement. Michelle turned her head and found Cam still lying on her side, her blue eyes twinkling just like the stars as she stared at Michelle.

"You know I love you, right?" Michelle said reverently.

"Yes."

"Good." She reached and brought her fingers to Cam's face, lightly tracing her jawline. "Let's enjoy tonight."

"And then get married," Cam stated, her lips ghosting against their match.

"Yes."

If you have enjoyed Next, please leave your review on Amazon.

Here is a taste of Claire Highton-Stevenson's next book in the Camryn Thomas series.

Coming Soon

Yes

Wedding bells are finally ringing. Cam and Michelle are tying the knot.

With a honeymoon to be planned, it's a simple solution for Camryn: an uninhabited idyllic desert island would be just perfect! But Michelle has other ideas, and our girls are London-bound.

How much of Camryn's past will come back to haunt her this time? What happens when an unexpected face returns? And will Camryn and Michelle come to a decision that will change both of their lives forever!?

Read on for the first chapter to Yes!

Chapter One

"I don't care where, I am only concerned with when. So, when you have decided where you want us to get married, just let me know and I will be there," the blonde woman making coffee threw over her shoulder.

Camryn Thomas was being stubborn, and it was irritating Michelle Hamilton no end.

"Jesus Christ Camryn, this is your wedding too!" the irate brunette all but screamed, her sultry voice turning a little hoarser as her vocals reached a higher decibel. The actress was in no mood for her fiancée's indifference.

Taking a deep breath, Cam pivoted to face Michelle. She didn't want to continue this and end up with an argument when there were so many other, more important things they could be doing, like taking their clothes off and going back to bed. She moved swiftly and closed the space to where the darker of the two sat at the island. Reaching out, she took her hand between her own and kissed her knuckles tenderly.

"Babe, I love you. I really, really love you, and I want nothing more than to be your wife and for you to wear my ring, but I just want to do it! Where we do it will make no difference to me because the only thing I will have my eyes on is you. Not the venue, not the scenery, and not the guests. Just you!"

"I hate it when you do that," Michelle growled, her brown eyes fixed firmly upon her lover's as her arms flailed theatrically. It was a cloudy winter's day, and her eyes did no more than complement it with the storm brewing in their depths.

"What? When I do what?" Cam asked, perplexed yet

again. Sometimes she just had to admire the way Michelle could quite easily flip into her over dramatic alter ego, Shelly Hamlin; a little too easily when she wanted her own way.

Camryn just wanted to get married. She had thought that was what Michelle wanted too, but since informing her mother, along with her agent and friend, Janice Rashbrook, the wedding had taken on a life of its own and was now threatening to turn into the celebrity version of a royal wedding. That was something Cam really didn't want, but would go along with if it made her lover happy. She would do just about anything to make Michelle happy.

As they'd met just a few months earlier, a lot of people might have thought they were rushing into it, but Cam didn't care what they thought. She knew what she wanted, and when she wanted something, she would generally do all she could to get it. Being married to Michelle was no exception.

Michelle had similar feelings. Being a TV star had put enough limitations on her life already. Now she was finally in the place she wanted to be – loved and settled – and nobody was taking it away from her. It was still too fresh in her mind just how close she had come to losing Camryn. The attack, by Cam's ex-girlfriend from back home in the UK, had left her half dead, lying in a pool of her own blood, and it had left deep scars on both of them. In Camryn's case it was both figuratively and physically.

Jessica Montgomery had set about terrorising Michelle in an attempt to split them up and have Cam return to England with her. It failed, of course. Unaware that Jessica was Michelle's stalker, Camryn had made it clear to her ex on several occasions that she wasn't interested in her, but she just wouldn't take the hint. Then, just after Christmas, she had attacked Camryn.

The anger and venom with which Jessica attacked was shocking enough in itself, but that she did it while Cam was in charge of entertaining Michelle's brother's kids had made things a whole lot worse. They still had no idea on her whereabouts, but they weren't going to let it spoil their future. When that attempt failed, she tried again. It was astonishing that Cam was even thinking about a wedding right now.

"When you say something so fucking beautiful and yet still manage to be so fucking annoying." Michelle's face at this moment was stuck between wanting to smile and wanting to scream. She was just beautiful, and Cam couldn't help but smile as she leant in to kiss her soft, supple lips. She sucked the bottom one between her own as she pulled away, leaving Michelle wanting more.

"You are beautiful, you're all I want and need. I will marry you anywhere you want to do it; if it makes you happy, it makes me happy."

"I hate you."

"You love me." Cam smiled and stepped in close. "You love me and you know it."

"I do love you," she agreed before Cam enthusiastically kissed her again. Tongues that knew the dance so well quickly found the rhythm they both enjoyed. "I know what you're doing." Michelle said, breaking the kiss, her arms locked firmly around Cam's neck.

"Hmm and what would that be?" Cam replied as her mouth moved from its original target to its next, her neck. She always did love her neck. The way it curved up from her shoulder into her hairline was just too enticing to ignore.

"You're trying to distract me with sex," the actress said, a slight whimper accompanying her words.

"Sex?" she inquired as her tongue licked a path downward from ear to collarbone, delighting in the small hollow she knew would be waiting for her. "Distract you from what?" Cam kissed her way across her pulse point, sucking gently before continuing up until she found a lonely ear lobe needing attention.

"Oh God, you know what that does to me?" Michelle shivered as goosebumps speckled her skin and her stomach clenched with arousal. Nobody had ever had this effect on her before.

"I do, it is true. I love how it affects you...how *I* affect you." She smiled against her skin. This was what she was born to do: to spend as long as possible teasing and tempting Michelle Hamilton.

"And distracts me."

"Distracts you?"

"Hmm hmm." Michelle hoped she would never get used to the effect Cam had on her. Her body was just in tune with her: Cam's fingers, her mouth, and her voice. She just had to look at her with those blue eyes, clear as crystal, that would bore into her, and Michelle would feel an urge to just submit to anything her fiancée wanted of her. Yes, Camryn Thomas had a way about her that Michelle Hamilton couldn't get enough of.

"So, what was it you were telling me?" Cam asked, trying

to concentrate and give her undivided attention to her fiancée. She extricated herself and went back to the task she had started earlier, making coffee for them both, leaving Michelle aroused but grateful to be back on track with the wedding plans.

"I was *asking* you what your opinion of the Padua Hills theatre was for the wedding." She passed a brochure over to Cam, who placed it down on the table, and tried desperately not to imagine Camryn pulling her clothes off. "Please don't make instant, it really is horrible when you do it."

Cam glared for a second before grinning. Apparently her coffee-making skills where lacking. "Okay, firstly are you asking me because it is somewhere you really like, or because Janice and your mother like it?" she asked, turning her attention to the machine that made perfectly flawless coffee.

"Well, I admit it was Janice that suggested it. However, I think it's quite nice."

"Quite nice? Not amazing or fantastic, just quite nice? Are you happy enough with quite nice?" she teased gently. "Though to be fair, you did call our first kiss 'nice,' so I'm not sure how to take it when you say 'quite nice?'" She laughed before she continued, dodging a playful spank to her butt. "Seriously babe, I just want you to have the best, not 'quite nice'. I want to see your face light up when you show me something because when that happens, I will be ecstatic. So, can we agree to chill out a bit, take our time and find the place that's 'us'?"

"But Camryn, what you fail to understand is that a lot of these places are all booked years in advance, and it will be hard to find somewhere at such short notice!" Michelle whined, actually whined like a child, but the grin that went with it suggested she knew what she was doing.

"Ok listen, I want to marry you as soon as possible, but I am willing to hold off if it means you getting your dream wedding."

"Will you please just look at the brochures though. I want your input. We could pick three and then go and visit them and see when the earliest is we can book."

"Ok."

"Ok?"

"Yes, on one condition," Cam said in all seriousness, her head nodding slowly as a sly grin developed on her lips.

Narrowing her eyes suspiciously, Michelle asked the question. "And what would that be exactly?"

"Well." She waggled her eyebrows.

Michelle took a moment. She knew exactly what Cam was wanting from her. With a smirk, she grabbed the hem of her top and lifted it up and over her head. "You have got 15 minutes, and then we are going to look through these brochures, got it?"

"Yes my love," she answered, unhooking the red satin bra that stood between her and her prize. "I love your boobs," she added as she bent slightly to take a hardened nipple between her lips.

"You are so rude," Michelle gasped. She loved this feeling. She hadn't always enjoyed the attention a lover lavished on her breasts, but Cam was different, tender in her movements. No less aggressive or passionate when required, but always tender.

"What is it with the name-calling? I am hurt." Cam feigned sadness, her bottom lip jutting out and quivering before turning into a giant smile. "Now if you could be a love and remove the rest of your clothing I would be a very happy girlfriend."

Michelle took her time to extricate herself from her tight-fit jeans and underwear. She slowed her movements, enjoying the slight fidget Cam had going on as she took a step back to relish the show.

With her arousal being fuelled to the extreme by this mini-strip, Cam wasted no time in grabbing hold of Michelle by the waist and pressing her up against the kitchen counter. She took hold of her buttocks as she moved in for a kiss, a kiss so thorough that Michelle barely noticed she was being hoisted up onto the worktop. The marble was cold against her bare skin and she gasped out loud, as Cam slid her to the edge of the counter. Camryn broke the kiss, the need for air and to move lower encompassing all of her thoughts. Her mouth found its goal in an instant.

"Oh Jesus, Cam, so good." Michelle's voice was low and smoky as she relaxed into the sensations coursing through her right now. She had no control over her hips as they moved by their own will to create the perfect rhythm that would take her where she wanted to go.

This was one of Cam's favourite things to do: tasting her lover, hearing the way she moaned and feeling how she writhed as her hands flew to Cam's hair and held her in place. Cam was more turned on than she had ever been before, with anyone!

"Baby you're going to make me come," Michelle gasped as Cam's tongue swept around her heated core, teasing and nudging her toward a pleasure she was well aware she wanted.

"That's the plan," Cam boasted, as she swapped her tongue for fingers, rocking into her when their lips crashed together in a searing kiss once more.

"So…close…baby please… Oh God Camryn, please." Cam heard her pleas and doubled her efforts. Her bicep burned, but she refused to give in. Her training had been building her muscle strength up, and she was determined to get back to where they were before Jessica tried to ruin everything.

"Fuck yes!! Right there baby!" Michelle cried out, shuddered, and collapsed forwards, her hands wrapped tightly around Cam. She loved to climax like that, knowing that Cam knew her so well and cared enough to want her to climax like that. None of her other lovers had ever spent so much time and effort trying to understand what got her off, but Camryn did. Cam would try anything and everything to make sure Michelle was spent, sated. She would gorge on her, her body would be left drained and exhausted, and she would wake feeling more content that she had ever done.

Cam took Michelle's face in her hands and kissed her gently. She let her hands wander down Michelle's torso and under her thighs. Wrapping them around her own waist, she lifted her and carried her to the couch. She lowered Michelle to lie down, then climbed on the couch with her and pulled their bodies close together.

"Damn you, Camryn!" Michelle muttered, twisting

herself around to burrow into her lover's side.

"What have I done now? Ya know most people's girlfriends would be grateful for the orgasm you just had!"

"Oh, you can trust me, lover, I am very grateful and very, *very*, satisfied. However, I now just want to sleep, snuggled with you here for a while when *we* should be looking through brochures."

"Ah I see, how cruel of me?" She smiled and made a grab for the blanket that lay along the back of the couch. She tucked the blanket around them both and thought about how, just a few days ago, they were so far apart emotionally and physically. They both worried Cam would never come out of the funk she had found herself in with regard to how her body now looked. "I like this, just us," she whispered, then added, "What about Vegas?"

"Camryn Thomas!" Michelle said without opening her eyes. "I had better be dreaming that you just suggested Las Vegas as a destination for our wedding!"

Camryn kissed her cheek, smiling and said nothing more. Everything was just how it should be.

ABOUT THE AUTHOR

Claire Highton-Stevenson lives in West Sussex with her wife and fur babies. Two cats: Tumble and Murphy, as well as two dogs: Scouse and Eliot.

Her first novel: Out was published in August 2017 and there are plans for several more next year!

She is a huge Liverpool FC fan, her dream would be to play at Anfield. She is an award winning photographer. Her work can be found on her website: www.clairestevensonphotography.com.

Next year she aims to travel more!

Made in the USA
Columbia, SC
02 April 2018